NOT
ACCOUNTING
FOR
MURDER

NOT ACCOUNTING FOR MURDER

A WALL STREET MYSTERY

REBECCA SALTZER

LEVEL
BEST BOOKS

First published by Level Best Books 2024

This novel is entirely a work of fiction. The names, characters and incidents portrayed in it are the work of the author's imagination. Any resemblance to actual persons, living or dead, events or localities is entirely coincidental.

Rebecca Saltzer asserts the moral right to be identified as the author of this work.

First edition

ISBN: 978-1-68512-676-6

Cover art by Level Best Designs

This book was professionally typeset on Reedsy.
Find out more at reedsy.com

To my grandmother, Maxine Cobbs Hughes

Contents

Praise for Not Accounting for Murder

"Anne Scott, the plucky heroine of Rebecca Saltzer's latest, provides an up-close look at the world of the one percent—which, despite appearances, isn't pretty. As she navigates that treacherous world, facing both professional and personal peril, Anne offers all of us one all-important lesson: Money is murder."—Tom Coffey, author of *Public Morals*

"*Not Accounting For Murder* will grip you from the start, echoing the suspense and attention to detail reminiscent of Hitchcock's finest works. Against the backdrop of Wall Street's cutthroat trading and the glittering facade of high society, this classic mystery will have you wondering which of the many suspects could be the murderer, and what of the many reasons why will be the motive for murder. With each twist in the plot, suspicion shifts, leaving readers on edge. *Not Accounting For Murder* is the second book in Rebecca Saltzer's Anne Scott Series, and I, for one, am eagerly awaiting the next thrilling installment."—Desmond P. Ryan, Toronto Police Detective (Ret'd), author of The Mike O'Shea Crime Fiction Series and The Mary-Margaret Cozy Series

"As the youngest manager for Spencer Brothers' Centaurus stock fund, Anne Scott just wants to do right by her investors. But when she decides to dump the fund's shares of Energix, a Wall Street darling reporting profits through the roof, she doesn't realize her move will endanger the fortunes of people close to her and entangle her in a murder mystery—where she's the prime suspect. Author Rebecca Saltzer draws on her background in the financial industry to weave a smart, page-turning tale of deception and intrigue. Always follow the money."—Sharon Marchisello, author of *Trap, Neuter, Die*

SHORT SELLING

Short Selling: a way of betting that the stock price will decline. An investor sells shares they do not own by borrowing them from a broker. At some agreed-upon time, the investor returns those shares by purchasing them on the open market when (hopefully) the price has dropped, keeping the difference as a profit. If the market moves up, instead of down, the investor will have to buy the stock back at a higher price and take a loss on the transaction.

1

The Aftermath

The Hamptons

July 1990

The day had begun with manicures and pedicures and ended with the death of Richard Fernsby.

Within minutes of the body being discovered, three policemen from the East Hampton Village precinct responded to the call. They immediately taped off the stairs leading down to the dock and began taking statements. Guests awaited their turn, huddled in the hushed tent that just thirty minutes before had been alive with music and dancing.

"Ma'am?" The short, stocky officer motioned for Anne to come over.

As she made her way past the empty tables and chairs, a heavy rain drummed on the canopy hanging above.

"Your name?" He flipped to a new sheet of paper.

"Anne Scott."

"Friend of the bride or the groom?"

Neither, if she were totally honest. "The bride," she answered. "My fiancé, Alex, is her brother."

"Family." He gestured toward the gray shingled house, which sat some distance back from the bluff edge, alone, its nearest neighbor nowhere in sight. "Are you staying here or in town?"

"Here."

"Nice place," he said appreciatively.

Stunning, to be more precise. With an expansive porch and myriad of gabled windows, it stood gracefully near the top of a small hill, like a ship's captain surveying the great expanse of the bay. Anne could only guess what it was worth. Nothing *her* family could ever have afforded. Not the type of place she had ever imagined she might one day actually be invited to visit or vacation in.

He paused as if trying to figure out how to ask the next question. "Did you talk with Richard Fernsby at all this evening?"

She nodded. "Briefly."

"What time was that?"

"Around 9 pm." She knew because she had checked her watch, wondering how much longer she would have to wait until she could politely leave what had turned into a dreadful party.

"Where did the conversation happen?"

She thought for a moment and then pointed about 20 feet over to her right. "Right around there."

"How did he seem?"

Wound up. Bitter. Rude. She quickly evaluated possible responses and settled on the easiest one, something others were also likely to say. "I think he'd had a bit too much to drink."

"Hmmm." The officer scribbled something down. "What gave you that impression?"

"He was…belligerent. And looked a bit unsteady on his feet."

"Anything happen after that?"

"He left. I think he was going to get some coffee with Kevin."

"The groom?"

She nodded.

"Was that the last time you saw him?"

"Yes…well, until…" she stammered and then nodded toward the boat anchored below. "Until he was found down there."

"Thank you." The policeman clicked his notebook shut and motioned to the next person to come forward. "That will be all."

In the dim light, Anne could see her fiancé, Alex, standing alongside his parents and the newlyweds, all looking stricken. They had formed what looked like a reception line near the entrance to the tent, where they were solemnly shaking hands with the departing guests. When the last of them had exited, Anne breathed a sigh of relief. Finally, she and Alex could get away from everybody and everything and talk privately about what had happened.

They ran across the lawn, pelted by the driving rain, and arrived at the house a sopping mess. She kicked off her wet heels and gave her shoulder-length hair a quick shake to avoid leaving a trail of water through the house. Even so, small drops marked her path from the entrance hall, up the stairs, and the rest of the way to his room.

"We look like drowned rats." Alex handed her a towel and threw his damp jacket on the bed.

Normally, she would have joked with him, maybe suggested they warm up together in the shower, but he was moving and speaking stiffly, as if he could barely hold himself together. She touched his arm. "How are you doing?"

"I don't know." He loosened his tie and unfastened his cummerbund, setting them in a loose pile on the dresser. "I guess I'm in shock."

So was she, to be honest. It wasn't every day someone kicked the bucket at a wedding. "That's natural."

"Richard was only sixty-two years old. And fit. I wouldn't have expected… but, I guess the stress of everything just caught up with him."

She pulled a hanger out of the closet. "Did the paramedics say it was a heart attack?"

"Or stroke. I don't know how you tell the difference. And no one actually said." His fingers slowly unbuttoned his shirt. "I assume they'll do an autopsy."

"What do you think he was doing in the boat?" She pulled off her stockings and hung them over the desk chair to dry.

"Maybe he wanted to leave a small gift for Kevin and Paige...although, in all the commotion, I didn't see anything lying around." Alex paused, a pained expression on his face. "More likely, he was so drunk he just passed out."

And then went into cardiac arrest and died. Unless... Could he have killed himself? She unzipped her dress and pulled it over her head. "I'm wondering if I should have told the officer about Richard's choice words for me."

"Not if he didn't ask."

"What if it indicated he was suicidal?"

"Richard? No. Those were the words of an angry bulldog who was three sheets to the wind." Alex shook his head. "He was totally out of line. If I'd been there—"

But he'd been elsewhere, in his role as a groomsman, helping out with his sister's wedding. And even if he had been physically present, what could he have really done?

She slipped her arms into Alex's robe and hung her wet dress on the now vacant hook. "It shows his state of mind, which was definitely unsettled and—"

"Anne." He put a hand up to stop her. "Listen to me. As an attorney—"

There was no need for him to finish. She already knew what was coming next.

"—whenever you're dealing with law enforcement, NEVER volunteer random information. You don't know how it might come back to bite you."

Which was exactly why she hadn't mentioned it.

"Besides. You hardly even knew him. You met him, what? Once? At a quarterly investor meeting?"

She nodded. Even then, she had found Richard Fernsby arrogant and obnoxious, almost itching for a battle. And all she had done was ask a simple question. But that question had illuminated a crack, which quickly turned into a gaping chasm that ultimately led to her standing with a group of near strangers on a windy bluff and his body lying lifeless on the dock below.

2

Quarterly Investor Meeting

New York City

June 1990 – A month before the wedding

"Tt's an untapped market," the CEO of Energix waxed on to the assembled investors. "I expect our stock price to rise by twenty or thirty dollars by year-end."

Anne bit her lip. The suggestion was preposterous. There was a glut of capacity, and the shares of other companies in that very same industry he was touting had been falling precipitously.

She raised her hand. He glanced in her direction and nodded. Anne felt a bolt of nervous energy and began to stand.

"Great presentation, as always," a voice boomed in her ear.

She turned to look at the man standing diagonally behind her, notepad in hand. He furrowed his brow, as if pondering a deep thought, and then opened his mouth wide, obviously planning to continue.

Anne quickly sat back down.

"What about your projections on the energy trading side of things?"

"I'm glad you asked." Richard Fernsby looked like the cat who had just swallowed a canary as he launched into a drawn-out sales pitch, effusively extolling the potential upside of the business. A lot of big talk and sweeping generalizations, but nothing concrete that convinced her the company was fundamentally poised to be a great investment. Anne tried not to fidget while waiting for him to finish his spiel. "As you know, we always hit our targets."

She raised her hand again and was passed over for someone on the other side of the room who asked yet another softball question. Anne glanced down at her watch, wondering if this was typical for how these meetings went.

The man sitting to her left whispered. "Let me give it a try," and raised his hand the next time Richard Fernsby began winding down. Almost immediately, her neighbor was selected. He turned to her and smiled. "All yours."

She stood up and faced the podium squarely, her feet planted firmly on the ground. "Anne Scott, from Spencer Brothers."

The CEO gave a slight nod that she took as an acknowledgment.

"I was a little surprised when you said that you won't be providing a balance sheet today because typically—"

"That's right," he cut her off and then shrugged, suggesting there was nothing in the least bit odd about it. "We haven't finished putting it together."

"When do you expect to have the information available?"

"Soon." He squinted, as if trying to see her better. "Spencer Brothers, did you say?"

She nodded, feeling a small thrill as she replied, "I manage the Centaurus Fund."

At thirty-one years old, she was unusually young for such a senior position. It had been a big promotion three months earlier, and a major change from her first eight years with the bank as a bond analyst, where she advised traders from her small cubicle on the edge of the floor. Now, she was in charge of a multi-million-dollar stock fund, making her own decisions as to whether to buy and sell. And when. The responsibility was both exciting and terrifying at the same time.

"So, you're the new kid on the block." He leaned over the podium and winked. "The one and only thing you need to know is that we always hit our targets."

There was something creepy about the way he smiled at her as he repeated his trademark sentence, as if he thought she would be swept up by his charm and distracted from asking any more questions.

"And your target date for releasing the financials?" she pressed, making sure to emphasize the word *target*.

His lips came together and twitched a couple of times before he replied. "They'll be released when we file with the SEC." He glanced over at his Chief Financial Officer, who was hunched over a pad of paper, busily writing. "The numbers are still being netted right now."

The CFO looked up from his scribbling to nod in agreement.

"If they're still being tallied, how do you know what your earnings are?" Anne looked back and forth between the CEO and CFO, silently observing her. "How do you *know* you've met your targets?"

The CEO crossed his arms and gave an exasperated sigh. "Because we know our positions on a daily basis and are capable of doing simple math. We're traders, for God's sake."

"Exactly," Anne replied, feeling all eyes in the room watching her, "which is why—"

"Look," he cut her off with a sharp sweep of his hand. "I'm just saying that we're holding off on releasing detailed financial information until we've finished our accounting." With every word, his tone became more condescending. "That shouldn't be too hard to understand."

Anne blinked and slowly sank back down into her chair. She hadn't intended to antagonize the guy. Her firm had made a lot of money by both underwriting Energix's stock and restructuring various pieces of the company's debt. The last thing she wanted was to throw a wrench into that relationship. But at the same time, it was odd that no financial information was being released at what was supposed to be a quarterly investor meeting. Even odder was that none of the other analysts in the room seemed to object.

"If there are no more questions, I think we're done here." He stepped away from the microphone and headed over to confer with his CFO. Immediately, the room erupted in a beehive of activity, analysts and investors streaming in every direction. She grabbed her pocketbook and Burberry trench coat hanging off the back of the chair and joined the throng headed toward the exit.

"Good job sticking to your guns back there," a silver-haired man addressed her as they stood waiting for the next elevator to arrive. "Richard Fernsby always struts around like he owns the place, and most people just accept whatever he throws in their general direction." He smiled at her. "It was entertaining to watch him squirm."

Anne studied the man for a moment as she thought about how to reply. "Was that meeting typical? Lots of hype? Exceedingly light on details?"

He chuckled. "They're always like that. But in the end, Energix always comes through with great returns. Reliably. It's a total winner." The elevator dinged, and the doors began to open. "It makes my investors happy, which keeps my boss happy. Pretty hard to argue with that."

Indeed. She had just seen how hard.

* * *

"Nobody except for you will even remember that he spoke to you like that," her co-worker Jennifer said confidently.

They were sitting in Anne's new office, which consisted of little more than a desk and two small chairs in a cramped space. Nonetheless, it was a big step up from the cubicle she had inhabited previously while supporting the trading desk. A large, floor-to-ceiling window let in plenty of cheery light. Most importantly, she could shut the door when she needed to concentrate or wanted a bit of privacy.

"And anyway, everyone knows he's a total jerk."

The man certainly had a reputation for being ruthless. One of the first things he had done after becoming CEO of Energix was to fire the entire management team and replace it with people he knew from his MBA days at the Harvard Business School.

Jennifer flipped her long, wavy brown hair behind her back and rested her elbow on one side of the chair. "But even if Richard Fernsby is a mealy-mouthed little toad, the company he runs is a rock star in the financial community. Energix's stock price has climbed steadily for the last few years. They must be doing something right."

Something right? Or something that simply satisfied the short-term appetites of Wall Street analysts and traders? Something that might not necessarily play well in the long run.

"Maybe," Anne allowed, "but I don't know of any other financial institution that refuses to provide a balance sheet and earnings statement at their quarterly investor meetings."

"Agreed." Jennifer leaned over to pull a Hershey's chocolate bar out of the side of her bag and snapped it in two, placing one half on the desk in front of Anne and peeling the wrapper off the remaining piece.

Anne nodded toward the chocolate. "Thanks. The really strange thing is that no one else questioned him about it. The other analysts blithely accepted his arm-waving statements about how Energix is generating huge sales without any understanding of how they're actually doing it."

"Fernsby probably doesn't want his competitors to know the secret of Energix's success. Kind of like a trade secret. And as long as he consistently produces great returns, then everybody wins. It sounds like everyone's bought in. Except for you."

"As an investor, I want to make sure I understand what's driving the profits. And it's also important to know which sectors of the business are losing money and, therefore, being propped up by profits elsewhere. Without financial statements, the whole thing is a black box."

"It's a trust-me story." Jennifer took a bite of chocolate.

"Which works as long as something doesn't go wrong," Anne snorted. "Next thing you know, shareholders may find that their investments have vanished." She flung her fingers wide. "Poof! Like smoke into thin air."

Jennifer laughed. "That's not going to happen with a huge company like Energix. But it's possible their growth could slow down, in which case you might like to invest in a different company that has more potential."

"Or a nicer CEO."

Jennifer wrinkled her nose. "Probably not something that should enter the equation." The smile on her face disappeared, and her tone became serious. "You know that we recently helped Energix restructure some of their debt. Right?"

Of course Anne knew. That was part of what made this whole situation so stressful. Spencer Brothers had earned tons of commissions on deals with this company. It had been extremely lucrative for all involved. She nodded. "But my job is to manage this fund and if the stock isn't likely to perform, I need to dump it." Anne took a small bite and let the chocolate melt in her mouth.

"Absolutely. But at the same time, be careful. Make sure you have all of the facts. He has a lot of friends around here."

"Not just here." As Anne said the words, the realization of what was bothering her suddenly became clear.

Jennifer gave her a quizzical look. "What do you mean?"

Anne drew back in her chair, casting about for how to respond. She didn't want to explain that her fiancé's parents belonged to the same country club as the Fernsbys, that they often attended parties together in the Hamptons where they both had summer homes, and that his sister was best friends with Richard Fernsby's daughter. But as she saw Jennifer studying her, she knew she had to say something. "Alex's parents travel in the same social circles as Richard Fernsby and his wife."

In fact, it was only a matter of time before she, too, crossed paths with the man socially.

"Your Alex?" Jennifer pointed at the ceiling, a reference to his office five floors above them in the legal department of Spencer Brothers.

Anne took a deep breath and nodded.

"Oh." Jennifer's eyes widened. "That complicates matters."

It did, indeed. Not only would Richard Fernsby and his elegant wife be attending her future sister-in-law's wedding in one month's time, but his daughter was the maid of honor.

3

Paige's Bridal Shower

The Hamptons

June 1990

Anne took one look at the other women in the room and knew she should have chosen a different dress to wear, something softer, with a hint of romance, rather than the straight-lined, navy shift she had purchased from Ann Taylor.

"I was wondering when you'd get here," Paige bubbled warmly. As the guest of honor, she was sitting alone on the couch, gifts arrayed on the table in front of her, with a second pile on the floor nearby. She motioned with her champagne glass. "Girls, this is my brother's girlfriend—" she caught herself, "I mean fiancée, Anne. She works at Spencer Brothers."

"So that's how you met," said a cheerful woman leaning against an expansive stone fireplace that anchored one end of the room. She wore a pink floral dress with a string of large pearls around her neck, a triple-strand pearl bracelet, and matching pearl earrings. "Are you a lawyer, too?"

Anne shook her head. "Portfolio manager. For one of the funds."

"Oh." She looked surprised. "A number cruncher."

"She can help Alex manage his finances," a woman's voice deepened by alcohol and cigarettes floated across the room. Anne turned to see a tanned, athletic woman standing near the windows that, along with some French doors, spanned the entire back side of the room. "He's always hated anything that has to do with math. And horses. Has he told you about the time he went riding in Central Park?"

No doubt this was the girl Alex had dated briefly in high school. He had described her as an avid equestrian. Even for this party, she was dressed like a rider, wearing a plaid blazer, button-down shirt, tan & white leggings, and knee-high leather boots.

Anne smiled. "I understand it didn't go very well."

Horse-Lover giggled with what sounded almost like a neigh. "That's one way of putting it."

"Didn't he get thrown," said a woman with an unusually wide mouth and two rows of blindingly white, perfect teeth, "and break his arm?"

"Just his tailbone," Horse-Lover said dismissively.

"And his pride," yet another added with a theatrical shudder as she walked toward Anne with a glass in hand. "Evidently, he landed in a big pile of manure."

Quite hard, in his version of the tale, after the horse had reared up, startled by a passing jogger who had emerged unexpectedly from behind a tree.

"Mimosa?"

Anne nodded and met the outstretched hand.

"I'm Käthe, by the way. Marketing executive by day. Purveyor of fine food and wine at night. And steadfast Maid of Honor."

The hostess. And daughter of Energix CEO, Richard Fernsby.

Anne gestured toward the room. "Such a lovely home."

"I'll be sure to tell my mother you said so."

Perhaps it was the diamond studded earrings, matching diamond pendant, and diamond tennis bracelet that elevated the outfit. Or perhaps it was just the way Käthe stood that exuded an air of someone who knew she had everything she could ever want and firmly believed she was entitled to it. All Anne knew was that the two of them wore dresses very similar in style, and yet Käthe looked considerably more polished. And confident.

"So, when are you and Alex walking down the aisle?" Pearls-Galore plopped herself down in a nearby wingback chair.

"We haven't set a date."

"Don't wait too long," Perfect-Teeth warned. "Someone else might try to grab him."

"God knows, enough people have tried." Käthe winked. "We'll have to hear how you actually succeeded. But first things first." She turned toward the bride-to-be and waved in the general direction of the coffee table. "Are you ever going to open these presents?"

Paige leaned forward and lifted a small turquoise box tied with white ribbon and gave it a tiny shake. "Someone knows I love Tiffany's."

A woman wearing a lavender Laura Ashley dress, matching shoes, and headband frowned. "There's no card." She had taken a seat nearby, ready to keep a list of who had given Paige what.

"It's from my mother." Käthe took a large sip of her drink.

"She shouldn't have!" Paige smiled broadly while at the same time shaking her head. "She already gave me that beautiful teapot at the April party."

The first shower. The one with at least thirty people, including many of Paige's mother's friends. The one Anne hadn't been invited to because the family was still blissfully unaware that she and Alex were engaged. His mother had talked about the event endlessly afterwards, a constant reminder that Anne was nothing more than a two-bit player floating in the periphery of their exciting lives.

"Oh, you know how she is." Käthe looked fondly at her best friend. "You're like a second daughter to her. She's so happy for you."

Anne felt a pang of envy, as if she had been physically stabbed in the heart. It would be nice to be accepted like that by Alex's mother. Instead, the tall, commanding British woman had looked visibly shocked by the news that Anne and Alex had decided to tie the knot, going so far as to pull him aside and suggest he reconsider.

"Open it!" Pearls-Galore began to reach for the box and then retracted her hand, evidently catching herself. "I'm dying to see what it is."

As the ribbon was being removed, Horse-Lover sidled up next to Anne.

"Do you think you'll get married in the Hamptons as well?"

Anne waved her hands helplessly and smiled. "No idea." Short. Hopefully, not perceived as curt, but definitely discouraging further discussion on the topic. Paige had made it clear she didn't want Anne and Alex's engagement to steal her thunder and Anne wanted to do what she could to keep Alex's sister on her side.

"But surely—"

"We just got engaged a few weeks ago."

In fact, that was the only reason Anne had been invited to this shower at all. Paige had insisted that Anne, as a future sister-in-law, come to this event being hosted by the bridal party, presumably with the idea that it would help induct her into their greater social circle.

Horse-Lover leaned toward her and whispered. "I gather it was quite a surprise to the family. Paige says they had no idea how serious things were between the two of you."

That was an understatement. Alex had deliberately kept his parents in the dark, making it crystal clear that he did not feel any need to obtain their approval.

"Are you pregnant too?"

"What?" Anne stared at the woman's sly smile for a moment, bristling at the implication that Alex might only be marrying her because he felt obligated, but also surprised at the directness of the question.

Horse-Lover raised both hands in a show of surrender. "We've all been kind of wondering..."

Anne shook her head slowly, "No."

In retrospect, she realized the question hadn't come completely out of left field. Paige's announcement that she was pregnant a few weeks earlier had set off a furor about how to best time her dress fitting for the upcoming wedding. It wouldn't be a huge reach for her friends to wonder if Alex had found himself in a similar predicament.

"Hmmm." Horse-Lover pursed her lips as if she didn't quite believe her.

Despite all of the social training this woman had undoubtedly had, and the pretense she made of engaging in the art of polite conversation, she was surprisingly rude. And a snob. Anne waited until Horse-Lover had averted her gaze before looking over at Paige who was holding up a silver baby spoon for all to admire.

"It's lovely," Anne managed to say.

As the conversation turned toward wedding plans, Anne looked out the window toward the ocean in the distance, where the sun glistened on the water. Both Käthe and Paige had spent their high school summers in this Long Island seaside enclave, playing tennis, sailing, and hanging out on long stretches of private beach. Anne had always felt financially advantaged as the daughter of a medical doctor, and yet she could only imagine a lifetime of privilege like this.

"On Cape Cod?" Anne heard Pearls-Galore exclaim.

"Well, I'm going to be selling some of my Energix stock next week and need to figure out what to do with the proceeds." Käthe began ticking off the assets she already owned or had access to (the so-called cottage in the Hamptons where this party was being held, a penthouse apartment in the city with fabulous skyline views, her parent's ski place in Vail, and their swanky home in Short Hills). "I don't know. I was thinking that maybe a secluded retreat on Martha's Vineyard or Nantucket would be nice."

"The perfect romantic getaway," Horse-Lover said with a conspiratorial smile. "But why are you selling? Energix is such a great investment."

Käthe gave a casual shrug. "I don't think it's a good idea to have all my eggs in one basket."

Anne agreed entirely and might not have thought much about it except for the comment that came immediately after.

"My father's the one who suggested I reduce my holdings. That I diversify. He's gotten rid of a ton of his Energix stock recently, and I'm pretty sure he plans to continue selling more."

Whoa. Anne felt her nerves go taut. Why would the CEO of a company that's supposedly going to increase in share value spectacularly by year-end be dumping his stock? And, even more concerning, telling his daughter to do the same?

"What about a flat in London? Or Paris?" Paige paused in unwrapping

15

her gifts. "My parents love their home in the Cotswolds. It gives them a comfortable base for traveling around Europe."

Anne had seen pictures of the ivy-covered stone house nestled in the English countryside, less than two hours by train from London. In fact, she and Alex were planning to spend a week there themselves, at the end of the summer, touring nearby castles and rambling on footpaths through quaint villages and grassy hills.

Käthe leaned forward as if bringing them in on a great secret. "My father has his eye on an apartment in the heart of Paris that my mother's really excited about. Plus, he's talking about buying a luxury yacht that's staffed with a permanent crew."

Anne watched everyone nod as if this were an everyday occurrence.

"He wants to cruise around the Pacific for a month or two sometime next year. I'm thinking that if I ever get married, I could have a beach wedding in the Virgin Islands and then take my guests sailing around the Caribbean for a few days."

"That would be so much fun!" Pearls-Galore exclaimed.

It would, indeed. But much more intriguing to Anne was how much stock the Diamond Goddess's father must have dumped in order to support all of these new purchases. It had to have been worth millions of dollars. Many millions.

Käthe's face clouded over. "I just don't know when he'll actually be able to take any vacation. We've lost a couple of senior managers in the last few weeks, which has made him so stressed. My mother says he's hardly sleeping."

Anne took a deep breath and tried to look nonchalant. None of this had been disclosed at the shareholder meeting on Friday.

"But this morning, she told me they're close to hiring someone who should be a great fit. And they've promoted a couple of people internally who will quickly get things back under control. In fact—" She locked eyes with Paige and then raised her glass in a toast, "Kevin was promoted yesterday as a result of some of the changes, so it's working out really well for some people."

Kevin? As in the groom? The guy soon to be married to Paige?

Anne glanced over at the couch and saw Paige positively beaming. "He's going to be the right-hand man to the CFO. I'm so thrilled for him!"

As the bridal party twittered away in excitement about Kevin's promotion, Anne looked around the room feeling numb. The more she learned about Energix, the more concerned she became. With high-level managers selling their stock and key senior people resigning left and right, it was even more urgent that she understand the company's financial situation. First thing Monday morning, she would get her hands on the most recent financial statements.

"Anne?" She was abruptly jerked out of her thoughts.

"So cute!"

"Where did you get it?"

"It's Royal Doulton, right?"

Paige was holding up the Peter Rabbit plate, cup, and saucer that Anne had brought as a shower gift. She felt a wave of relief. At least her present had turned out to be a winner.

* * *

"How long has Kevin worked at Energix?" Anne asked after she and Alex had returned to the apartment they shared in the city.

He paused in emptying the dishwasher. "About ten years. Before that he did a stint in investment banking. Down in Atlanta of all places."

Not exactly the financial capital of the world, but one could be a big fish in a little pond and use it as a stepping-stone, ultimately ending up in senior management at a major corporation like Energix.

She pulled a few more carrots out of the bag and began chopping. "But he has an MBA?"

"Oh yes." There was a loud clunk as Alex set a pile of plates in the cabinet. "From Harvard, of course."

Of course. Richard Fernsby's alma mater. The sole place from which he recruited people to serve on his senior management tcam.

She added the carrots to the other vegetables sizzling in the pan. "Evidently, he got a big promotion last week and now reports directly to the CFO. I had no idea he was so senior."

"Kevin's climbed through the ranks fairly quickly. But don't forget, he's at least ten years older than Paige."

Twelve, to be exact, which meant he was fourteen years older than Anne and Alex. Thanks to random chit-chat during the bridal shower, Anne had learned his age (forty-four), marital history (divorced with three children, after a decade-long marriage that had ended bitterly), and favorite drink (dry martini on the rocks, although he also enjoyed an occasional beer with the boys). And, of course, she now also knew that he was involved in the financial accounting of Energix, reporting directly to the CFO, a corporation that she was evaluating.

Alex set two plates on the island, next to the wine glasses and cutlery. "My father mentioned something about him getting a huge chunk of stock as part of a new job. It sounds like Paige is planning to spend it on a lavish house in Short Hills."

Another senior executive selling his stock? Although in his case, perhaps it wasn't significant given that he was about to marry, and his prospective wife was already expecting.

"Makes sense, I guess." She added some Thai seasoning to the mix and gave everything a big stir. "Once the baby arrives, she'd probably prefer to be closer to your parents."

"Hopefully, not too close." He snapped the dishwasher door shut and pulled a bottle of wine off the rack. "She might find it difficult to maintain her autonomy."

Especially with your mother. Anne watched him fuss with the corkscrew as he began to open the bottle. Usually, he was a master with the gadget, but tonight he seemed to struggle with it, as if his mind wasn't fully on the task.

"Finally!" He put the corkscrew away and began pouring the first glass.

"Is something bothering you?"

He finished pouring the second glass of wine and then turned to face her. "My father mentioned that Paige and Kevin signed a prenuptial agreement last week. He thinks you and I should do the same."

Anne had been wondering when an idea like this would be floated. Once it became clear that Alex was determined to proceed with getting married, she figured his parents' next move would focus on protecting his assets. From her. The street urchin who had somehow tricked him into marriage. Probably by casting a magic spell.

"Given that this is the second time around for Kevin," she began.

"Exactly. He comes with children, alimony, and all the rest." Alex paused and bit his lip before moving toward the fundamental issue at stake. "And Paige has significant assets."

At last. He was finally ready to address the elephant in the room. The trust fund that had been set up for his sister when she was first born. And the similarly hefty one that had been set up for him. It was a topic Anne and Alex had deftly danced around in the past.

Until now.

"With all of that in the background, I can see where it makes sense for the two of them to have a legal agreement that spells things out," Alex said. "But in our case..."

The phone rang loudly and insistently, causing them both to start.

Damn! She felt a rush of adrenaline. She wanted to hear his thoughts on the prenuptial agreement as it pertained to the two of them. As a lawyer, he probably would be in favor of the idea. But as her fiancé, he had made it clear that his family's money was something he never wanted to lean on. He didn't want it to govern his decisions or negatively intrude on his life. Most importantly, he didn't want to ever let his parents use it as a lever to control him.

"The answering machine can get it." Alex picked up the glasses of wine and handed one to her.

She nodded and took a sip. A rich red with just a hint of fruit. It was surprisingly bracing.

"I told my father I'd think about it."

Her legs felt oddly heavy, as if she'd been on her feet all day. She took another sip of wine and leaned against the counter. In a flash, she realized that she felt let down because he was undecided on the matter. On some level

19

she had hoped he felt sufficiently confident in their love for one another that he would unilaterally reject the idea. Dismiss a legal instrument as unnecessary. But, of course, that wasn't very realistic.

"Okay," she said evenly, not wanting to betray any hint of her disappointment. She had no intention of pressuring him in any direction on the subject.

"But honestly, there's no question in my mind."

Nor was there in hers. She had no designs on his money and was willing to sign a prenuptial agreement. She just didn't like what the document symbolized. Potential failure. Anger. Heartbreak. And divorce. She loved him with the very fiber of her being and couldn't imagine the marriage failing. But if it did, she would pick up the pieces and move on. Without him. And without his financial help.

"Okay," she said again, resigned to the inevitable. She'd sign the damn piece of paper, and hopefully, his money would never be an issue.

Alex looked earnestly at her. "The only reason I told my father I'd think about it was to hold him off. As far as I'm concerned, we don't need one, and I don't want one. What do you think?"

She took a deep breath and studied him carefully. "Are you sure? Because I don't want your parents' money, and I'm happy to let them know that."

He gave a single, firm nod. "Case closed."

A waft of Thai spices reminded her that their dinner was getting cold. "We should probably eat."

"But first—" he clinked his wineglass against hers. "No more talk about my fusspot family or anything related to work. It's still the weekend. For a few more hours at least."

"Deal." Energix could wait until she was back in the office. Couldn't it?

4

Red Flags

New York City

The day after the Bridal Shower

First thing Monday morning, Anne ran up to the corporate library without even bothering to take off her coat.

"As you probably know, we subscribe to a service that provides us with all corporate-related SEC filings on a monthly basis," the librarian told her. "We got the latest set last week. I'm not sure if our intern has finished filing them. That subscription dumps more paper on us than Alaska gets snow."

Anne tried not to fidget as the woman leisurely stood up, cleaned a smudge off of her glasses, and then lumbered slowly over to a large file cabinet near the corner.

"Hmmm." A frown creased the librarian's brow. "I don't see anything from the last two months here for Energix."

"Is it possible—"

"Let me check her desk."

Exactly what Anne had been about to suggest. Based on what Käthe had said at the bridal shower, Richard Fernsby should have filed an SEC Form 4, listing the amount and price of any shares he sold. It was a form that was required to be filed within two days of any stock transaction by a company insider, such as a CEO, CFO, or other senior manager.

"My goodness," the librarian muttered. "I could have sworn—"

"Mrs. Beasley?" A young woman strode toward them, her eyes heavily ringed with black eyeliner and spiky hair dyed a bright shade of red. "What are you—"

"The SEC filings." The librarian squinted through her glasses. "I thought you had finished putting them away, but—"

Punk-Rocker shook her head. "Almost, but not quite. I still have the last two months remaining." She reached around the stout older woman and pulled the bottom drawer open. "Which company are you looking for?"

When Anne returned to her office a few minutes later, she had a small pile of documents firmly in hand. She closed the door, kicked off her shoes, and began studying them in earnest.

Four large stock sales in the last two months by Richard Fernsby totaling $12.6 million. And those numbers didn't include stock sold by the CFO ($8.2 million), two executive vice presidents ($5.4 million and $7.3 million), and the CFO's secretary ($1.1 million). *Seriously?* Anne remembered the young, pretty secretary sitting near the CFO during the quarterly investor meeting. She had worn bright red stilettos that matched a very short skirt. Every time the woman got up to do anything, it seemed like the majority of (male) heads in the room would turn to follow her. *Ugh.*

Anne leaned back in her chair and put her hands behind her head. The red flags on Energix were starting to wave wildly, but she knew she had to slow down, study the remaining documents, and hold off on jumping to conclusions. In addition to the technical analysis of the numbers, there were political ramifications to consider. A large sale of stock by her fund could jeopardize millions of dollars in commissions her firm had enjoyed as an underwriter for Energix. Her colleagues who profited from those transactions would be furious. Not that she would allow political considerations to stop her from acting, but she needed to be absolutely certain that owning the stock, in fact, posed a large risk to her fund before pulling the trigger. And that the benefit to her fund outweighed the cost of lost business.

She set the stock sale forms to the side and pulled out the company's financial statements from the prior year, their so-called 10K filings, another required document that all public corporations provide annually to the SEC. As she became engrossed in the pages, her morning tea grew cold beside her.

"How was the bridal shower?" Her co-worker, Jennifer, opened the door without knocking and glided into the chair opposite Anne's desk. "Were they all a bunch of snobs?"

Anne hesitated, not wanting to divert her attention from the documents sitting in front of her, but also feeling a desire to vent. "They live in an alternate universe," she replied. "No concept of what things are like for the rest of us."

Jennifer grimaced. "Can't say I'm surprised."

"The cottage," Anne made air quotes, "is a gabled, English-country-style manor house hidden behind a tall boxwood hedge. It's very private and secluded with a spectacular view of the ocean."

"Wow. I'll bet the landscaping—"

"It's beautiful. Flowers everywhere. Stone steps leading to a tennis court on one side and a pool on the other. Big, tall trees judiciously scattered around the property. The kind of thing you see in Architectural Digest."

"How about the party itself?"

Jennifer's eyes widened when she learned who had hosted the event. "Hang on. You didn't say anything about Richard Fernsby's daughter being the maid of honor. No wonder you were so rattled after the investor meeting last week."

Anne sank into her chair. "I didn't want to make a big deal about it."

"That makes no sense!" Jennifer sounded exasperated. "You're going to have to face these people again and again at various social events. Of course it's a big deal! You should have told me. I can't give good advice without complete information." She leaned back in her chair and crossed her arms. "Is there anything else I should know?"

Strictly speaking, the answer was no. Jennifer worked in a completely different department. But she was also a trusted colleague and friend, someone whose opinion Anne valued, often providing a great sounding board.

"I've been studying some of Energix's recent SEC filings."

"And?"

"Take a look at this weird disclosure on related party transactions. At the bottom of the page, printed in the tiniest font ever."

Jennifer squinted through her glasses and began to read.

"In 1990, Energix entered into a series of financial transactions with Cayman Islands LP, a private investment company that focuses on energy-related investments." She looked up briefly. "Energix is doing deals with an energy investment company in the Caribbean?"

Anne nodded toward the document. "Keep reading."

"In these transactions, Energix sold approximately $520 million of assets."

Jennifer looked up again, a puzzled expression on her face. "That's a lot of money for some no-name outfit in the Caribbean to lay their grubby little hands on. Any idea where those dollars came from?"

Anne most certainly did, and it was something she found rather concerning. "They got a loan from Energix. From what I can tell, the Caribbean company has no assets of its own."

"Whoa!" Jennifer knitted her brows, her face a show of consternation. "So, they paid Energix with their own money? It's really just a paper transaction, then."

Anne nodded, her lips pursed. "And not only that, a senior executive of Energix is the managing partner of this Caribbean firm. In effect, Energix is doing business with itself."

Jennifer did a double-take. "Wait a minute. So Energix is selling a half billion of assets to some Fly-By-Night in the Caribbean that's controlled by one of their own executives. And this same executive is borrowing money from Energix in order to make the purchase in the first place? Have I missed anything?"

"At the very end, it says Energix booked a $120 million profit on the transaction."

"You've got to be kidding." Jennifer shook her head. "That means this Caribbean outfit paid way too much for what they got. And yet, the senior executive in charge of the deal had to have known it was way overpriced. Why would he—" she rolled her eyes, "I assume it's a he?"

Anne shrugged. "Probably." The only professional woman she'd seen associated with the firm was Richard Fernsby's own daughter, tucked away in the marketing department, light years away from the core business itself. All other people of the feminine persuasion had been young, attractive secretaries.

"Why would anyone in their right mind go forward with the transaction? It doesn't make financial sense."

Exactly what Anne had been wondering before Jennifer appeared at her door.

"Unless…" Jennifer paused. "Could it be a kickback to the executive in charge of the business?"

"How? The Caribbean company is left completely in the red. The only winner in this deal is Energix."

She shook her head. "Which leaves us where we started. It makes no sense for a private investment company to agree to these terms."

"Unless this no-name operation isn't real," Anne said slowly, the idea taking shape as she spoke the words out loud.

"What do you mean?"

"What if it's a shell corporation, set up for the sole purpose of giving Energix a place to shift poorly performing assets?" She paused and then finished flatly. "And their rosy financial picture is just an illusion, created by a series of financial manipulations."

"That would mean that the whole thing is just an accounting trick to make Energix's finances look better than they really are."

"Exactly," Anne bit her lip. "They're using a sham corporation to *beautify* their balance sheet. No cash ever flowed from this Caribbean company to Energix because there were never any real transactions. They were just numbers on a ledger. And that $120 million in profits that Energix booked?

It's all made up as well."

"Wow." Jennifer made a face. "They could be hiding huge losses behind that Caribbean curtain."

"You think?"

"How much Energix stock does your fund own?"

Anne slumped forward onto her desk with a dramatic sigh. "Probably time to run this by Alex."

It was times like this when it was handy to be engaged to one of the firm's corporate lawyers.

* * *

"You have to admit it's pretty clever," he said as they were eating dinner that evening.

"But is it legal?"

Alex picked up his wine glass and smiled. "That depends."

Anne rolled her eyes. Lawyers could never answer a question with a simple yes or no.

He took a sip and leaned back in his chair. "There's nothing inherently unlawful about selling or transferring assets from one business to another."

"But if they're using this Caribbean outfit to misrepresent their profits—" Anne cut in, anxious to get to the heart of the issue.

"That's the concerning part. It suggests an intent to deceive." He took a bite of his steak.

"Which is the definition of securities fraud." Anne stood up to refill her water glass. "Right?"

"If they are deliberately dumping rubbish assets into this Caribbean company to hide financial problems with Energix, then yes, a case could be made. On the other hand, they might have some perfectly legitimate reason for making the transfers."

"Like what?"

Alex speared several asparagus tips onto his fork. "Perhaps they're doing business with a government that requires they invest a certain dollar amount within the country. Or maybe they're taking advantage of a tax loophole of some sort. Without more information, there's no way to know."

Anne pulled the rolls out of the oven and carried them back to the table along with her water. "Several of the company's top executives have also dumped a ton of Energix stock recently, including Fernsby."

He grabbed a roll from the plate and began buttering it. "Which could be nothing more than a rebalancing of portfolios. Perfectly innocent. Or, it's possible they know something and are cashing out while they still can, in which case it would constitute insider trading."

"Fernsby told Käthe to lighten her load as well."

Alex looked up sharply. "How do you know that?"

"She mentioned it at the bridal shower. She's thinking about using the proceeds to buy a cottage for herself on Cape Cod."

His lips curved up in a wry smile. "To hide her latest boy-toy from her parents, I imagine."

"Could be." Anne shrugged, not wanting to get off on a conversation about the men in Käthe's enchanted life. "All I know for sure is that I'm seeing one red flag after another, which makes me think that Energix might be in fairly serious financial trouble. Or at least headed that way."

"Objection, your Honor. Speculation."

She raised her arms in a mock gesture of frustration. "My whole job is to speculate based on tidbits picked up here and there. And then to invest accordingly."

"True." Alex ran his fingers through his sandy brown hair. "And taken together, I agree the whole thing sounds dodgy. I'm just trying to wrap my head around the idea that Richard would knowingly participate in a scheme like this. It just doesn't fit with his character."

"Because he's so scrupulously honest?" She instantly regretted the sarcastic tone of her voice when she saw the look of surprise on Alex's face.

"Because he's the type of guy who likes to win fair and square," Alex said calmly, in a lawyerly-reasoning sort of way. "I've played tennis with him numerous times over the years. If there's even a question that his shot is over the line, he's the first one to refuse the point." He popped the remaining piece of steak into his mouth and began chewing.

"I'm not sure that good sportsmanship necessarily translates into business integrity," Anne said slowly, picking her words more carefully. "They have different stakes. In one case, you risk losing friends. In the other, you're grappling for money."

"I don't agree." Alex leaned back and took another sip of wine. "We're talking about someone who's ultra-competitive. Absolutely hates to lose. After missing a shot one time, he threw his racket down so hard it broke. He'd never give away a point just to make someone happy. Or because he wants to look good. He does it because he wants to win honestly. That doesn't seem at all like the type of person who would *cook the books*."

"Maybe the fact that he's a family friend—" Anne began.

"He's more than that." Alex set his glass down. "He was like a father to me the year we moved across the pond."

The year Alex was kicked out of two private schools in quick succession and had to enroll in the local, public high school, much to his parents' chagrin.

He fixed his steel blue eyes on her. "Do you remember the wild beach party I told you about? In the Hamptons?"

"The one with the illegal bonfire? And fireworks that were reported as gunfire?"

"Yeah." He grimaced. "That one."

"What does that have to do with Richard Fernsby?"

"He's the one who bailed me out."

"What? Why didn't your parents—"

"They were in England, taking care of my Grandfather's estate. I'll never forget the loud echo as the cell door banged shut, and I realized I was stuck in a space the size of my closet."

"What about everyone else?"

"They all ran."

Not that Anne thought it was a great idea for a bunch of drunk teenagers to wake up their neighbors at all hours of the night, but it didn't seem fair that Alex was the only one who had been caught and faced any consequences.

"Why didn't you run, too?"

"Because I'd sprained my ankle the week before, playing soccer."

He had told her the story over dinner one evening, when recounting what he called his *lost year*. The year he turned fifteen, moved to the States, and found numerous ways to get into trouble. But it had been a while, so the details were fuzzy, and he had referred to Richard as a family friend, so she hadn't made the connection with Energix. Until now.

"When the constables arrived, I tried to make light of the situation, thinking they would let me off with a warning." He shook his head. "But the open can of beer in my hand, in addition to the million empties scattered on the sand nearby, didn't help matters. Next thing I knew, I was in handcuffs."

"Seems a bit harsh."

"That's what Richard said."

"Hmmm." Evidently, Richard Fernsby wasn't entirely heartless, despite what his detractors in the media occasionally said.

"He drove over in the middle of the night, as soon as he heard. Said he thought the police were being overzealous. And then he told me a few stories of things he did when he was a teenager."

"Wait. Is he the one who arranged for the charges to disappear as well?"

Alex gave a cryptic smile.

Anne threw both hands up in the air. "How did he manage that?"

"He had a lawyer-friend who got a clerk to pull the case from the court docket shortly before I was scheduled to appear before the judge."

And poof. In an instant, history had been erased. It was as if the whole thing had never happened. Thanks to Richard Fernsby, Alex's record had remained squeaky clean.

He must have seen the look on her face.

"I know what you're thinking. It sounds like Richard isn't above bending the rules."

Anne twisted her wineglass back and forth in her fingers. "You have to admit—"

"Helping a wayward high school kid is completely different than misrepresenting the financial condition of a Fortune 500 company."

She let go of the glass and put her hands up in surrender. "We're getting off on a tangent. Even if Richard Fernsby has the ethical constitution of a saint, it's possible that someone else at Energix is fiddling with the numbers, in which case I should dump the stock as soon as possible."

"And if you're wrong?"

"I'll miss out on huge returns." She paused and took a deep breath. "And it could cost Spencer Brothers millions in underwriting business."

"I'm glad I'm not in your shoes." Alex placed the cork on top of the wine bottle and gave it a firm tap. "But that's why they pay you the big bucks."

Not exactly. She was paid well, but not nearly as well as the previous fund manager. She knew, because he had left a pile of salary stubs kicking around in the drawer when he quit to start his own investment firm. She arched an eyebrow.

"I know the guy you replaced made a bit—"

She cut him off with a single sweep of her hand. "Let's not get into it." As one of the first women to be put in a high-level money management position at Spencer Brothers, she was a trailblazer. And an anomaly. They both knew she would have to do everything ten times better than her predecessor in order to be paid the same amount and taken seriously. When she took the assignment, she had made a deal with herself to simply do the best job she could and let the chips fall where they may. Her mother's words echoed in her mind: *never let the fear of failure drive your decision-making.* And instantly, she knew what she was going to do.

5

The Big Dump

New York City

The next day

"Sold. At \$97 per share." Anne took a deep breath. After a long night of tossing and turning, she had marched into the office and placed the order. The Centaurus Fund no longer owned any Energix stock. At all.

She felt a small flutter in her chest. The assistant taking her order had sounded surprised. *Are you sure?* Anne looked out the windows of her office at the Hudson River twenty floors below, wondering whether there was any chance she had made the wrong call. Perhaps missed something crucial? She started reviewing the evidence in her mind. The ruminations continued until her secretary knocked on the door and reported that Peter Eckert, head of the Fixed Income division, wanted to meet with her.

Immediately.

She slipped her feet into her pumps, stood up and re-tucked her shirt so that it lay smoothly below her skirt, and headed toward the elevator.

"You can't be serious." The senior vice president waved his hands dismissively after she confirmed the sale. "Energix is *the* largest seller of gas in North America. And you just dumped their stock?" He sighed loudly, cocked his head to the side, and began studying the stapler sitting on his desk. "It's on everyone's buy list." He enunciated the words slowly and precisely, making it abundantly clear he thought she was a total idiot. "Everyone's."

Out of the corner of her eye, Anne saw the head trader, Nick Angelini, standing stock-still by the large glass window that overlooked the trading floor. A fidgety person by nature, he normally paced about the room, doing his best to wear out the carpet. Instead, he was simply staring at her.

"That's true." She straightened her shoulders and shifted her position so that her back was firmly supported by the chair. "But something's off about their profit statements."

Peter's head shot up, no longer focused on the stapler, his eyebrows leading the action. "Off?" he barked. "Maybe you just missed something. Did that ever occur to you?"

His comment sailed straight toward her fear of having made a critical mistake. She felt a bolt of adrenaline course through her body as she began to imagine her fledgling career as a fund manager destroyed by a single, bad decision. Everything she had worked for, wiped away in an instant. She fought to keep her voice even and her demeanor calm. "Let me lay out what I'm seeing."

"Okay." He waved his hand in a limp, resigned manner.

She decided to start with the positives. "Energix is regarded as innovative and highly profitable. Everyone loves the stock because they consistently meet their earnings targets. In fact, they often beat them."

"That's why I own it," he said, a smug smirk on his face.

Peter owned Energix stock? Personally? No wonder he was being such a jerk. The panic within her began to subside. "But those earnings may not be real."

Nick took several quick steps toward Peter's desk and leaned forward, his six-foot frame towering over her. It felt like he was sucking up all of the air. "What are you talking about? Their financial statements have been approved by the auditors and filed with the SEC."

Did he own it personally as well? Or was he just concerned about the firm's exposure? Either way, these guys were clearly reacting more strongly, more viscerally, than she had expected when she first walked into the room. She picked her words carefully. "I'm not saying they're doing anything illegal, but their choice of accounting is *unusual.*"

"What does that mean?" Nick was now studying her face as intently as Peter had been studying the stapler.

"It's very aggressive. They're assuming that oil and gas prices will shoot up really high in the future, and they're booking those expected profits today, even though they haven't actually realized them. It's called mark-to-market accounting."

Nick crossed his arms and straightened up. "How come no one else is concerned about this?"

Because they haven't bothered to look, she felt like shouting at his sneering face. *Like you, they've been blinded by the meteoric rise in stock price.* Instead, she shrugged coolly, playing the part of the dispassionate financial analyst. "It's buried pretty deeply in the tiny footnotes at the back. I'm not sure how many people have noticed." She paused to look at Peter, who was picking lint off of his sleeve. *Was he even listening to her?*

Anne cleared her throat and continued. "Which takes me to the next thing I find concerning. Energix is an energy trading company. For all intents and purposes, that makes them similar to an energy hedge fund, and yet they earned a measly 7% return on capital."

"Just 7%?" Nick looked at her with a puzzled expression on his face. "Are you sure?"

She nodded. "It's awfully low given the type of firm they are, their market dominance, and seriously aggressive accounting methods."

Peter slowly sat back in his chair and rested his intertwined fingers on the desk in front of him. "Go on."

"Their cost of capital has to be close to 9%, but if they're earning just 7% in returns then they are actually operating at a 2% loss, despite reporting record profits to their shareholders. Those supposed profits are all due to this mark-to-market accounting they are doing. Meanwhile, their stock is trading at eight times book value. I think it's poised to take a huge fall."

Peter carefully removed his glasses and began to slowly wipe them with a small cloth that had been neatly folded in his shirt pocket. "What about their ability to pay off debt?"

"I don't think they're in imminent danger of default, if that's what you're asking. Just that the stock is over-priced right now, which means it isn't a good fit for the Centaurus Fund."

"Hmmm." He put his glasses back on and began tapping his fingers lightly on the desk. "What are they assuming as the price per barrel of oil?"

"$200."

Peter's fingers became still.

"That's ridiculous!" Nick snorted.

Anne completely agreed. "And for future gas prices, it's even worse. They're assum—"

"$200?" Peter cut her off, his tone accusatory and, at the same time, incredulous. "Are you sure?"

His eyes narrowed as she nodded and referenced the footnotes at the end of the financial statements.

"Enough." Peter stopped her just as she began to launch into the odd transfers to the Fly-By-Night company in the Caribbean. "We get the picture."

Nick began pacing back and forth in front of the floor-to-ceiling glass window that separated Peter's office from the rest of the trading floor. "Peter. If the company goes south, we have a lot of exposure on those swap deals."

"Energix isn't going anywhere." Peter's tone was confident, cocky even.

Perhaps. But if it were up to her, she'd start weaseling out of whatever swap deals Nick was talking about. Or try to sell them to somebody else, pronto.

"Even so, we might want to think about pulling back—"

Peter put a hand up to silence Nick. "I'm not ready to modify our strategy, yet." He paused and shifted his gaze back to Anne, "but I am intrigued."

The mood in the room suddenly felt different, lighter, but more ominous at the same time. It was something about the way he had said the word *intrigued*. Anne felt like a mouse being dropped into a cage, unsure if she was about to get devoured by a snake.

Peter cocked his head sideways. "You sold more stock than the fund actually owns. Is that right?"

She eyed him warily. "Yes."

"That means you're going to be following the company very closely."

Indeed. In shorting the stock, she had bet that the price would decline in the future. If she was wrong, she would lose the gamble, and her fund would owe a ton of money. Until she closed those positions out, she would be scouring every tidbit of information she could find to make sure she picked up on anything pertinent about the company.

Peter peered over his glasses at her. "Keep us informed of any changes. Anything at all."

"Are we done here?" Nick was anxiously looking out at the trading floor.

Peter nodded, and Anne stood up to go.

"Be careful what you say about Energix outside of this room," Nick said as he brushed past her through the door. "Is that clear?"

"Crystal," she said to his retreating head.

"Anne." She turned back to face Peter, whose mouth had widened into a smile that reminded her of a wolf. "You should be aware that Fernsby is a personal friend of Steve's."

Who? Her confusion must have been obvious by the look on her face.

"The guy who signs our paychecks?" Peter's face twitched. "The CEO of Spencer Brothers?"

Her heart began thudding, and she felt a rush of blood to her face. Peter's boss was a close personal friend of the guy who ran Energix? If there was any chance she was wrong, her career at Spencer Brothers would be over. Even if she was right, her future might still be toast.

"Yeah. They golf together." His face twitched again. "A lot."

"Got it," she said, mustering her confident, everything-is-completely-under control voice as she exited and shut the office door.

6

A Little Birdie Told Us

The Wall Street Chronicle
Thursday, June 28, 1990

Is Energix Losing Steam?

Sources tell us that the new manager of Spencer Brothers Centaurus Fund, Anne Scott, has jettisoned its Energix holdings. Shares of the energy giant (EGX) fell 89 cents, to $96.05 in afternoon trading on Wednesday. When asked for a comment, CEO Richard Fernsby blasted her as "an incompetent neophyte with virtually no experience" and offered this piece of advice to Centaurus investors: "Run! Don't walk, for the hills."

Alex set the newspaper down next to Anne's cup of tea and kissed her lightly on the top of her head. "This could make dinner a little awkward on Saturday night."

She glanced down and froze.

"Sources?"

"Probably one of the traders." Alex shrugged. "They have the biggest mouths."

She barely registered his words as she continued reading, her dismay growing exponentially with each sentence. "Incompetent neophyte?"

"He's going on the offensive."

She gave Alex a death stare. "Run for the hills?"

He chuckled. "I think you struck a nerve."

She leaned forward, rested her elbows on the table, and buried her face in her hands. In fact, she hadn't really thought about what would happen after selling the stock. She'd been so fixated on making the right decision that she had intentionally put all thoughts about potential repercussions completely out of her mind. Now, here it was, splashed across the front page for everyone to see, including Paige's husband-to-be. And Alex's parents. Her heart began thumping. "What is your family going to say?"

He put a hand on her shoulder and gave it a small squeeze. "Don't worry about them."

"But Kevin works for Energix."

"And you work for Spencer Brothers as the portfolio manager of a major investment fund. It's your fiduciary responsibility to make good financial decisions that benefit the investors. Period."

"I better get to the office." Anne's mind was racing, wondering how people at work were reacting to the news.

"Or you could start by fortifying yourself with some scrambled eggs." He pulled a frypan out of the cabinet and set it on the stove. "Everyone will still be buzzing away as usual, regardless of when you arrive."

She hesitated for a moment, balancing his relaxed, common-sense reply against her natural tendency to always assume the worst. "Okay. While you do that, I'll nuke some bacon as well. It's not like anything earth-shattering is going to happen in the span of fifteen minutes."

* * *

"Where have you been?" Her secretary greeted her with a frantic wave of her arms. "Steve Warnock wants to see you at 8:30. I didn't know what to say."

Anne glanced down at her watch and saw that she had ten minutes before the appointed time. "Say that I'll be there." As she spoke, her throat felt dry, and she didn't recognize the raspy-sounding voice. She loosened the belt of her coat while she walked the remaining few steps into her office and then stood for a moment behind the door, feeling surprisingly calm. It was as if she was looking at herself from afar, an impartial observer, registering the facts but feeling no emotion. She wondered, shouldn't she be more concerned that the president of Spencer Brothers wanted to meet with her?

And yet she simply felt numb.

She began to wonder what she would do if she were fired. Return to her office and pick up her coat and scarf? Or head directly to Alex's office? She shook her head. Most likely, she would be escorted from the premises. That's what had happened to her old boss when he was let go, although they had given him an hour or so to pack up his things. Anne slowly untied the laces of her sneakers and pulled her black pumps out of the drawer, ignoring the phone ringing nearby.

"Anne?" Her secretary poked her head through the door. "There's a reporter on the line from—"

"Take a message, please."

"No problem."

She disappeared, leaving Anne alone with her thoughts, which were now racing. Had she sold the stock too quickly? Was there any chance she was wrong about Energix? Was she about to get fired? And then the rational part of her brain kicked into high gear, listing the many problems she had found. Mark-to-market accounting inflating the profits with pie-in-the-sky oil price forecasts. Odd transactions with the Fly-By-Night company in the Caribbean buried in the tiny footnotes. The total lack of transparency. She stood up, financial reports in hand, and took a deep breath. As she slowly exhaled, she told herself that she knew exactly what she was doing and simply needed to explain it.

"Please cancel my nine o'clock appointment," Anne said while sailing past her secretary's desk on the way to the elevators.

* * *

The ride up to the executive suite took an eternity. When the doors finally opened, she heard nothing except the clicking of her heels on the cool marble floor as she walked toward the receptionist sitting behind a gleaming, mahogany desk at the far end of the corridor.

"May I help you?"

Anne tried to sound confident as she gave her name.

The woman motioned at a nearby alcove. "I'll let you know when he's ready."

She sat down on the smooth leather couch, took a deep breath, and waited. As the clock behind the receptionist's head slowly ticked, Anne noted the quiet gurgling of the fountain in the corner, the slightly wilted plant sitting on the coffee table that looked like it might need a little water or perhaps more sun, and the wingback chairs that flanked either side of the couch. When she tilted her head to one side, she could see that one had a partially detached tag peeking out from under the seat.

Eventually two men she recognized as senior vice presidents emerged from the glass doors that led into the executive suite. They walked silently to the elevators, their faces grim. She glanced down at her watch. Twenty minutes had elapsed.

And then she waited some more.

Had he forgotten she was there? She looked over at the receptionist, trying to catch her eye. But the woman kept her head buried, studying something of great interest on her desk, until at last, the phone rang. She murmured into the receiver and then looked over at Anne.

"Miss Scott?"

Finally. She stood up, brushed her hands against her skirt, and marched toward the gallows.

* * *

She was ushered into the president's office, where she was greeted by a tall, trim man wearing a crisply ironed light-blue shirt and navy suspenders. "Nice to meet you," he said, giving her a firm handshake and flashing a quick smile.

He motioned for her to sit while he remained standing over by the large picture window, his face serious, arms hanging stiffly by his side. As she tried to get comfortable, she glanced at the empty, executive-style leather chair directly opposite and noticed his pinstripe suit jacket casually hung over the back, completely at odds with his controlled demeanor. She took a deep breath and waited for him to begin.

"Richard Fernsby is very unhappy that the Centaurus Fund sold its Energix holdings. He's threatening to withdraw all of his other business and give it to one of our competitors." He focused his piercing gray eyes on her. "What made you decide to pull the plug?"

She breathed a sigh of relief at the straightforward start. "I'm skeptical of their accounting strategy. When they invest in an asset, like a pipeline, they immediately book the expected profit, even though the company hasn't actually made a dime. While legal, it's risky."

The president cocked his head. "But it's possible they'll meet their projections."

"Possible," she shrugged, "but unlikely."

He regarded her for a moment; his brows knit tightly together. "Historically, their performance has been outstanding, which suggests their financial forecasts are fine."

She nodded. "So it appears. But I've noticed that they have a pattern of transferring assets that aren't performing well to a corporation in the Caribbean that just so happens to be managed by one of their own executives. It enables Energix to write off unprofitable activities without hurting the bottom line. Quite ingenious, actually. But in the end, they're playing a dangerous shell game. At some point, all of these financial manipulations are going to catch up with them. When that happens, I expect the stock price to fall. Big time."

"Hmmm." He walked over to his chair and sat down. "Richard claims you made snide remarks at his most recent investor meeting. He thinks you were trying to embarrass the company in front of the other analysts. That you were grandstanding."

Anne felt a rush of blood to her face. "I simply asked when he would be able to provide a current balance sheet. He was claiming they'd had a great quarter and yet wouldn't provide any financial results because they were supposedly still netting the numbers. There was nothing rude—" She caught herself becoming defensive and realized how flustered she must appear. The pitch of her voice sounded unnaturally high, and she was talking way too fast. She shifted in the too-large chair, unable to find a comfortable position, and willed herself to remain calm and collected. Or at least appear that way. "It was a valid question to ask," she continued evenly. "When he began to balk at providing any more details, I backed down immediately."

"Sounds reasonable to me." He peered at her over his glasses. "I assume you know who Joe Peacock is?"

The head of the equity underwriting division. He oversaw all new stock sales. He was one of the men she had seen walk out shortly before she was called in. Anne's muscles tensed as she gave a quick nod.

"He's upset about a big stock offering coming up. All of the other investment banks involved in underwriting it have *buy* ratings for Energix. They're running around saying it's the greatest thing since sliced bread. And then there's you, who seems to be saying something completely different."

She nodded, her lips drawn in a thin, tight line.

"Fernsby told Joe he could forget about participating in the upcoming deal, or any others in the future, because you dumped their stock. He said we aren't showing confidence in his company."

Anne raised her hands in a show of exasperation. "But it doesn't make sense for the Centaurus Fund to own it if the price is about to fall."

"True. But what if you're wrong?"

"Time will tell." Despite the pounding of her heart, her voice sounded firm and confident.

"Joe wrote a memo suggesting we replace you." He picked up a piece of paper and squinted as he read. *"Let's get her out of here, pronto, and get our Energix business back."* He flicked his wrist, and Anne watched the blistering missive float slowly back to his desk. "He says you should never have been put in charge of the Centaurus Fund. That you're not up to the job."

Anne took a sharp breath. If the president also believed that about her, his next step would be to send her packing. She squared her shoulders and looked him straight in the eye. "Joe's wrong. Nobody bats a thousand all of the time, but I've demonstrated time and again that I know how to analyze the financial condition of businesses and make good decisions. That's why I was put in charge of the fund." Her gaze remained steady as she braced for the hatchet.

The president appeared to study her for a moment. "That's exactly what I told him."

She sat back, stunned. Then why was she sitting here having to explain herself?

He cracked a smile. "The simple fact of the matter is that you're each trying to maximize profits for Spencer Brothers in different ways. He does it by generating fees and commissions, while you do it by making good investments. Unfortunately, the situation with Energix has put your two teams in opposition to one another. Fernsby is simply trying to exploit the situation to his own benefit."

It was a relief to see that the head of Spencer Brothers understood the political realities of the place, although not so great that Fernsby did as well.

"As long as we make money in the end, then nobody will be hurt. But if you're wrong about Energix—"

He left the rest unsaid, but Anne knew exactly where he was heading. If she cost the firm lucrative fees, for what ended up being no good reason, the head of equities would be gunning for her, and there would be no place to hide.

"Glad I got a chance to meet you." He stood up and put out his hand. "Keep up the good work."

And with that, she was dismissed.

* * *

"That was it?" Jennifer looked incredulous. "He didn't say anything else?"

Anne shook her head.

"I can't believe Joe Peacock tried to throw you under the bus."

Seriously? Anne gave her co-worker a you've-got-to-be-kidding-me look. Crushing the competition was par for the course at a place like Spencer Brothers. Sink or swim. Kill or be killed. It had been like that since day one at the firm.

"I mean, it seems totally over the top." Jennifer rolled her eyes. "Getting you hauled up to the executive suite. All because Richard Fernsby threw a temper tantrum."

"The fees in these deals must be huge." Anne slid her formal black pumps off and kicked them to the side.

"But even so, it's still a jerky move. And I don't understand why Richard Fernsby thinks he should be able to dictate how *you* manage *your* fund. Last time I checked, he didn't even work for Spencer Brothers."

That was something that Anne had been wondering about as well.

"The fact of the matter is that people buy and sell stock all the time." Jennifer flicked her hand dismissively. "It's called the *stock market* for a reason."

"I think it's more about the message it sends. Fernsby's concerned that it looks bad."

"Clearly. And his response is to act like a schoolyard bully, calling people names, using threats to strong-arm spineless bankers like Joe Peacock into compliance. It's so unprofessional."

It was desperate.

"You know what?" Jennifer leaned back and crossed her arms. "I think Fernsby's afraid you're onto something and that other investors will find out, too."

Anne tended to agree.

"Except nobody on the street cares what a random fund manager at Spencer Brothers has to say," Jennifer chuckled. "It's so absurd."

Anne nodded and smiled along with her friend and yet wondered, *was it such a laughable idea?*

* * *

A week later, she looked up from her scribbling to see Jennifer waltzing through the door.

"I take it back." Her co-worker looked pointedly at the newspaper she was holding in one hand. "You've started a trend."

The Wall Street Chronicle
Thursday, June 28, 1990

Energix Continues to Slide

Greenwich Select and Advantage Investments have both sold their holdings of Energix stock amid rumors that the company is facing significant losses in its most recent quarter. At the close of trading, Energix shares (EGX) had fallen to $89.90, a decline of more than 6% in the last week. When asked for a comment, CEO Richard Fernsby said unequivocally that the rumors were false and that the company is poised to be more profitable than ever.

Anne had breathed a sigh of relief after seeing the front-page story that morning. She was no longer the lone voice in the wilderness questioning whether Energix had strong financial legs. Instead, the burden of proof was steadily shifting over to Richard Fernsby who, despite receiving a marked increase in investor requests for financial clarity, had yet to release the most recent quarterly results.

"That'll teach Joe Peacock not to mess with you." Jennifer placed some Hershey's chocolate kisses on Anne's desk. "Here's a little something to celebrate your victory."

"Thanks." Anne picked up one of the chocolate candies and began removing the silver foil.

"Hopefully, he never tries to go after you again."

Anne shrugged. "It wasn't personal. Joe lost out on a profitable underwriting opportunity that would have been great for his bottom line. But honestly," she shook her head and frowned, "given the circumstances, I'm not sure Spencer Brothers should even be involved in helping Energix bring more stock to market. It seems a bit irresponsible to me."

Jennifer snorted. "As if doing the right thing ever amounted to a hill of beans around here. It's always about the bottom line on Wall Street. The minute you lose sight of that, you've lost the game."

Wasn't that the truth. Nonetheless, Anne didn't want to spend all of her waking hours worrying about being stabbed in the back either. She leaned down to pick up her purse. "Let's get something to drink."

As they fought with the soda machine at the end of the hall continually rejecting her last quarter, she heard someone calling her name.

Jennifer squinted at the short, stout figure walking briskly toward them. "I think it's your secretary."

Normally, the woman moved at a snail's pace, conserving every bit of energy for painting the town red at night, but right now, she was clearly on a mission.

"Alex is on line one!" she called out, slowing down once she knew she had their attention. "He says it's urgent."

Anne locked eyes with Jennifer. "I wonder if his father has had a heart attack or something."

"Take this one with you." Jennifer handed her the Coke. "I'll figure out what's going on here."

She ran back to her office, the cold soda bouncing in her hand. "What's up?" she greeted him breathlessly.

"I just got off the phone with Richard Fernsby."

Her chest tightened at the sound of his agitated voice.

"He's threatening to sue you, personally."

"Me?" She stared at the red metallic can sweating on her desk. "For what?"

"For causing Energix's stock price to fall."

Anne leaned back in her chair as the information slowly sank in. "That's ridiculous. I don't control the market."

"But you do control what you say to investors in the market."

She paused as she tried to remember who she had spoken with in the last couple of weeks. "I haven't said anything to anyone outside of Spencer Brothers."

"I tried to tell him that. He wasn't exactly in a listening mood. While he was ranting and raving about stock price manipulation, he said he'd go after Spencer Brothers as well."

"Can he do that?"

"Sue? Of course. He just has to file a complaint. The question is whether he can convince a judge that he has a legitimate case."

* * *

That afternoon, Anne found herself in the president's office for the second time in just as many weeks.

"So, we meet again." He motioned for her to sit in the open chair directly across from him, the same one she had sat in previously. "Alex has just been briefing me."

She glanced over at her fiancé in the adjacent chair. He gave her a tiny wink, his private way of trying to let her know everything would be fine. But having seen the stern look on Steve Warnock's face, she wasn't so sure.

"Fernsby is clearly rattled," the senior executive began. "Any idea what he wants?"

Alex intertwined his fingers and leaned back in his seat. "It's pretty clear he would like Spencer Brothers to make a public statement that we have full confidence in his company." He paused and tapped his thumbs together. "And for Anne to be sacked. Immediately."

"Really." Steve's face was inscrutable, the word delivered in an even tone of voice. She wondered what he was actually thinking.

"And your legal advice?"

"Ignore him."

The president looked over at Anne and appeared to study her, his grey eyes unblinking and unyielding.

"Anne hasn't spoken with anyone publicly about the company," Alex continued, "so Fernsby can't make a case for slander against either her or Spencer Brothers."

"What about the claims of price manipulation?"

Alex shook his head. "He'd have to prove that Anne ran around telling people the stock was a horrible investment and that she made those comments *after* she shorted it so that she would be able to buy it back again, later, at a lower price. And just like with the slander argument, he doesn't have a leg to stand on because she has been radio-silent on the matter."

Steve peered over his glasses at her. "Is that correct? No off-the-record conversations with any reporters? No quiet whispers to a good friend at another firm? Nothing? Whatsoever?"

She looked him squarely in the eye. "Nothing."

He watched her for a moment across the vast expanse of his desk. "Any idea who leaked the stock sale a few weeks ago?"

She hesitated for a nanosecond. *Idea?* Of course she had some ideas. One of the trading assistants had probably said something to a friend over a beer. But she knew that wasn't what he was asking. She kept her gaze steady. "No."

"His claims are baseless," Alex said firmly. "We should ignore him and continue going about our business. I think his over-sized reaction suggests that Humpty Dumpty is about to take a huge fall."

The head of Spencer Brothers shifted his gaze back to Alex, and his mouth widened into a smile. "My thoughts exactly."

* * *

Anne felt a mixture of relief and anger as they exited the corporate suite, her heels echoing loudly on the shiny marble floor. On the one hand, it was reassuring that the CEO of Spencer Brothers wasn't overly concerned about Richard Fernsby's latest stunt. Nonetheless, it was annoying that any threats had been issued at all. In retrospect, she would have been better served by remaining silent at that quarterly investor meeting. She might have avoided his ire altogether. At a minimum, it would have given him less ammunition to use against her.

"That went well enough," Alex said while they waited for the elevator to arrive.

She shrugged noncommittally, holding back until they were safely inside the car with the doors closed before saying what was really on her mind.

"I can't believe we even had to have that meeting," she huffed. "This whole situation with Richard is completely out of control. First, there were those newspaper articles calling me an *incompetent neophyte,* and now he's threatening to sue."

"It just means you've gotten under his skin. He's under pressure and starting to crack."

The elevator began racing down toward his floor.

"Who else do you think knows?"

Alex cocked his head at her. "That he's trying to intimidate you with a lawsuit?"

She nodded.

"He probably spouted off to a few of his lieutenants." Alex shrugged. "But who cares?"

"I hope your soon-to-be brother-in-law wasn't one of them. We'll be seeing him on Saturday night, for dinner." She bit her lip.

The elevator slowed down and came to a halt at his floor.

"Kevin knows better than to bring something like that up at a family event," Alex snorted. He exited the car, putting his hand out to keep the doors from closing. "I mean—" he paused, no longer looking or sounding nearly as certain, "—at least I hope he does."

7

An Awkward Dinner

Short Hills, NJ

That weekend

"For the send-off," Paige said with a big smile, "everyone will gather on the bluff for a final toast."

Alex's sister was leaving nothing to chance for her upcoming wedding. Everything was being planned to the nth detail.

She turned to look at her mother. "What do you think about having some sparklers on hand for the guests?"

"Lovely idea. I'll add it to the list."

They were having dinner at Alex's parents' house in Short Hills, New Jersey, a wealthy enclave, about forty-five minutes' drive from the city. His parents sat at either end of the antique mahogany table, like bookends, with their two children and significant others filling the space in between. Except for the constant talk about the upcoming wedding, the dinner had been lovely: a creamy bisque soup to start, mixed greens with a lemon vinaigrette dressing, and lobster for the main course with crusty French bread rolls on the side, all paired with a crisp, fruit-forward chardonnay.

"And for the coup de grâce," Paige lifted her arms dramatically, "the band will play *Sailing* as the boat heads off across the bay."

Anne stifled a groan. This whole send-off idea was too choreographed. Too controlled. Verging on tacky. She glanced at Alex, in the chair beside her, expecting to see him roll his eyes. Instead, he looked confused.

"You're not talking about taking the catamaran, are you?"

"No." It was clear from the exasperated look on Paige's face that she thought the answer was obvious. "The Bayliner."

"That's what I thought. But—" He stopped when he saw Kevin shaking his head.

"What?" His sister looked back and forth at the two men, neither one saying a word.

"It's a motorboat," Alex said, a pained look on his face. "With a big engine and no sails. It doesn't really match the song."

Paige sighed loudly. "Do you always have to be so literal?"

Kevin shook his head again as if to say, *I told you.*

As Alex began backpedaling, Anne studied the tall cylindrical vase in the center of the table. It had an eye-catching mixture of red, orange, and yellow flowers interspersed with long, green leaves that flowed over the edge, drawing the eye toward the center where there was a dramatic red circular flower. She knew that his mother belonged to the garden club and occasionally won prizes for her floral arrangements. Presumably, this was one of her creations.

"Fireworks would be even nicer," Paige prattled on. "But we know those aren't allowed anywhere near the beach."

The illegal bonfire story rears its ugly little head. Anne looked up in time to see Paige smirk at her brother.

"You know what?" Superficially, Alex looked serious, but not overly upset. Under the table, however, Anne saw his hands clenched tightly near his lap. Clearly, he did not like being reminded about his brush with the law in high school. "I think it's time to leave that little incident in the past."

"Little?"

His lips tightened into a thin red line.

"Whatever." Paige gave a small shrug. "My point is that it's the ambiance

I'm going for." She looked at Anne, one eyebrow pointedly raised. "Something you might want to consider for your wedding as well."

Alex's mother coughed loudly. "Is everyone ready for dessert?"

As they dug into the chocolate mousse pie, Paige finally shifted gears and began talking about the new house the couple was in the midst of purchasing. "With everything going on at work, Kevin has barely had time to sign the mortgage application." She rolled her eyes. "They're so busy arguing about write-offs that they can't even—"

"Paige. Let's not bore everyone with my dreary job." He laughed. "As long as it pays the bills, that's all that matters."

"What do you mean? It's not boring at all. You've found all sorts of—"

"Honey!" He gave her a quick nudge. "We haven't heard anything about Anne and Alex's wedding plans."

Alex's mother stiffened.

Kevin's brown eyes were suddenly laser-focused on Anne. "Have you set a date?"

"Not yet," she replied brightly. "We're waiting until we make it through your big day before beginning to even start thinking about ours."

Alex took Anne's hand under the table and gave it a small squeeze. Not only did they want a much lower-key affair, but his sister had been adamant that their nuptials not overshadow her wedding in any way, whatsoever.

"I've been wondering." The tone of Kevin's voice shifted slightly. "How long have you managed the Centaurus Fund for Spencer Brothers?"

Anne felt herself go on alert. "Since March." She took a sip of her port and looked at Alex's father. "This is very nice."

The sixty-year old patriarch smiled, and she was struck by the strong resemblance between father and son. Same gentle eyes, generous spirit, and relaxed manner.

"It's a vintage port from an exceptionally good year. My favorite. I save it for special occasions, like this dinner tonight." He lifted his glass, as if to toast. "I'm glad you like it."

But Kevin was undeterred by her quick change of topic. "You're fairly young to be managing such a large fund."

She slowly turned back to face him. "I have eight years in the business."

"Advising traders on the bond side, right?"

He had obviously done his homework. She gave a small nod.

"But now you're an equity fund manager, buying and selling stocks," he persisted. "That's a lot of responsibility and quite a different ball of wax."

She took a bite of her dessert, using the time to craft her reply. "It's been exciting to shift into a new part of the business. I've learned a lot in the last few months."

"But typically—"

"She's a top-notch analyst," Alex said proudly. "They're lucky to have her."

She glanced over at him and smiled. It was nice having someone so strongly in her corner. Growing up, she had always had to fight every battle for herself. Her parents didn't believe in helping with homework or college essays, which had put her at a huge disadvantage relative to her peers. At the time, she had resented their philosophy. It had seemed incredibly unfair, even uncaring. But more recently, she had begun to appreciate that it had taught her to be an independent thinker and resilient to failure, qualities that had helped her to excel academically in college and accelerated her rise through the ranks at Spencer Brothers.

"I'm sure," Kevin said smoothly. "In fact, I think it's quite impressive. Spencer Brothers is known for being something of an old boy's club, and yet they promoted a woman to lead a very prominent fund. It's good to see them finally moving into the 20th century."

"It certainly is," Anne said evenly, ignoring the implication that she might have gotten the job simply because of her gender.

"It's interesting that one of the first things you did was to sell your Energix holdings." He cocked his head sideways and squinted at her. "What made you decide to do that?"

The last of her dessert, hung midair on the exquisite silver fork, just waiting to be finished off. "I can't get into the details of our thinking, but it came down to a question of what made the most sense for the fund." She quickly popped it into her mouth.

"Of course." He gave her a tight smile. "It's just that when people start a new job, they generally take their time to get the lay of the land, before making any big changes."

I'm not most people, she felt like saying. Instead, she kept her face expressionless and said nothing, refusing to rise to the bait.

"I think everyone would agree that Energix has been a great investment ever since Richard Fernsby became CEO." He opened his palms and looked around the table like a politician trying to drum up support from a crowd. "Which makes me curious." He leaned forward and cast his eyes on Anne. "Why sell now? Better yet, why sell at all?"

"Maybe we should save this discussion for another time," Alex said amiably, although Anne sensed an edge to his tone.

"The reason I ask," Kevin said, without budging his gaze, "is because it's had kind of a domino effect on the market. First you sold, then a couple of other funds followed suit. It's actually creating liquidity problems for us."

As if any of that was her fault. Resisting the urge to say that Energix had only themselves to blame for their current financial predicament, Anne scouted around for a noncommittal reply. "The markets can be fickle."

"They sure can. We're going to be stuck paying more for our newest debt securities than we ever would have expected. It's almost like we stepped on somebody's toes, and we're persona non grata from the *in-group*."

Welcome to the real world. She gave what she hoped was a sympathetic-looking smile.

"When Fernsby saw the rates we're looking at, well—" Kevin glanced over at Alex's mother. "I won't repeat what he said here. But he was fit to be tied."

Anne wondered if Kevin had any idea that his boss had threatened to sue her.

"It's been exhausting trying to pull skittish investors back into the fold." He sank back in his chair.

She studied his face more closely. His eyes were ringed with black circles, and tiny lines creased his skin. Just twelve years older than Paige, he looked thin and brittle, old enough to be her father.

"In three weeks' time, you'll get a break from all of this," Paige said cheerfully, as if a bit of rest was all he required. "You just need to make it through the wedding."

* * *

"Alex!" his mother hissed. "You've got to have a prenuptial agreement!"

Anne was standing by the fireplace in the expansive living room while Alex's father showed Kevin a baseball that had been autographed by Babe Ruth. The two of them were so deeply engrossed in studying the signature that they were missing the conversation happening in the hallway, just outside the kitchen. But Anne could hear it clearly.

"Mother. I'm not discussing it."

"But Alex, what if Richard actually follows through with a lawsuit? If he were to win, he could tap into your assets."

"He doesn't have a case."

"How can you be so sure?"

"I'm a lawyer. Remember?"

Anne peeked around the wall, hoping to see the expression on Alex's face, but the large circular staircase completely obscured her view.

"A prenup isn't some insidious negative thing," Paige jumped into the fray. "It simply lays everything out in the open. Before there are any hard feelings. Kevin and I have one."

"But your circumstances are different," Alex replied. "Kevin has to pay alimony and child support. His ex-wife could easily come after him for more."

"And what makes you think the same wouldn't happen with Anne?"

He laughed. "Well, she's never been married, for one thing. So, there's no ex in her background to come crawling out of the woodwork."

"That's not what I meant," his sister retorted. "And you know it. If things fall apart with you two, she could go after your money just as easily as Kevin could go after mine."

Anne glanced over at Kevin, gesturing at something in the bookcase. It was filled with signed, first editions the family had collected over the years. Neither he nor Alex's father seemed to be aware that she was even in the same room. She took a step closer to the hallway and continued listening.

"—so pig-headed!" Paige exclaimed.

"How much do you know about her background?" His mother asked slowly, distrust permeating every word.

"Not now." He sounded tired.

"What does her father do again?"

He sighed. "He's a family physician, and her mother's a biomedical researcher. They're self-made people. Like she is."

"You've met them?"

"Of course."

"How would we know?" His sister snapped. "You've hardly told us anything. It's a miracle we've even met Anne."

"Gee," he spat back. "I wonder why!"

Anne heard angry footsteps echoing down the hall.

"Where are you going?" His mother demanded shrilly.

"To the living room."

She spun around and began studying an intricate Chinese vase displayed on a nearby table.

"Alex!"

"We're done here."

* * *

"What an evening," Alex said the moment he turned the key in the ignition. "I couldn't wait to get out of there. How about you?"

He shifted into first gear, leaving a spray of gravel behind them as his BMW roadster sped down the tree-lined driveway.

"After dinner," he continued without giving her a chance to reply, "my mother cornered me in the kitchen, concerned about the lawsuit-that-hasn't-happened." He turned left and began winding through the dark suburban streets, the car's headlights casting eerie shadows on the trees. "There's only one way she could have known about it."

"Paige."

"Who else?"

Anne swallowed, realizing she had been secretly holding on to the fruitless hope of a good relationship with his parents. A rosy vision that, as they got to know her, they would see she was fun and smart, the perfect match for their son. But the truth of the matter was that they didn't approve of her for reasons that were beyond her control. Now, thanks to Alex's sister, the Battle-Axe had yet another reason to be uneasy. "I can't say I'm totally surprised."

"A person in Kevin's position should know better than to repeat information like that." Alex paused to adjust his mirror. "And despite the specter of litigation pending in the background, the man had no qualms about discussing the company's financial woes. Over dinner, no less." The car began accelerating down the hill. "What was he thinking?"

That I'm naïve and gullible? That I have no idea when someone is pumping me for information? That I would be so flattered by his attention I would lay out my investment strategy at the first opportunity? Anne took a deep breath to quell her rising anger. It was possible that the company was imploding around the guy, and he was simply desperate for answers. "I was surprised at how direct he was in his questioning."

"Me too. I thought about shutting him down, but you handled it so well there was no need. Polite, but nothing substantive. If I didn't know better, I'd think you were an attorney." The car came to a sharp stop as they rounded the corner, the traffic light glowing bright red.

"Just in love with one." She felt a flush of warmth as she turned to look at him.

He reached over and squeezed her hand. "This lawyer-guy of yours must be really good at what he does."

"He is." She laughed. "But his sister could sure do with some legal coaching. I couldn't believe it when she announced that they're arguing about write-offs at Energix."

Alex groaned. "I don't think she realized that it was inside information."

"Good thing Kevin cut her off."

"Not in time."

"Don't forget," Anne said, "she's a graphic artist, not a financial professional."

"Which is why Kevin should never have blabbed any of that stuff to her in the first place."

"But he probably had to explain why he's been so busy."

"Well, then, he should have been VERY clear that that sort of information isn't for public consumption."

A fair point.

"And it's definitely something that should NOT come up in casual conversation with anyone who might invest in the stock." Alex lifted his hands from the steering wheel and tensed them as if he wanted to strangle someone. "Which includes pretty much EVERYONE in their entire social circle!"

"I think the light's about to turn."

"Right." He shifted into first gear and placed his hands back on the wheel.

"The one upside I can see is that it confirms what I suspected all along." Anne couldn't help but feel a prick of self-satisfaction that she had been the first to recognize Energix's story was too good to be true. And had gotten out before the price began to fall.

"Indeed." Alex released the clutch, and the car began to pick up speed. "Hopefully, Energix doesn't completely come apart between now and when Kevin walks down the aisle."

"Oh, come on, Mr. Negativity." She laughed. "The wedding's in three weeks. It couldn't possibly unravel that fast." She watched a pair of oncoming headlights fly past them, narrowly missing a pedestrian as it zipped through the intersection at breakneck speed. *Could it?*

8

A Slow Death Spiral

New York City

A week later

"Anne!"

She turned to see Peter Eckert coming toward her, two large muffins balanced precariously in one hand and a Styrofoam cup of coffee held in the other.

"Wait up!" He handed the cashier a ten-dollar bill and stood by for his change.

She drummed her foot on the ground, wondering what the head of the fixed income division wanted to discuss. *Energix?* It had to be. Two days earlier the company had reported a net loss of $600 million for the quarter, blaming write-offs associated with Caribbean investments gone bad. Alex thought it likely that things would start to calm down for Kevin and that Paige could safely talk about Energix in the company of friends and family now that the information had been made public. Unless, of course, there were more bombshells still to come.

Peter grabbed a plastic spoon along with a handful of sugar packets, and the two of them walked in lockstep toward the elevators. "You got out of

Energix just in time."

Sure did, she felt like saying. The revelations had hit their stock price hard. At last check, it was trading in the neighborhood of sixty-five dollars per share, down significantly from the ninety-seven dollar price she had gotten when she dumped her holdings the month before. And yet he had acted like she was an imbecile when he first learned of the sale. She gave a tight-lipped smile, waiting for him to get to whatever his real point was.

"What do you think about their ability to pay off their debt?"

"It depends," she replied carefully. "From the way they've been fudging the numbers, it's hard to tell how profitable the company really is."

They came to a stop at the elevator bank and turned to face one another.

"That's what's concerning me." His gray eyes darted back and forth. "I'm beginning to wonder if Energix is sliding into a death spiral."

Anne had been wondering the same that morning as well. It would be great news for her fund because she had sold the stock short. The lower the share price went, the more money she would rake in. In fact, at the rate things were going, it was starting to look like she would make a killing. But it seemed that Peter was in the opposite position from her. His trading operation likely held some of Energix's bonds. Or were owed money through the swaps that Nick had mentioned. For them, a demise in Energix's financial condition would be costly.

She pushed the Up button. "If these write-offs truly clear the decks, then hopefully Energix can focus on their core business and turn a solid profit."

For this reason, she had been debating whether to hedge her bets by cashing out a portion of her short holdings immediately, in order to lock in some of her gains.

"But if there's more to come..." She left the rest unsaid as the elevator doors opened and they stepped inside. "We should get a clearer picture in the next couple of months."

"By then, it will be too late." His mouth twitched.

Too late? She looked at the two suspendered yuppies sharing the elevator with them and tried to choose her words carefully. "When do the swap deals come due?"

He stiffened. "Six months from now." The elevator came to a stop at his floor.

"Are they collateralized?"

He ignored her question as he stepped off. "I know you're following the company's financials closely. So am I. Two pairs of eyes are better than one, so let me know if you see anything that should get me worried."

* * *

"I think this qualifies as something that should worry him." Jennifer nodded at the paper sitting on Anne's desk. A mere two days had elapsed since Energix's initial announcement of large second-quarter losses, and the chips were beginning to fall.

The Wall Street Chronicle
July 12, 1990

Energix Fires CFO, Donald Chalmer

Battered by a sudden loss of investor confidence, Energix's board ousted its chief financial officer after learning that he had received $12 million in so-called "management fees" in the prior year. Energix shares fell $10.38 to $55.42 in late afternoon trading. The price has dropped nearly in half in just the last month, triggering an announcement by the SEC that they will start an investigation into a series of Caribbean investments that caused nearly $1 billion in write-offs.

"It's never a good situation when the regulators get involved. They're bound to find something."

Anne nodded in agreement. "I'm actually wondering what it means for Paige's husband-to-be. I think the CFO was his boss."

Jennifer shot her a pitying look. "Hopefully, he isn't next. It doesn't sound like she's the type to deal very well with a spouse being *terminated*."

Financially, they would be fine. Paige had more than enough money for the two of them. But socially, the blow would likely be devastating. "I shudder to think." Anne gave a theatrical shake of her shoulders.

"Although, come to think of it," Jennifer said with a mischievous grin, "given the British stiff upper lip and all, it's possible Paige would weather things better than we're giving her credit for."

Anne intertwined her fingers and tapped her thumbs against one another. "The more interesting question is how much her husband-to-be knows about the financial shenanigans happening left and right all around him."

"He's fairly senior in the organization. It's hard to believe he doesn't have much of a clue."

"If there end up being criminal indictments…"

Jennifer clicked her tongue. "Things could get ugly."

Anne leaned back slowly in her chair and let out a big breath of air. "I wonder if there's a chance the company could go completely under."

"That would throw a wrench in Peter Eckert's swap deals."

Anne sat up sharply. "What do you know about those?"

"Not much." Jennifer unzipped her bag and pulled out a chocolate bar. "Only that they involve some oil barges he bought at the end of last year."

Anne raised an eyebrow. "Barges? As in ships that sail around the globe?"

Jennifer nodded slowly. "That's what one of the traders told me. Weird, huh?"

It was beyond weird. Spencer Brothers was a Wall Street trading operation, not an energy corporation. "But—" Anne began, still trying to make sense of what she was hearing.

"Energix is supposed to buy them back early next year some time."

"If they're still in business." Anne made a face.

Jennifer laughed. "I don't think that thought crossed anyone's mind at the time they made the deal. I mean, obviously, they stuck some verbiage in the contract to cover the possibility, but no one actually expected to use it." She broke the candy bar in half and handed one of the pieces to Anne. "What I don't understand is why Peter is so worried. It's not like we're holding uncollateralized bonds that would become worthless. If push comes to shove, we can always sell the barges to someone else. Energix isn't the only game in town."

Anne froze as the significance of her friend's words swept over her. There was no obvious reason for Peter Eckert to be worried about the barge deals, unless there was more to them than a simple swap.

Jennifer's eyes widened. "Wait a minute."

Anne nodded. "We've been assuming—"

"We're missing something!" Jennifer spat the words.

"Something crucial." Anne bit her lip. "But what?"

She got a clue, a week later, at Paige's bachelorette party.

* * *

Bar hopping in Manhattan

Anne pulled the pink and yellow umbrella out of her Mai Tai and slipped it into the side of her hair. It was the least she could do to give some semblance of fitting in. She glanced around the table at the women who had been friends for years, now at their third dive-bar of the evening. *Slumming,* Paige had said when asked what they would be doing.

"Cute." Pearls-Galore took a long slurp of her piña colada. "Too bad Alex isn't here to see it."

"I don't think he'd approve," Paige said with a small burp.

"Wa-a-ay too wild for that strait-laced lawyer," Perfect-Teeth batted her eyelashes around the table.

Anne wondered what exactly she thought she was communicating with the flapping eyelids. Some sort of weird imitation of flirting? Evidently, it was meant to be funny since Horse-Lover was practically in hysterics.

Käthe stood up and took a big bow. As usual, she was dripping in diamonds that constantly flashed when she moved around in the low light. "And now it's time for the maid of honor to make a toast."

"Wait!" Pearls-Galore banged her hand on the table, causing her water glass to spill. "We need a picture first." She reached behind her chair to grab the camera and scanned the room in search of a waiter.

"I can't find my shades," Horse-Lover slurred. She looked on the floor around her chair.

Perfect-Teeth erupted in giggles.

"What?"

"You're wearing them."

Horse-Lover's hand flew to her face.

The heart-shaped sunglasses had been Käthe's idea. She'd passed them out when the group first climbed into the limousine, insisting that everyone wear them for the evening.

"Has anyone seen that handsome waiter?" Horse-Lover stood up unsteadily. "I'm ready for another drink."

"Probably time to cut her off," Pearls-Galore whispered to Anne.

Anne nodded in agreement, but abruptly stilled her moving head just as Alex's old flame glanced in their direction. Horse-Lover had started the evening with two shots of tequila followed by at least four other cocktails and several glasses of champagne in the car. As the limousine had crawled through the Manhattan city streets, bringing them to their current destination, she'd unbuttoned her blouse and stood up through the sun-roof, dancing semi-topless for all the passing world to see.

"Hey!" Pearls-Galore called out. "Let's go to the Russian Tea Room next. I'm ready for some dessert."

Anne groaned inwardly. They'd had so much high-carb food already. Batter-fried chicken wings. French fries. Onion rings and nachos. And now she wanted a sugar bomb to top everything off?

Their waiter glided up to the table, deftly avoiding Horse-Lover's roving hands. "Another round of drinks?"

As he trundled off with their order, Käthe raised her glass in the air and tapped it lightly with a spoon. "Your attention, please. Paige is about to take a huge step." She paused dramatically. "Off the cliff." Another pause and the glass went higher, with a large angular tilt. "Into the abyss of marriage!" The pineapple perched on the rim of her glass suddenly slid off, landing with a loud splat on the table.

Horse-Lover studied the fallen piece of fruit for a moment before grabbing a nearby toothpick and flicking it mercilessly to the floor.

What did Alex ever see in her? Of course, it had been a fairly short relationship when both were merely teenagers. But still. She didn't seem to have many redeeming qualities. Even more puzzling was why she was included within Paige's bevy of friends.

"Whatever happens," the Diamond Goddess ignored the sticky yellow mess congealing within nearby stepping distance of her open-toed Prada shoes. "We'll always be here. Through thick and thin." She focused her gaze on Paige. "A true constant in your life!"

Paige jumped up to hug Käthe, her gold bangle bracelets clanking loudly against one another. "Nothing will change between us. I promise." She leaned over and whispered something in Käthe's ear.

"I hope you're right," Käthe murmured in return. "They accepted my offer on that cottage."

The house on Martha's Vineyard she had been eyeing? Anne raised an eyebrow. She must have sold the Energix shares she had been talking about at the bridal shower.

"You bought it!" Pearls-Galore looked at Käthe expectantly.

Käthe gave a terse nod.

"Then why the long face?"

"There have been some complications," she mumbled.

Perfect-Teeth gave her an appraising look. "Something to do with that mystery man of yours?"

"Something like that." Käthe sank down in her chair and studied her drink.

Horse-Lover twisted back and forth in her chair, suddenly looking cagey. "When are you going to let us meet him?"

"Girls!" Paige eyed her friends sternly. "When she's ready."

Käthe had remained completely still throughout the exchange, but then something shifted. She slowly straightened up, like an unfurling kite. "It's fine," she laughed gaily. "Soon!"

The transformation from crumpled balloon to puffed-up dirigible was complete. She smiled widely. Fiercely. Like a warrior princess ready to take on the world. "In fact, I propose a toast to me!"

"Here, here!" Paige thumped the table.

"The owner of something worth nothing." Käthe took a long sip through her straw.

Nothing? Anne looked around the table. Everyone looked as confused as she was. Surely, she didn't mean her secret lover.

"You mean...the house you just bought?" Pearls-Galore asked slowly.

Käthe gave a sly smile. "The company I took over last week." She spread her arms wide, like a diva greeting her fans. "You're looking at the president."

President? Of what? Anne had a bad feeling about what she was about to hear.

Pearls-Galore grabbed the last quesadilla off of the snack platter. "I want to get on this gravy train."

"It requires special connections." Käthe winked. "Unfortunately, the company didn't come with any employees to order around. But it did come with some rusty barges."

Barges? Anne breathed in sharply.

"So, I've been thinking—"

"Wait a minute—" Horse-Lover began.

Käthe put a hand up to stop her. "—it's based in the Caribbean." She tilted her head back dramatically. "Therefore, a business trip is in order! To get a firsthand look at the operation!"

A cold shiver ran down Anne's spine. Käthe was on the paperwork of the Caribbean entities being investigated by the SEC? She probably had no idea what she had signed on to or the extent of Energix's financial problems. Did she bother to read the newspaper? Or watch the evening news?

"Count me in!" Pearls-Galore gave a thumbs up.

"Me too," Paige announced. "After I get back from my honeymoon. Well, maybe not immediately. I mean, Kevin will need to—"

"No need to plan anything tonight." Käthe flicked her sparkly wrist. "Just pencil the idea in!"

Anne hid behind her sunglasses, blinking. Was Käthe truly oblivious that she was being used as a pawn? Or was she as calculating as her father?

9

The Rehearsal Dinner

The Hamptons

The night before the wedding

"What's the backup plan if it rains?" Alex looked back and forth at his mother and sister.

"It won't," Paige said firmly.

"But the weather forecast—"

She put her hand up. "Alex. It won't rain."

He glanced over at the bridesmaids and groomsmen who were lined up on either side of the floral canopy, framed by the gray frothing bay waters in the distance. "Just in case?" he asked, his voice nearly drowned out by a squawking seagull that swooped down in a gust of wind.

"I'm nervous enough without you stressing me out even more!" His sister glared at him.

He lifted his hands in a show of submission and stepped back a few paces.

Kevin put his arm around the anxious bride and gave her a quick squeeze.

"Any other questions?" she addressed the crowd, a strained smile on her face.

Everyone shook their heads.

"Excellent," Alex's mother gave a single clap. "Let's get ready for the rehearsal dinner."

* * *

"I'm afraid their marriage won't survive," Käthe said tearfully. "My mother spoke with a divorce lawyer yesterday to understand her options."

Anne came to an abrupt stop and hovered, just out of sight, wondering whether to continue into the ladies' room. The sinks, where the women were talking, stood between her and the bathroom stalls where she was headed.

"Maybe she's just trying to protect their assets," Paige replied. "To get some of them shifted into her name alone."

"But where will that leave my father?" Käthe blew her nose loudly.

Anne stepped back outside and waited a moment, debating what to do. She hated to interrupt them, but she had drunk a large quantity of water over the course of the evening and really needed to use the facilities. She pulled the door open for a second time and stepped in.

"...not over," Paige said in a hushed voice. "Kevin told me that Energix is going to have to restate their earnings from the last five years in order to correct some sort of accounting violations."

Anne took a sharp breath. More inside information that the blabbermouth should never have shared with anyone. Financial revisions of that nature would cause the stock price to drop even lower than it already had.

"You've got to be kidding me. That will send my mother—"

Anne pulled her shoulders back and marched into the room. "Hi." She gave a small wave and walked briskly past the women.

"Hi," they replied in unison, tight smiles plastered on their faces.

She locked the door and hung her purse on the brass hook.

"That's the other thing," Käthe's sniffling whisper echoed off of the shiny marble floors straight into the toilet cubicle. "She's so angry at Donald."

Donald? Anne had to think for a moment. *Chalmers.* The CFO, fired from Energix the week before. She grabbed some toilet paper and dried her perspiring hands.

"She blames him for everything that's gone wrong with the company. But he's just a scapegoat."

A scapegoat? If he wasn't the mastermind behind all the clever accounting, then he had to have at least been complicit.

"I thought—" Paige began.

"He says the barge idea came from Peter Eckert, who *assured* them that Spencer Brothers does these kinds of transactions all the time."

Anne froze, clutching the toilet paper into a tiny wad. The head of fixed income investments at her own firm had advised Energix on these shady transactions?

"His mistake was to trust that slimy bastard." Käthe sniffed. "I'm thinking Donald should march himself over to—"

Without thinking, Anne had thrown the lumpy ball of paper into the toilet and depressed the lever causing a loud whoosh.

"Shh!" Paige shut her down, probably realizing there was a chance Anne could hear them. There was a pause, the sound of a small cosmetic case being snapped shut, and then their footsteps receded from the room.

After she was sure they were gone, Anne emerged from the stall and walked over to the row of sinks. She stared at the reflection of herself in the mirror, her heart pounding while thoughts whirled around in her head. *How are Peter's swap deals tied to the Caribbean Fly-By-Night business? Why does Käthe care if her mother blames the CFO? And what action does she think Donald Chalmers should take?*

She pulled a washcloth out of the wicker dispenser, ran it under some hot water, and held it up against her skin. Unable to come up with any answers, she found herself fixating on how sallow and pale she looked under the harsh lights. *What am I doing here? I am so out of my league.*

* * *

"Is everything alright?" Alex studied her when she returned to the table.

"Later," she whispered through clenched teeth.

"Let's go." He pushed his chair back and stood up. "Things are wrapping up."

"Alex!" His mother beckoned from the rustic stone fireplace. "Let's get some pictures before you leave."

He gave Anne a quick peck on her cheek. "This won't take long."

Yeah, right. She'd heard that one before. "I'll join you in a sec." She whipped out her lip gloss while he forged ahead. After checking her appearance in a small compact mirror, she took a deep breath and strode confidently across the room.

"Just family," her future mother-in-law said as she approached the group.

Anne stopped short, feeling a mixture of surprise and anger, noting that Alex's mother wouldn't look her in the eye.

"I'm sure you understand."

Not really. Although it sent a message loud and clear. She glanced over at Alex, who was caught up in a conversation with his father, completely unaware.

Sorry, Paige mouthed with what she probably thought was a sympathetic smile.

Obviously, not that sorry. Nonetheless, Anne wasn't about to make a scene. She knew that the bride-to-be was a bundle of nerves, and that the Battle-Axe was a longer-term problem that should be addressed some other time. "Okay," she said, doing her best to sound polite and appear unruffled.

Except she wasn't.

A swell of anger rose like a tide within her. She watched the two women fussing about how to arrange themselves, seemingly oblivious to the hurt they had just caused and realized there was no reason to remain standing on the sidelines like a discarded gum wrapper. She walked outside and stood by the patio railing. As she listened to the rhythmic crashing of waves on the beach below, she began to consider the possibility that Alex's family might never accept her.

"Lovely night," Käthe said, floating into her periphery, her diamond jewelry sparkling under the evening lights. "There's something about the sea breeze that I find very calming."

"Me too." Anne gazed up at the bright moon, high in the sky, and was surprised to feel some of the accumulated tension from the evening evaporate. It was amazing how a few minutes in nature could completely change one's perspective.

"I hope the weather holds for tomorrow." Käthe threw the words out lightly, but there was a pensive air about her, and her puffy face betrayed her earlier teary state.

Anne smiled. As they both well knew, Bridezilla had cut Alex down at the knees when he had inquired about the back-up plan for such a possibility. "I'm sure the day will be lovely no matter what happens with the weather."

As she stood next to the Diamond Goddess, Anne was struck again by how similar the two were in appearance. Both were about the same height and weight, with wavy, shoulder-length light-brown hair and wore understated but lovely sheath dresses that skimmed their bodies in a flattering silhouette. And yet, she felt like the understudy in a play, the offstage performer who would never measure up to the star.

"I hope there aren't any fireworks."

"I don't think they're allowed on the beach," Anne opted to interpret the statement literally while guessing that the maid of honor was hinting at something darker.

Käthe gave a small laugh. "Make sure Alex remembers that."

As if he could ever forget.

"Kevin's old boss will be at the wedding tomorrow." Käthe twisted a lock of hair back and forth in her fingers. "He's been keeping a low profile since being dismissed last week, but he can't hide forever. I imagine his wife told him he needed to dust off his trousers and pull himself together."

Anne hadn't seen the guest list, so this was the first she was learning that the disgraced CFO would be in attendance. "That could be a bit awkward if your father is there too," she said carefully.

Käthe sighed. "They all belong to the same country club, so they're going to have to learn how to deal with one another at some point."

Unless one of them decides to take their toys to a different sandbox. Unsure what to say, Anne simply nodded.

"Might as well be now." Käthe lifted her arms in the air like a ballerina, gracefully stretching herself up toward the sky.

"We're done." Alex came up behind Anne and slid his hand around her waist.

The Diamond Goddess glanced at the fireplace where Paige and Kevin were posing for additional pictures with various friends and relatives and then back at Anne, a quizzical expression on her face. "You're not—"

"Family only," Anne said flatly.

She looked genuinely sympathetic. "See you tomorrow."

"You too." Despite the heaviness in the pit of her stomach, Anne managed to muster a smile. Not a single picture of her at the rehearsal dinner. She wasn't a family member, and she wasn't a friend. She was simply a plus-one. Had Alex even noticed?

"Sleep well tonight," he said jovially. "Tomorrow's going to be a long day."

* * *

They drove in silence, the short distance to his parents' summer house.

"What's wrong?" Alex asked her as soon as they were safely in his bedroom with the door shut.

Where to even start? Your mother excluded me from the photographs, and I don't think you even noticed? Anne took a deep breath and reconsidered. *Probably not a great opening line.* As she slowly let the air flow out between her lips, she took a moment to look at Alex's face and saw worry lines around his eyes, the type he got when he was tired and stressed. She knew he found his family difficult to deal with on a good day and that this one had been particularly hard with his sister in her amped-up state.

He touched her shoulder gently. "Did something happen in the ladies' room tonight?"

Let's go there instead. I'll wait on bringing up the photo business until after the wedding and we can calmly discuss the awkward family dynamics. She nodded. "Käthe had a bit of a meltdown. Her mother's contemplating divorce."

"What?"

"It sounds like—"

"But Brigitte and Richard are such a solid couple."

Anne raised her hands in a don't shoot-the-messenger kind of way. "Evidently, the woman is worried that she's going to become financially destitute if Energix goes down the tubes. She seems to think that divorce might be a way to protect their assets, but—"

"You're kidding me. If there's fraud involved, money can often be clawed back anyway. Brigitte must know that."

"Well, your sister tried to say—"

"Oh no," he groaned. "Paige, the legal expert, weighed in?"

Anne threw her hands up. "She meant well. But the thing that concerned me—"

"Actually, I'm not surprised that Brigitte would be terrified of losing everything. Given her background and all."

Anne drew up in surprise. "What do you mean?"

"She escaped from East Germany as a child by climbing out of a window in Berlin and dropping over the wall to the west side." He gave her a sideways look. "I thought you knew."

How would she? It wasn't like they had spent hours talking about the Fernsbys. Anne shook her head, annoyed by his inability to fill her in on what inevitably turned out to be important information.

"She was just seventeen and completely on her own." He unzipped his toiletry bag and pulled out his toothbrush. "I remember her telling my mother that she thought she was going to starve, but in the end, she managed to make her way to the States with a scholarship of some sort. That's how she met Richard, actually. He was getting his MBA at Harvard, and she was at MIT, getting a PhD in chemistry."

Anne did a quick calculation. "That must have been in the early sixties. Pretty unusual for a woman at that time."

"When Brigitte sets her sights on something—" he sliced the air with his hand, "—she goes for it. Like a bulldozer. She'll flatten anything in her way."

With two parents as smart and determined as that, it was hard to believe that their daughter was flopping around in the dark, completely clueless as to what was going on with Energix. "Where did Käthe go to school?"

"Yale." He squeezed some toothpaste out and handed the tube to Anne so she could do the same. "She majored in economics with a minor in math."

Anne's eyes narrowed. Clearly, the new president of the Caribbean Fly-By-Night entity was capable of working with numbers. "And yet, she works in the marketing department." Anne turned on the water and began brushing her teeth.

"She doesn't have to work at all," he snorted. "The only reason Käthe got that job at Energix was so she'd have something to do. After she went to rehab—"

"Rehab?" Anne spat a mouthful of toothpaste into the sink, along with the word.

"She had a pretty serious cocaine problem."

Anne looked at him, dumbfounded. She might have expected this of Horse-Lover, but not the Diamond Goddess.

He raised an eyebrow. "She doesn't advertise it."

"That's understandable," Anne murmured, still trying to reconcile the idea of elegant, poised, always-perfectly-dressed Käthe struggling with drug addiction.

"In the end, the family did some sort of intervention." He flicked his toothbrush in and out of the running water. "She went away to one of those expensive clinics for a few months and returned with the idea that she wanted to work in corporate America."

And luckily for her, Daddy was the CEO at Energix. With the snap of his fingers, her wish had been granted. Once again, Anne was struck by the power of good connections. The only person she knew with a drug problem was a cousin who had had to file for bankruptcy after depleting his family's entire savings on methamphetamines. The repercussions of his poor choices continued to follow him years later as he struggled to regain financial stability. Nobody wanted to hire anyone with a history like that.

"Has she relapsed at all?"

He shook his head. "But I know her mother worries about it. Of course, it doesn't help that Brigitte is a worrier in general." He tapped his toothbrush on the side of the sink and placed it in a nearby cup to dry. "Her parents lost everything after World War II, when East Germany became part of the Soviet bloc, simply because they were intellectuals in what had become a communist state."

No wonder the woman was consulting with an attorney. With the daily revelations about Energix hitting the paper, her financial prospects appeared to be hanging on by a thin, precarious thread.

"Even so, I always thought she and Richard were a good match. He tends to be a dreamer, full of big ideas, while she's pragmatic, keeping him firmly tethered to solid ground. They balance each other. But you know what?" He wrapped his arms around Anne, holding her tight. "You can judge for yourself tomorrow. They'll both be at the wedding."

She groaned inwardly at the reminder that she would be socializing with the man who had mercilessly dragged her name through the mud.

As if reading her mind, Alex added, "I expect you'll find he's a completely different person outside of Energix."

10

The Wedding

The Hamptons

Morning, July 21, 1990

Anne woke to the smell of fresh coffee and the sound of plates and cutlery being pulled out of cabinets and drawers. She peered at the clock and sighed. Seven-thirty. Time to get up and face the family.

"Let's just stay here for a few more minutes." Alex reached out and tugged at her arm. "Once we go downstairs, we're going to get swept into the wedding frenzy."

She hesitated and then slid back under the covers, snuggling against his chest. He was right. Why rush into the lion's den?

"I've been wondering." He drew ever-widening spirals on her shoulder. "Why didn't you stick around for the photos last night?"

She sighed. "I was going to wait until after we got back to the apartment to discuss it."

His hand stopped moving. "Let's talk about it now. There's going to be a photographer again today. It would be nice if you were in a few of the pictures with me." His eyebrows quirked playfully. "Is there some reason my beautiful fiancée wants to stay incognito?"

She sat up, wrapped the corner of the blanket around her shoulders, and relayed his mother's edict: *Just family.*

He squinted his eyes as if he didn't quite understand. "Is there any chance you misinterpreted what she meant?"

If only it were that easy. Anne pulled the blanket more tightly and shook her head slowly. "Paige tried to apologize, but the fact remains—"

"I'm sorry." He bit his lip. "I'll talk to my mother this morning. It won't happen again."

"Look." Anne shifted slightly, trying to find a more comfortable position. "I don't want to force anyone to include me in their beloved portraits, but I'm getting concerned that she has a real problem with us. Me. Our engagement."

He gave her shoulder a gentle squeeze and pulled her down toward him. "Whatever is going on with my mother ends today. We're a package deal." He kissed the top of her head as he held her against his chest. "It's as simple as that."

She was hearing the right words and genuine-sounding emotion. But was it realistic? And would he actually step up to the plate? He had made a point of keeping their relationship under wraps until recently, presumably to avoid confrontation. On the other hand, he had remained strong on the whole prenup thing, demonstrating that he was willing to take a stand when required. "One thing to consider—"

A loud knock on the door disrupted their conversation. "Anne!" It was Paige, already frantic, even though the day had hardly begun. "Don't forget. Mani-pedis in one hour, sharp!"

"Sharp!" Alex whispered, giving Anne a small pinch on her arm.

She hopped out of bed and reviewed the card listing the schedule of events. Highlighted in pink was the directive: *Wear something comfortable and loose fitting in the morning.* At least the shoulder massage would be relaxing, and her nails would look nicely shaped and polished. She pulled a t-shirt and shorts out of her travel bag and headed for the shower.

"Want any help?" Alex clambered behind her.

"Nope." She gave him a quick kiss and turned on the water. It was going to be an action-packed day, and she wanted time to grab breakfast before heading out.

In fact, the bridal lunch ended up being surprisingly pleasant as well. It was held in a small, private room at the country club, filled with flowers, tasty light bites, and windows streaming natural light. As she laughed and cracked jokes with the other women, she felt like one of the group. Perhaps she was finally learning how to navigate the social waters of this community.

It wasn't until Richard Fernsby's arrival at the wedding reception that the first hint of a problem surfaced.

* * *

"That looks like Richard's car," Alex pointed at a red Mercedes convertible that had just come to a quick stop.

Anne took a sharp breath as a portly man climbed out and handed his key to the valet. He appeared to have aged ten years since the investor meeting the month before, his paunch protruding over a scrunched-up cummerbund, his face haggard and worn. *Hopefully, he doesn't recognize me.*

"Alex. My boy." His mouth widened into a smile as he stepped forward to shake hands. "How are you doing?"

"Really well." Alex pumped his hand vigorously. "I'd like to introduce you to my fiancée, Anne Scott."

A dark look passed over Richard's face that was quickly replaced by a false-friendly smile. There was no doubt in Anne's mind that he had just made the connection between his nemesis at Spencer Brothers and the woman standing before him. The question was how he would handle the revelation.

"We've met," he said evenly, giving her hand a firm shake.

She breathed a sigh of relief that he had decided to play friendly, at least for the day. "It's nice to see you again."

An older and more beautiful version of The Diamond Goddess glided over to join them. Like her daughter, she was dripping in diamonds and exuded an air of graceful ease. Alex gave her a quick kiss on each cheek, kicking off another round of introductions.

"Mrs. Fernsby—" Anne began.

"Please. Call me Brigitte."

"But first." Alex glanced around the foursome. "Would anyone like some champagne?"

Everyone nodded in unison, and Brigitte raised a finger. "I'll help you carry the glasses." She spoke with a distinctly German accent. "We can catch up. Yes?"

As soon as the two of them broke away, Richard began scouting around for better company. "Peter! Hey, Eckert!" he called out, his eyes fixated on a dark suit emerging from a bright blue Porsche. "A word?"

Anne watched in horror as the head of fixed income at Spencer Brothers strode toward them, his gray comb-over standing upright thanks to the brisk wind. Hanging off of his arm was his twenty-something secretary. She wore a skintight, glittery-pink dress that barely covered the tops of her thighs. Tottering across the uneven lawn in stilettos, she looked in grave danger of tripping as she struggled to match his fast pace.

Peter briefly greeted Anne and promptly disappeared with Richard, leaving her alone with his gum-chewing date.

"Small world!" The young woman popped one last bubble before spitting the wad onto the ground, just missing the giant sparkly bow on her shoe. "I didn't think I'd know anyone else here." She pulled out a cigarette and tilted the box toward Anne. "Do you smoke?"

At least she was polite.

"Absolutely not!" Peter said loudly, causing the two of them to turn. Anne couldn't make out the rest of what he said except for the word *barges*.

His date took a long drag on her cigarette and blew the smoke out to one side. "This is a really nice place. Do you know the bride personally?"

Anne was saved from further conversation when Alex and Brigitte returned, each holding two glasses of champagne.

"Where did Richard go?" Alex handed Anne one of the drinks.

She nodded toward a large rhododendron, thirty feet to her right, where Peter was gesturing angrily.

"There's no leeway..." Peter's voice was drowned out by a plane flying overhead.

Twinkle-Toes turned to Mrs. Fernsby. "I can take one of those glasses of bubbly off your hands."

Brigitte studied the woman for a moment and then smiled enigmatically. "That would be lovely, dear."

"If I go down, so do you!" Richard turned on his heel and slammed into a tall, thin man, knocking the beanpole into a bed of hydrangeas.

"Sorry," Richard muttered, looking anything but.

"Isn't that—" Anne began.

"Donald!" Peter rushed over and reached out a hand. "Are you okay?"

Indeed, it was Donald Chalmers, the recently-fired CFO of Energix.

"I'm fine." He stood up and brushed off his suit, all the while glaring at his former boss.

"What happened?" Käthe joined the ever-growing crowd.

The ex-CFO locked eyes with her, a look of panic on his face. Meanwhile, Richard stood sullenly to the side, simply frowning.

"Are you alright?" Peter asked again.

"I'm fine," he said brusquely and nodded at his wife.

"We're moving on," she announced, waving a flounce-sleeved arm in the air like a queen dismissing mere commoners.

"What was he doing there?" Richard eyed the retreating man.

"Escorting his wife to the sushi table." Peter sounded exasperated. "Or maybe the one with prime rib. Like any normal person."

Käthe flashed her mother a look of consternation, seemingly mortified by her father's attitude toward his former employee.

Brigitte shrugged slightly in return. "Richard must be in one of his moods. Ja?"

What does that mean? Is he going to be banging into people all afternoon? "Good thing Don wasn't hurt," Anne whispered to Alex. "He got bumped pretty hard."

"How about if you all come closer together?" A photographer motioned with his hands. "Let's get a photo."

Anne groaned inwardly as they gave their best smiles for the camera. Richard Fernsby was the last person with whom she wanted to rub shoulders.

"Actually," the cameraman paused his clicking to address Peter Eckert and his date. "I think it would be better if you and your daughter moved further to the right."

Alex coughed as the smoke from her cancer stick wafted around their fake smiles.

"And you might want to try to hide that cigarette."

* * *

Evening

Between the salad and main course that evening, Alex whispered in Anne's ear. "Let's elope. We can hit the Elvis Chapel in Vegas and skip all this fuss."

She laughed.

"I'm serious. It would be so much easier." He leaned back while a waiter refilled his water glass.

"I think my mother might be upset if we did that. But maybe we could do something small."

"With my family, that'll never happen. Small will grow to just a bit bigger, and next thing you know, half the country club will be invited." He took a bite of lobster. "But you can't invite just half the country club…"

She looked around the tent. "You have to admit this is an exquisite affair." Every table had an eye-catching flower arrangement on it. The food was delicious. The sound of waves rolling in and out on the beach below could be heard in the background. In some ways it would be nice to do something similar when they got married. And yet.

"I think we should just slip away without telling anyone and then celebrate afterwards with our friends." He swirled the wine gently in his glass before taking a sip. "Come to think of it, that's what Brigitte said she wished she and Richard had done."

Anne glanced over at the table where the Fernsbys sat with his parents, laughing and talking as if they didn't have a care in the world. "I wonder why."

"She's very pragmatic. Probably thought it wasn't worth all the effort." He shrugged. "Or cost."

A groomsman sitting at the next table over, reclined precariously in his chair and tapped Alex on the shoulder. "We need a bow for the dog so your sister can get another picture with her."

Alex squinted at the slightly disheveled man. "She's already wearing one."

"Not anymore." His chair wobbled when he shook his head. "What's left of it's in pieces all over the kitchen floor." It wobbled again and, this time, tipped backwards onto the ground.

Alex put out a hand to help the guy up. "Right. I'll find another one after we finish dinner."

Consequently, Anne was on her own at the end of the meal, milling around the edge of the party as it shifted into full swing. She was swaying back and forth in time to the music, looking around for someone to chat with next, when she spotted Richard Fernsby. He stood alone near the drinks table, about twenty feet away, staring at her with an angry scowl on his face.

She forced a smile and gave a small wave in an effort to be friendly.

His head rolled back and then snapped forward, as if he was having difficulty controlling his movements.

Is he drunk?

He began heading toward her, his gait unsteady.

"Anne," his thick, gravelly voice boomed in greeting. "Our upcoming little star." He sneered as he extended an arm outward, pretending to introduce her to the crowd, and immediately lurched to the side, struggling to maintain his balance.

Her heart began pounding.

"I just want you to know one thing." He crept closer to her with each utterance, his face mottled red. "One simple thing."

Anne stared at the CEO, reeking with sweat, towering over her.

"This isn't over."

A chill went down her spine as she took a step back. Out of the corner of her eye, she saw Kevin rushing over.

"You'll pay for what you've done." His face contorted with fury. "You miserable little bitch."

And then he spat on the ground.

In front of at least a dozen nearby guests.

The conversations in the area encircling them immediately ceased as everyone within earshot paused to see what would happen next in the battle between Richard Fernsby, big-time CEO of Energix, and Anne Scott, wet-behind-the-ears money manager at Spencer Brothers. Probably unemployed after his good friend and golf buddy (the president of her company) got wind of this.

Kevin grabbed Richard's arm. "Come on. Let's go up to the house."

* * *

"Do you have any idea where my daughter might be?" Brigitte's azure eyes sparkled under the lanterns that hung in long rows, illuminating the outline of the big party tent.

Anne eyed her warily. She was still reeling after being publicly chewed out by the woman's husband just an hour earlier. *What's her game?*

"I haven't seen Käthe in quite a while," Anne managed. *Or anyone at all,* she might have added. After Richard's out-of-the-blue attack, she had taken a long walk around the grounds to calm down and re-center herself. "Maybe she's busy doing maid-of-honor things."

Brigitte appeared to study her for a moment. "I want to say how sorry I am for how my husband acted earlier tonight. It was unforgivable." She rested a diamond-studded hand on her heart. "I wish there were something I could do to make up for it."

It was a nice sentiment. But the words couldn't be taken back. And Anne couldn't get them out of her mind. *This isn't over. You miserable little bitch. You'll pay for what you've done.* They kept rattling around, refusing to settle down, a constant reminder of how tenuous her position in both the financial and social worlds was. She was an outsider, barely tolerated, who could be kicked out on a whim.

"If it's any consolation, I told him to find his own way home tonight." Brigitte dangled a key in her hand.

Decisive and bold. Anne envied her response. The polar opposite of how she herself had reacted.

Brigitte opened her palms to the sky. "Seems only fair. Yes?"

Fair? It was an odd choice of word. More like *what he deserved.* But English wasn't this woman's first language. Anne nodded stiffly.

"Never let someone disrespect you like that." Brigitte's eyes looked hard. "And there's nothing weak about choosing to walk away."

That's probably what she should have done. Haughtily. As if she hadn't a care in the world. But she'd been so shocked, so caught off guard, that she'd stood transfixed, like a statue, unsure what to say or do while options ping-ponged in her mind. Defend herself? *I was only doing my job. It's your own damn fault you're in this pickle.* Laugh as if he'd just cracked a very bad joke? Told him where to shove it? Instead, she'd simply frozen, with god-only-knows-what sort of look on her face. She cringed just thinking about it.

Brigitte looked pained. "I'm not sure what came over him."

Anne wondered if she had any idea that he had also threatened to sue her.

"I just wanted to let you know how appalled I am." She gave a small nod and began to turn away. "Actually." She paused and came back to face Anne. "I'd like to give you some advice on something else. Ja?"

Advice?

"I heard what happened last night at the rehearsal dinner."

Anne tensed. Was she about to get a lecture about eavesdropping in the ladies' room? It wasn't like she had hidden in the stall. Paige and Käthe had been fully aware that she was in there. They chose to continue the conversation. She braced for the onslaught, but this time, she wasn't going to stand by like a limp fish. If Brigitte tried to take her to task, she was going to let the woman have it.

"Don't let Alex's mother intimidate you."

Anne blinked and felt her jaw go slack.

"I don't think she's approved of anyone he's ever dated. And I have to

84

say, excluding you from the photographs at the rehearsal dinner last night was...how do you say?...despicable." She shuddered. "And tacky."

A dam of emotions threatened to burst inside of Anne. She had begun the conversation assuming that Brigitte was a stuck-up society wife about to put her in her place but found that she was completely the opposite. Sympathetic. So different than her husband. And strong. Someone who understood how discouraging the situation with Alex's parents was. Anne had been ready to take the woman down when all she wanted to do was offer some kind words and friendly support. She gripped her wineglass, feeling like an idiot. And yet, she found herself wondering, *how did someone as nice as this end up with someone as obnoxious as Richard?*

"I'll let you in on a little secret." Brigitte leaned toward her conspiratorially. "Richard and I went through a similar thing. His parents didn't want to meet me before we got married. In fact, we didn't know if they were even going to attend the wedding. But you know what took the cake?"

Anne stared at the stunningly beautiful, poised woman standing next to her, wondering what awful thing was about to be exposed.

"His mother called me a 'worn-out shoe' because I had been married briefly before I made my way over to the States. A hasty, silly marriage that lasted just a year."

And all along Anne had thought that *Alex's* mother was a nasty piece of work.

"She was upset also that I was five years older than Richard, even though she is twenty years younger than that worthless sack of potatoes she calls a husband. It makes no sense."

Anne nodded. The woman was totally right. *No wonder there are so many in-law jokes. And family feuds.*

Brigitte wiggled her fingers in mock horror. "The idea of the older woman with the younger man was anathema to both of them. They didn't care that I was in the PhD program at an elite institution. Or that I love their son. All they were concerned about was my age and German accent." She narrowed her eyes. "So shallow. And very short-sighted, because we married anyway. Their behavior drove a deep wedge between them and Richard that never went away."

The Battle-Axe in Anne's life looked like a walk in the park compared to this monster-in-law.

"The thing to remember is that her rudeness speaks volumes about her. It says nothing about you."

And I suppose the same could be said about your husband being no reflection of you. "Wow. I really appreciate—"

Kevin suddenly appeared. He was panting heavily, and his bowtie was askew. "Sorry to interrupt. Have either of you seen Käthe anywhere? It's almost time for the send-off. We need the maid of honor to do something with… I forget what…sparklers? I don't know. I'm just the messenger."

Brigitte locked eyes with Anne. "I better go find my daughter." She headed toward the pulsing crowd of new-wave dance-punk enthusiasts just as they screamed *Rock Lobster* and began wiggling down toward the ground.

"I'll look as well," Anne told Kevin. "Why don't you just get yourself to the boat?"

Alex intercepted her before she had made it halfway across the tent. "I'm so sorry we haven't had a chance to talk." He shook his head. "I heard what happened with Richard."

"He totally lost it! Right in front of—"

"Alex!" One of the groomsmen waved his arms.

He groaned.

She took a deep breath. "We can talk later."

"I'm sorry." He raised his hands in exasperation. "My mother's having a cow. We need to get everyone to the bluff for the send-off before the weather gets worse."

Anne glanced up at the clouds gathering in the sky. The air felt heavy. It wouldn't be long before the first drops of rain began to fall.

"Have you seen Kevin?"

She pointed toward a hunched figure in the distance, dragging himself slowly across the grass in the general direction of the dock. "I think the festivities may have done him in."

"I'm not surprised," Alex chuckled. "I'm exhausted, too. And I haven't had to deal with half as much as that poor guy has."

Stuff with Alex's mother? Or is Paige starting to go off the rails? Anne leaned in for a hug and felt him respond by pulling her toward him. "Would you like me to do anything?"

He rocked her gently back and forth. "Just stay here while I grab the best man. Earlier in the evening, he said something about wanting to drive the boat. With the wind picking up, I'm not sure it's a great idea. I should probably have a quick chat with him before we get to the bluff to make sure he still wants to do it."

Anne pulled back and nodded toward a guy holding what looked like a martini in one hand as he pretended to sing with the band. "You mean him?"

Alex turned just as the man stumbled and fell against the speaker, splattering the remainder of his drink across the front of Horse-Lover's peach taffeta dress. No way was he getting behind the wheel.

Alex sighed. "Yet another reason to pass on the idea." He gave her a peck on the cheek and headed toward the stage.

After a word with the band and some prodding of the guests, the mood shifted along with the music. Gone were the entitled loud voices, inebriated laughing, and shallow gossip as the partygoers drifted out of the tent and made their way to the bluff above the dock. In their place were the hushed conversations of staff cleaning the litter left behind and the sounds of the big tent canopy creaking and flapping in the wind.

* * *

The send-off. It was supposed to be the final chapter of the day. Some congratulatory words to the happy couple. A quick farewell wave. Anne glanced over at Alex, walking beside her, his sandy hair blown every which way.

"I can tell you're still worrying about that wanker," he said in a lecturing manner.

Despite everything, she smiled. Wanker. His choice of word was so perfectly disparaging. So apt. And she loved the way the final r almost disappeared off of his British tongue.

"Fernsby was completely out of line, and everyone knows it." Alex slowed down and turned to face her. If I'd been there—"

But he'd been elsewhere, in his role as a groomsman, helping out with his sister's wedding. Fortunately, Kevin had stepped in and escorted the jerk away.

"I just can't believe he went off on me like that." Her voice caught in her throat, and she felt the sting of tears, tears she desperately wanted to hold back.

"Me neither." Alex sounded strangely distant. "I used to actually respect the man. Thought he was a no-nonsense, pull-himself-up-by-the-bootstraps kind of guy. Like Brigitte." He shook his head in disbelief.

"I know he'd had a lot to drink." Anne pulled her arms tightly against her chest and shivered in the cool night air. "But even so..."

"It's no excuse." Alex brushed a tendril of hair off of her face. "He's got a lot to answer for."

"Your family..." her voice trailed off, refusing to admit what she was thinking. *They already thought I was a loser. Someone to be dumped as fast as humanly possible. What are they going to say now?*

Alex pulled her toward him, his warm arms blocking the wind as they encircled her, and she felt herself sink into his protective cocoon. "I already said something to my mother this morning about the rehearsal dinner business. I'm going to talk to her again, as well as my father, and get everything sorted." His voice was calm. Soothing. Almost believable. "Trust me. Everything will be fine."

But how? She had seen various people briefing the lord and lady afterwards, casting hurried glances in her direction and then huddling in tight circles. Even without this latest brouhaha, it was clear her future in-laws could barely tolerate her. And now this...Anne shook her head. They would never accept her no matter how hard she tried.

"We better get moving." He gave her a final squeeze before disentangling his arms.

Anne stepped carefully through the damp grass, wishing she could melt into the shadows and slink away from their reproving faces. Instead, she was about to join up with the group buzzing around the bride and groom, alive with boisterous laughter, enjoying champagne. Suddenly, Brigitte's advice popped into her head: *don't let them intimidate you*. She pulled her shoulders back and lifted her face to the wind.

"Not only that, I'm going to talk to Richard as well," he said firmly.

"But—"

"No buts. He had no business bringing this rubbish to my sister's wedding, and the way he treated you was disgraceful. I'm—"

"Alex?" A man's voice called from the edge of the bluff where the wedding party and a handful of other well-wishers were gathered.

"Coming!"

"About time!" There was the sound of a cork being popped followed by laughter and clinking glasses.

"Dearest brother!" The bride's voice sang out. "Do you have the flashlight?"

"But of course!" He gave a small bow and clicked it on briefly for good measure.

"We're off!" the groom announced, raising his hand in a final goodbye.

And with that, the trio turned in unison and began making their way toward the boat docked below. Alex led with the light, illuminating a dozen, weather-beaten wood steps, while the bride and groom followed immediately behind, all moving at a very quick pace.

"Such a cute couple!" an elderly woman said to no one in particular.

"Aren't they just," Anne replied, relieved that the affair was almost over. Her feet hurt from wearing heels all day and it felt like the blustery wind was cutting through to her bones.

"And such a lovely reception," the woman continued. "I only wish my late husband, Everett—"

The flashlight went flying, followed by a clattering thump. "Bloody hell!" Alex yelled, his voice nearly drowned by the pounding surf.

Anne tried to discern his form in the darkness but couldn't make anything definitive out.

"Everything okay?" one of the groomsmen shouted down.

There was a pause and then Alex's weary sounding voice called back, "We're fine. A rope must have come loose."

"That's strange," the best man muttered. "Geoff said he checked them this afternoon."

"I did!" the groomsman, who must have been Geoff, sounded indignant. "Twice!"

"It's blowing a gale out here," a third piped up. "It probably just worked itself off of the fitting."

"I guess," the first one said, not sounding very convinced.

The flashlight began moving again, casting eerie shadows on the dock and water. From the way it was angled, they appeared to be untying the remaining ropes. Anne caught a glimpse of the boat rocking in the roiling sea below. It was going to be a rough ride to their hotel on the other side of the bay. Thank goodness she had declined Alex's suggestion that she join them. She'd probably be hanging over the side hurling before they had even made it halfway."

Paige said something that Anne couldn't make out.

"Wait a minute!" Yet another groomsman sounded incredulous. "Did she just say there's a tarp on the floor?"

They began murmuring amongst themselves. "But we moved everything to the boathouse this afternoon." Until eventually, "Let's go down and see what's going on."

Anne followed the groomsmen as they began parading down the steps.

"Alex!" Paige's voice sounded slightly shrill. "Can you shine the light over here?"

A dark shape was illuminated for just a moment as Alex swung the flashlight in her general direction. After a moment, he shifted the beam downward and then stopped suddenly.

Anne took a sharp breath and grabbed the handrail.

"What the hell?"

"Oh my God!"

"Is that a body?"

The wanker was dead.

11

The Second Brigade

The Hamptons

The day after the wedding

The morning after the wedding, Anne awoke to bright sun streaming through the window. The fit of stormy weather had made way for what promised to be a beautiful day. And yet she was exhausted. It was after 3 a.m. before they got to bed. And even then, she had slept fitfully.

Alex stirred under the covers.

"Hey, handsome." She gave him a light tap on the shoulder.

He rolled over and kissed her. "I'm knackered." He rolled back and stared at the ceiling. "I still can't believe that Richard's dead."

Neither could she. Her archenemy had been vanquished. It was a relief that he could no longer take potshots at her. "Last night was such a shock. It may take a while for everything to sink in."

His hand reached out and found hers, giving it a light squeeze. "Let's take it easy today. Forget about tennis or anything else social. Maybe just the two of us could bike along the shore."

Fresh air. Distance from his parents and the house and everything that had happened at the wedding the day before. "Sounds great." She sat up and stretched. The aroma of bacon wafted through the air. "Do you feel up to getting some breakfast first?"

As they entered the dining room, they were greeted by the scent of cinnamon, vanilla, and jasmine. Anne inhaled deeply and headed over to the mahogany sideboard covered with eggs, bacon, croissants, and freshly made pancakes arranged on a series of silver chafing platters.

The door separating the dining room from the kitchen swung open, and an apron-clad woman materialized with a carafe of orange juice. "Freshly squeezed," she chirped as she set it on the table.

When Anne had first learned that a weekend maid had been hired to handle all-things-domestic, she had thought it extravagant, bordering on pretentious, with just four people staying at the house. But after seeing the number of guests traipsing in and out over the course of the weekend, she had to admit it made things much easier for Alex's parents, especially his mother. And it was pretty darn nice to have a dedicated person available at their beck and call, willing to find an extra spoon or towel and to ferry a cold pitcher of water over to the courts during a hard game of tennis.

"Good morning." Alex's father was already seated, the Sunday Times open to the crossword puzzle. "How is everyone doing this morning?"

Before they could answer, the doorbell rang.

He glanced down at his watch and then at his wife. "They're early. I thought Kevin and Paige didn't fly out until sometime this afternoon."

Alex's mother appeared equally perplexed. "Why didn't they just come in?" She stood up and headed into the foyer.

Anne picked up a croissant, took a quick bite, and began filling her plate with items from the sumptuous-looking buffet. She caught a whiff of basil and dill as she lifted the lid over the scrambled eggs and decided to take an extra spoonful.

"Don't forget the pico de gallo." Alex pointed toward a small bowl on the side.

At the rate she was piling food on her plate, she wouldn't need lunch.

"Anne?" His mother poked her head through the door. "The police are back. They'd like to have a word with you.

"Me?" She gave Alex a quizzical look.

"I'll go with you."

She put up her hand. "It's fine. I can handle it." The previous night with the local constabulary had been straightforward, with just a handful of lightweight questions. Presumably, this would be more of the same.

He studied her for a second and then relented with a shrug of his shoulders. "I'll be right here if you change your mind."

She headed into the living room, where the officers were waiting. After a brief introduction, the two men sat down on the couch, and she took a seat in a chair facing them. In the background she could just make out the sounds of voices in the dining room and still smell the bacon. Her stomach grumbled. She hoped the interview would be quick.

"We're following up on statements that were taken last night," the balding one said. He looked to be about fifty years old and slightly overweight, in contrast with his buff partner in trendy sunglasses who could probably run a marathon.

"It says here that the last time you saw Richard Fernsby was around 9 pm, under the tent where the main event was going on."

"That's right."

He paused for a moment and appeared to study her. "Did you go down to the boat at any point yesterday?"

She gave a small shiver. "No."

"You're certain."

She drew back in her chair, unsure why they were quizzing her on this point. "Positive. I was up on the bluff with the rest of the wedding party."

He must have sensed her unease. "Don't take this wrong." He opened his palms in a just-doing-my-job kind of way. "These are the kinds of things we need to check whenever someone dies unexpectedly. It's standard procedure."

She heard her stomach growl and thought of the eggs growing cold on her plate in the other room. She had a sinking feeling that this meeting was going to take longer than she had hoped.

"In the notes from last night, you described Richard Fernsby as *unsteady on his feet.* Would you say he was drunk?"

Plastered. She nodded.

"Did you notice anything that might have suggested he was having a medical issue? Difficulty breathing, for example? Clutching his chest in pain? Anything of that nature?"

She thought of the red, pulsing veins on his beefy neck as he towered over her, looking like he might lose the last vestiges of self-control at any moment. "He didn't appear to be in any sort of physical distress when I saw him. Just angry."

The officer watched her, unblinking. "I understand he had a few choice words for you."

That's one way of putting it. "He called me a bitch."

The buff guy leaned forward. "Any idea why he was so hopping mad?"

She looked directly at him. "I manage a mid-sized investment fund that owned a significant amount of stock in his company until fairly recently. When I sold it, he blamed me for causing the stock price to fall."

Captain Cool took off his glasses and began rubbing one of the lenses. "Why *you* in particular?"

Good question. "Because I was the first to sell. He thought I had spooked the other investors."

"And had you?"

She shrugged. "No idea. Investment managers don't generally share their strategies with one another."

He put the glasses in his pocket and cocked his head.

"We buy and sell stocks all the time," she added. "That's our job. All I know is that his stock wasn't a good fit for my fund."

He put his hands behind his head and spread his legs wide. It was a posture that Anne recognized from years of dealing with the bond traders at work. Cocky. Meant to convey confidence and dominance. *What's his deal?*

The older officer tapped a ballpoint pen against his meaty palm. "Getting attacked like that in public must have been pretty upsetting."

It had been humiliating. And uncalled for. She met his gaze. "It was."

"How did you respond?"

94

Like a panicked squirrel who can't decide which way to go, as a car barrels down the road straight toward it. She reminded herself to keep her answers simple. "I just stood there." She bit her lip. "Mortified."

He nodded. "That's understandable. You needed time to think."

As Anne shifted the perfectly matched throw pillow a bit higher behind her back, she took stock of the scene before her. Mr. Sympathetic leaned earnestly forward on one end of the couch while Alpha-Male sprawled back on the other. *Where is all of this going?* She rotated her shoulders and let the pillow drop just a hair. A living room was meant to be a place for sitting and yet she generally found the furniture downright uncomfortable, regardless of how much it cost.

"Between the time you had this altercation with the deceased and when he was found in the boat, did you remain at the reception the entire time? Within the tent, I mean."

She blinked. *He's asking about my movements.* Her heart began to beat faster. "I know I went up to the house to use the bathroom at one point." She paused and deliberately slowed her pace, carefully considering her words. "Why do you ask?"

He repeated the open palm gesture again, as if to signal that he was just a public servant following bureaucratic orders who would rather be at home drinking coffee, but someone had to pay the bills. "It helps to get a better idea of where various people were. Who might have seen what."

"I didn't see Richard Fernsby after Kevin escorted him away."

He glanced down at his notes again. "Can anyone attest to your whereabouts between the time he left with the groom and when you spoke with Brigitte Fernsby?"

She opened her mouth and then shut it again. Not entirely. Part of the time, she had been milling around the party with Alex, exchanging pleasantries with the family's country club friends. But there was also that long walk she had taken along the bluff to clear her head.

Alone.

She looked back and forth at the two men sitting across from her. The older one appeared relaxed and comfortable, but something about the younger one's posture bothered her. He seemed on edge and was scrutinizing her intently. Way too intently.

"I think I want my fiancé to join us." She turned toward the door. "Alex!"

"Ma'am—"

"Can you come in here, please?"

The men exchanged glances. "We prefer to speak one on one."

And at this point, she didn't think she should be speaking to them at all.

"We want to avoid having one person influence the other." The calm veneer was gone. The balding man spoke quickly, with a hint of panic, as if he was about to lose his star witness. "It tends to happen without people even realizing it. He remembers a blue shirt, and next thing you know—"

"What's up?" Alex appeared at the door.

"I'm sorry, sir." Sunglass guy stood up. "I'm going to have to ask you to step out of the room until we're finished."

Anne locked eyes with Alex. "They're asking whether anyone can confirm—"

"Ma'am!"

"—where I was between 9 and 10 pm. Shortly before Richard Fernsby's death."

No one spoke for a moment.

"Why?" He walked across the room to where she was sitting and rested his hand on the top of her chair. He appeared at ease, congenial even, but Anne recognized his stance from years of working together on financial issues with traders who had gone astray. He was in lawyer mode, on high alert.

Paunch guy gave a no-big-deal shrug. "Dotting the i's, Crossing the t's."

Alex's eyes narrowed ever so slightly. "Which department are you in?"

He stiffened. "Homicide."

Anne took a sharp breath.

"Look," the detective sighed. "It's standard practice for us to be called out any time someone dies unexpectedly. Stroke. Suicide. You name it. Our job is to find out what happened and document it." He paused to adjust his glasses. "Just a few more questions, and we'll be out of everyone's hair."

"Right. Can you explain why you're asking Ms. Scott to provide a detailed accounting of where *she* was last night?"

"Like I said—"

"Sir," Alex put his hand up. "I understand your job. I'm an attorney. Why are you pursuing this line of questioning?"

The man regarded Alex for a long moment, his eyes glinting, as if calculating odds on a high-stakes bet. "There are some aspects of Mr. Fernsby's death that are suspicious. We're simply—"

"This interview is over."

* * *

"Did they identify themselves as detectives when you began?" Alex asked after shutting the door behind the two departing men.

"No. They flashed their badges, but I didn't realize they were different from the local police who came by last night. I thought they were just circling back to finish up some paperwork...that the whole thing was routine."

"Is everything alright?" Alex's mother suddenly appeared in the hallway, fiddling with her pearls.

He turned to face her, a look of consternation on his face. "I'm not sure. The police are acting as if they think Richard was murdered."

"Good grief!" She planted a hand firmly on each hip. "Does that mean we're going to be living with crime-scene tape all over the place for months on end? I thought they put it up last night as just a formality."

Anne took a deep breath. *Too bad Fernsby didn't happen to keel over at the church after the wedding ceremony instead. It would have been so much more convenient.*

Alex shrugged his shoulders, cool as a cucumber. "You'll have to ask them."

In the dining room, Alex's father looked ashen upon hearing the news. "Suspicious death, they said? A rather vague way of putting things."

"That's the point." Alex broke his croissant into pieces and buttered the first generously. "They don't want to give up the game. They try to say just enough to get people to loosen up and talk. It's a standard fishing tactic. We need to warn Paige and Kevin, so they don't fall for it."

"Warn us about what?" Paige glided into the room with Kevin trailing a few steps behind.

"It's the newlyweds!" Alex's mother went over to give them both a welcoming hug.

"The police think Richard Fernsby was murdered." Alex's father gave a dismissive wave of his fork. "Next, they'll be arresting the caterer for clogging the man's arteries."

"But he died of a heart attack." Paige leaned over to give him a quick hello kiss on the cheek.

"My point exactly."

"Dad!" Alex looked surprisingly exasperated.

At work, he remained calm and unflustered at the most trying of times, but here, with his family, it seemed like he struggled to keep his cool. *They know how to push his buttons.*

"This isn't a joking matter."

"Of course not. But to suggest someone topped the man? At Paige's wedding, no less?"

"Maybe the medical examiner saw something unusual." The words were out of Anne's mouth before she thought about the wisdom of inserting herself into the conversation.

The room went still except for the ticking of the antique grandfather clock in the corner.

"It's a good point." Alex finally broke the silence. "No one actually said it was a heart attack last night. We just assumed."

"You can't be serious." His mother clanked her fork on the plate. "That would mean one of our guests was responsible."

"I can think of a former co-worker with an axe to grind," Kevin said drily.

"Donald?" Paige arched her brow. "You think he would be capable of killing someone?"

"Fernsby fired him less than a week ago and pretty much hung him out to dry. Plus, he's the ex-CFO of a major corporation that's being investigated by the SEC. It would be enough to make anyone go postal."

"Then why did we invite him to our wedding?"

"We didn't know he was going to be let go." Kevin furrowed his brow. "I wonder if this will affect who takes over as CEO?" He gazed out the window, no doubt constructing a list of potential candidates.

Alex tapped a water glass to get everyone's attention. "Before we get any further, I want to say one thing."

"Uh-oh," Paige crossed her arms. "It sounds like we're in trouble."

He waved his spoon at her. "Nobody's in trouble, but the situation has changed significantly from last night." He paused, and his face hardened. "Richard is a high-profile individual. The fact that they're even suggesting the possibility of foul play means they're going to be looking for anything that seems the least bit off. And they'll be under pressure to get to the bottom of things quickly."

Kevin broke away from the window and leaned casually against the wall. "Can we still go on our honeymoon, do you think?"

Paige looked at him pointedly. "I can't imagine they would make us cancel at this late date. It's been planned for ages."

As if that mattered under circumstances such as these.

"They can't stop you once you're on the plane." Her father smiled enigmatically. "If I were you, I'd make a break for the airport now."

Alex threw his hands up. "You just gave a perfect example of what I'm worried about. Someone could easily seize on a remark like that and twist it in some unexpected direction."

"Let's not be overly dramatic." Alex's mother dabbed at the corner of her mouth with a napkin. "Richard's death has been very upsetting. Your father was just trying to lighten the mood."

"The thing that law enforcement types don't always have is a sense of humor. We need to take this seriously." He eyeballed everyone in the room. "No one should talk to any of these investigators without a lawyer present. It doesn't matter how innocuous you think your individual comments might be. Even a simple joke about hightailing it out of the country could be problematic if taken out of context. Believe me, none of us wants to get caught in the crosshairs of this investigation."

"Don't worry," Paige said equally somberly. "We all learned that lesson with your little bonfire escapade. If you had just kept your mouth shut..."

"Exactly." His jaw tightened.

Paige sighed. "Richard was really helpful in getting that situation resolved." She smiled sadly and continued reminiscing. "Even though he could be a bit fiery on the tennis court, he could also be a very strong ally. I'm going to miss him."

Alex's mother pointed toward the kitchen. "I asked the maid to put a basket together with a quiche, some fruit, and a few of these scones from our breakfast. I'm planning to pop over later today and see how Brigitte is doing." She closed her eyes and brought her hand to her chest. "I can only imagine..."

"I wish I could go with you...but our flight..." Paige bit her lip. "I just don't think—"

"You don't have time." Kevin looked at her. "In fact, we should probably get our luggage out onto the porch so that we're ready to go when the car arrives."

Paige walked to the door and then turned around to face the room. "Before everything happened last night, Käthe was talking about the annual tennis party they always have. Richard ordered a giant judge's chair that is supposed to arrive this week. Do you think Brigitte will still go forward with the event?"

"It's been a tradition for years." Kevin patted Paige on her back. "I bet she continues it."

And what if she doesn't? Will the world stop spinning on its axis? Navigating random social obligations seemed like the least of the poor woman's worries. If she didn't know already, she was about to learn that the police suspected Richard didn't die of natural causes. One more shock on top of having her entire life upended.

"Let us know when you're heading out," Alex's father said. "We'll see you off."

Anne thought of Brigitte telling Richard to find his own way home last night and felt a stab of pity for her. They were probably her last words to him. Such a sad note on which to part ways with someone who had been a huge fixture in her life for thirty-plus years.

"Ready for that bike ride?" Alex leaned toward Anne and grabbed a small piece of bacon sitting on her plate.

"Hey! I was planning to eat that." She took a last sip of tea and stood up.

"They're still out there." Alex nodded toward the window where the detectives could be seen in the distance milling around the dock and boat, presumably collecting evidence. "After all that rain last night, I wonder what they hope to find."

Anne followed his gaze, a single question in her mind. *Am I a suspect?*

12

The Funeral

The Hamptons

A week after the wedding

As the mourners gathered around the open grave at the cemetery, Anne saw two men standing apart from the group wearing short-sleeve golf shirts and LL Bean-style khaki pants, clothes completely unlike the other attendees. *The homicide detectives.* Her eyes widened when the one sporting reflective sunglasses gave her a small nod. She nudged Alex and tilted her head in their general direction. "Look who's here."

He glanced quickly and sighed. "At least they're keeping a respectful distance."

Had they been at the funeral as well? She hadn't seen them in the church, but she and Alex's entire family had been seated in one of the front pews near Brigitte and Käthe. It was possible the men had been in the far back, and she hadn't noticed.

"I hope Brigitte doesn't see them," he whispered. "It's the last thing she needs to worry about today."

Why are they here? She tried to focus on the minister's final words, but her mind kept wandering to the two policemen hovering behind the group.

She glanced back again and saw the buff guy leaning nonchalantly against a large oak tree, his mirrored shades trained on her. Or at least it seemed that way. Anne suddenly felt very self-conscious, aware that they were probably monitoring her every move.

"Just ignore them," Alex murmured quietly, his eyes never straying from the casket.

"...Ashes to ashes," the minister intoned, "dust to dust..."

Kind of like Energix. A company that had been vibrant and full of promise at one time, now reduced to a smoldering heap, the stock selling at a fraction of the price it had been a month ago, and the SEC breathing down their necks. Anne glanced over at Peter Eckert, wondering if he appreciated the irony of the words, but his face was impassive, giving no indication that he even saw her.

As the polished mahogany casket was lowered inch-by-inch into the grave, a gust of wind rustled the leaves in the trees, another reminder of the two men watching the proceedings from afar. *What could they possibly hope to learn at Richard Fernsby's funeral of all places?*

Brigitte picked up a handful of dirt and stepped forward. Tall and unfaltering, she waited for Käthe to join her before extending one arm and letting the gravelly soil slowly filter through her fingers onto the coffin below. After a long moment, she nodded at her daughter. "It's time to let him go."

Käthe gently threw a small bouquet of purple and white flowers she'd been clutching in her hand. A rivulet of water ran down her face, and she shook as the flowers spread out in a wide arc before raining down into the burial pit. As sobs racked her body, Paige stepped out of the crowd to put an arm around her best friend. Brigitte remained standing nearby, like a statue, firm and resolute.

Anne hardly knew the two women and had openly battled with the man lying in the coffin, and yet she felt great sadness for the bereaved mother and daughter. Both had been showered with all the standard platitudes throughout the day—*Sorry for your loss. If there's anything I can do to help. He'll be greatly missed*—well-intended words that were just that, words. In the end, nothing could undo the fact that Richard Fernsby was dead, and they were now forced to navigate the world alone, without him.

Brigitte turned stiffly and then froze as her eyes fell on the two policemen. "Heartless bastards," she practically spat. Her eyes blazed through the thin, black veil that went over her stylish, wide-brimmed black hat. "They can't even let us grieve in peace."

Käthe looked toward the trees, confused. "What are *they* doing here?" The pain of loss was etched on her puffy, tear-streaked face.

"Don't worry about them," Paige murmured.

"But—"

"I'll walk you to the car." Paige propelled Käthe away from the grave, the mourners clearing a path for them to pass.

Brigitte followed silently behind, stopping suddenly when she reached her elderly mother. She leaned toward the pale wisp of a woman, hunched heavily on a cane, and said a few words in German. *Something about the trees.* Anne tried to recall her high school language studies. *Connect?* No. *Avoid.* Anne saw the detectives in the shade of the oaks. *Avoid the trees.* The old lady nodded, and the two began making their way through the parted crowd.

"Lovely service."

"He'll be missed."

The widow acknowledged the kind wishes with a tight nod and then suddenly stumbled. Alex reached out to steady her.

"Danke...Thank you." Brigitte took a deep breath, as if to regain her bearings, linked her arm in his, and the three continued to make their way slowly past the weathered headstones while Anne trailed a few feet behind. "Those men have no business being here." She sounded angry. "My husband died from the stress of his job. It's as simple as that. No?" She sighed.

"I'm not sure why they think there's anything suspicious about it," Alex replied.

"They're simpletons! Those police make things so difficult. I could hardly arrange the funeral. Dummköpfe! They wouldn't release his body! It was... how do you say?...Unimaginable...No...Unbelievable. Nonsense."

Nonsense? Well...they probably needed time to do an autopsy since his death was *unexpected...*Nonetheless, Anne appreciated the sentiment. The detectives milling in the background were incredibly distracting. And she could see how a delay in the burial would be upsetting.

"It's obvious his job killed him! Why don't they see that?" Brigitte's voice quivered, a raspy tremolo of emotion. "Instead, they're lurking in the shadows, just like the Stasi...hounding my friends."

That was the part Anne found unnerving. It meant the police still thought there was a killer in their midst and, equally terrifying, that she might be one of their suspects.

"If anything, they should do something about that worthless skunk of a CFO." Brigitte paused and looked directly at Alex, her posture erect and defiant. "He destroyed the company. Because of him, Richard lost everything he spent his entire life building!"

Except that Richard may have had a role to play in the tragedy as well...he might even have been the architect behind the scheme.

Alex shook his head. "Richard was more than Energix." His voice was gentle but firm. "He *founded* the Second Chance Charity for disadvantaged children, *spear-headed* the campaign for a new cancer wing at the hospital, and was the *primary* donor for that new animal shelter the county just built." He watched Brigitte take his words in. "No one can ever take that away from him."

Richard was behind all of that? Anne was struck by the disparate facets of the man. On the one hand, there was the unethical jerk who had fleeced investors and lined his own pockets to the tune of millions of dollars. At the same time, his philanthropic legacy was that of a compassionate person who helped disadvantaged children and improved the lives of abandoned animals. Clearly, he had been a complicated individual.

The group reached the convoy of cars parked on the narrow gravel road that snaked through the cemetery. "I'm so sorry you have to go through this." Alex helped the widow and her elderly mother into the car. "I wish there were something I could do to make things better." His voice broke on the last words and he looked away.

But, of course, the investigation was out of his control. Out of everyone's control, except for the detectives who were conducting it for whatever mysterious reason. Anne glanced back and saw that the officers had stepped out of the trees and were talking to Peter Eckert. He nodded a few times, said something, and then nodded again. Buff-guy jotted something down, and then all three looked over at her.

Anne's heart thumped loudly. *Why are they all staring at me?*

* * *

At the Fernsby house, servers carried alcohol-laden trays around to the somber guests. "Another drink, ma'am?"

Anne shook her head. She had not been to many funerals in her life, and the only gatherings afterwards had been quiet affairs with no alcohol at all. Getting drunk seemed like a poor way to deal with the sadness, in her view, but to each their own.

Paige handed her empty glass to the waiter and picked up a new one, continuing to rattle on without pause. "The water was crystal blue, and the beaches incredibly bright white. Caneel Bay is so romantic. Have you and Alex thought about honeymoon—"

"No." Anne cut her off. "We haven't even set a date. With everything that happened last weekend, we've barely been able to sit down, let alone think."

Paige gave Anne a knowing look. "My parents said the same thing. They were so exhausted after the wedding. And then to have the police crawling all over the place." She gave an exaggerated shudder. "It about did my mother in."

I'll bet. Her immaculate lawn trampled for days on end. The bright yellow crime scene tape was strewn around the dock for all the neighbors to see. It had to be galling to someone whose social life revolved around an elite club that prided itself on being above the regular Joe.

Anne smiled sympathetically. "Did they give any indication about when things might be wrapped up?"

"No! The whole thing is really strange. We still don't even know why they think Richard's death is suspicious." She rolled her eyes and gave a deep sigh.

"I mean, really! Why would someone kill him? Even if they were incredibly upset about the financial situation with the company, what good does it do to take the guy out after the fact?"

Unless someone was trying to get even.

Paige leaned forward, as if confiding a tightly guarded state secret. "And Brigitte is just beside herself." She glanced around to make sure no one was within earshot and then grimaced. "They insisted on doing an autopsy."

Anne rattled the ice cubes in her glass with a quick shake. "I think that's normal when someone dies unexpectedly."

"Probably," Paige allowed. "But it made it a lot more difficult to schedule the funeral because they didn't know when they'd be ready to release the body. On top of losing Richard, she had to deal with all of that." She took a sip of wine, an indignant look on her face.

And yet, the body had been released after a week, allowing the funeral to take place in a fairly timely manner. "I'm sure the whole thing has just been awful." Anne shook her head.

"I can't even imagine."

Truth be told, neither could Anne. If she were to lose Alex unexpectedly, she'd be devastated. And they hadn't spent a lifetime together building memories like Brigitte and Richard had. "The whole thing is sad."

Paige fiddled with a deep blue sapphire pendant hanging on what Anne assumed was a platinum chain. "I have to admit that it worked out well for us, though. I was afraid we'd have to decide whether to fly back early from our honeymoon." She laid a hand on her heart, signaling that the idea pained her deeply. "Fortunately, the delay meant we didn't have to cross that bridge." She sighed and looked toward the sky, as if a huge weight had been lifted from her shoulders.

"Brigitte seemed pretty upset to see the detectives this afternoon." Anne tried to sound casual. "But if there's the slightest chance he was murdered, wouldn't you think she'd want to know?"

"Of course." Paige drew herself up tall. "But they're wrong."

"How can you be so sure?"

"Oh please," she snorted. "There's no question he died from the stress of Energix going under. He wasn't sleeping. He wasn't eating. At the wedding…well," she gave Anne a pointed look. "You saw firsthand. He was picking fights with people…behaving erratically…it's no wonder he had a heart attack. In fact, when Kevin pulled him aside, he was ranting about Peter Eckert being jealous of his success and how you wanted to make a name for yourself at his expense. He seemed to think the two of you were in cahoots to take him down."

"That's ridiculous. Peter and I are in different departments. We don't even—"

Paige waved her hand dismissively. "He was so upset that he was just spewing whatever came to mind, like calling you a pair of snowy owls."

"What?"

"Oh…" she paused and clamped her lips together, as if suddenly realizing she might not want to explain. "Well…" she said after a long moment, "he said they have bright yellow eyes and no conscience…just like you."

Anne blinked. He had likened her to a cold-blooded hunter from the Arctic? The type that perches on a post, silently waiting and watching for its next meal before pouncing mercilessly? She felt a chill run down her arms.

Paige looked pained. "Obviously, he wasn't coping well."

You think? Out of the corner of her eye, Anne saw Horse-Lover hovering nearby. "It didn't help that he'd had a lot to drink."

"W-a-a-aay too much," Paige looked down at her wine. "I think it was the culmination of years of stress. His identity was so thoroughly wrapped up in his job that it became his entire life. He couldn't handle it when things began to unravel." She took a deep breath. "Then he turned to alcohol for support." She lifted her head and gazed across the room. "I need to make sure that Kevin doesn't fall into the same trap."

Horse-Lover saw her opening and trotted in. "That's something we *all* need to be careful about." She gave Paige an air kiss. "I'm dying to hear about the honeymoon. Was it just perfect? Was Kevin able to leave his work behind?"

"He tried." Paige sighed. "But it was hard. He ended up being on the phone half the time, trying to make sure Energix didn't implode while we were gone." Her face lit up. "But the other half was good. He managed to catch a few rays of sun, and we had wonderful, candlelit dinners every night."

"What can you do?" Horse-Lover sounded sympathetic, but bore an alertness about her, like a cat eyeing an unsuspecting mouse. "He's the acting CFO. And he's stepping into a whirlwind of a situation, to say the least."

It was a fair point, and yet Anne couldn't help but think there was some ulterior motive behind her comments. It was as if she was trying to draw Paige out, to get her to spill the beans on something. But why would she be interested in the financial condition of Energix?

"I think it's only going to get worse now that we're back, and he's in the thick of things," Paige confided. "Even as we were driving to the funeral, he was on the phone with someone or other talking about cash-flow shortfalls and strategies for shoring up the balance sheet." She took a large sip of her wine.

Which meant that Anne's short positions were continuing to get more and more profitable. In fact, she made a mental note to start cashing them in, pronto, to book some of her profits.

"And tomorrow morning, there's a big meeting with all of senior management at 8:00 am."

"I wonder if Käthe will stay on at Energix, now that her father is gone." Horse-Lover's eyes darted back and forth, as if she was calculating the weight of every word.

"I doubt she's even thought about it." Paige bit her lip. "She's devastated by her father's death."

"It might end up being the impetus for her to re-evaluate things. Reset her priorities. Ditch the corporate gig and run off with that secret lover of hers." Horse-Lover searched Paige's face. "I kind of wondered if he was one of the guests at the wedding."

Paige gave a small start. "What? Why?"

"I had to set up the sparklers for the send-off at the end of the evening when nobody could find her."

"Oh, really?" Paige looked flustered despite her attempt to smile. "That was nice of you."

"It was no problem." Horse-Lover flashed a wide smile, no doubt meant to look reassuring. "I just found it odd because she's always so organized. And then it occurred to me that maybe it had something to do with her mystery Romeo." She winked at Anne. "I guess his identity is on a need-to-know-basis. Hopefully, we'll get read in at some point."

"Hard to say." Paige waved her hand vaguely. "Käthe keeps things very close to the vest."

"Kind of like her mother." Horse-Lover raised an eyebrow. "Did you see how Brigitte steered Old Granny away from those detectives?"

Paige leaned forward and spoke in a hushed tone. "She doesn't want Oma to get deported back to East Germany."

"She's here illegally?" Anne glanced at the frail woman sitting quietly in the corner, nibbling on cheese and crackers.

"Sort of."

"There's no such thing as sort of," Horse-Lover admonished. "Either she is, or she isn't."

Paige rocked back and forth on her heels, obviously struggling with how to reply.

"I remember when they brought her over here last December, right after the Berlin Wall fell." Horse-Lover moved in for the kill, reducing the space between her and Paige to mere inches. "How did they get someone into the country without proper paperwork?"

"She had a visa when she first arrived." Paige glanced around surreptitiously and then continued in a whisper. "But it was only good for three months...so now..."

"It's expired," Anne finished for her. *And Brigitte doesn't want the authorities to find out.*

"Exactly." Paige took a step back and crossed her arms. "Every time those detectives poke their noses around, there's a chance they'll notice and decide to report her."

"Does Frau Illegal speak English?" Horse-Lover had a mischievous look.

"Not much." Paige cocked her head. "Why?"

"Just wondering if she could tell us anything more about Käthe's secret lover."

Paige rolled her eyes. "You never give up, do you?"

She grinned. "It's one of my many endearing qualities."

As if she had any. Although Alex must have seen something in the woman years ago when he had briefly dated her. *What could it have possibly been?*

"And I can't help but think that there must be something unusual about her paramour..." Horse-Lover paused. "Like he's a former mob boss who's now in the witness protection program...or works for the CIA...or maybe he's married." Her eyes bored through Paige, who remained impassive. "Why else would she keep him so under wraps?"

13

Tallying the Numbers

New York City

The following day

"Do you always get in this late?" Twinkle-Toes stood by Anne's office door, chatting with her secretary.

Anne juggled her purse in one hand and a bagel in the other wondering what Peter Eckert's girlfriend actually wanted. "Someone jumped in front of a train at the Canal Street station. It brought everything to a screeching halt."

"Bummer." Twinkle-Toes gave a cursory glance around the department as she popped a big bubble. "It's kind of dead around here. Don't you miss being on the trading floor?"

"Not really." Anne set her briefcase down and began to rummage through her handbag. "Were you looking for me?" She pulled out a set of keys and waited.

Peter's admin glanced casually at her fire-engine red, glittered fingernails. "The boss would like to talk to you at 9 am."

"Did he say why?" Anne unlocked her office and dropped the keys back into her bag.

"Nope. Now that I've found you, I better get back." She gave her pencil skirt a tug and sashayed toward the elevator. "See you in a few."

"She thinks her sugar daddy is going to propose any day now," Anne's secretary said the moment Twinkle-Toes was out of earshot.

That would be a big change from his normal M.O. Nearly forty years old, the man had dated a number of young women around the firm and not been ensnared in marriage with a single one yet. Of course, there was always a first time for everything. "Wouldn't that be nice," Anne said in what she hoped was a neutral tone.

"It'll never happen." Her admin smirked. "His last girlfriend thought the same thing." She handed Anne a small pile of pink-colored messages. "By the way, the guy on top has called three times already. He seemed really antsy." She picked up a pile of folders from her desk and trudged over to the long row of gray, waist-high file cabinets arrayed along the far wall.

Anne hung her trench coat behind the door and walked slowly to her desk, wondering what Peter Eckert wanted to discuss. *Has something happened with Energix?* As she pulled a pair of black pumps out of the bottom drawer, she glanced down at the newspaper resting on her credenza. *Nothing on the front page.* She untied her sneakers and then flipped to the business section. *Or there, either.*

Her secretary popped her head in the door. "I'm stepping away to get some coffee. Don't forget to give the antsy guy a call."

After reassuring the anxious investor, (rumors about her fund shifting away from the high-tech sector were completely false), a quick discussion with the CFO of a sportswear company (time to dump the stock since their financial condition was not improving), and another to a high-tech start-up in the outskirts of Boston (maybe take a small position in this enterprise and see how it performed), she headed down to the fifth floor, pen and paper in hand.

She found Peter's girlfriend leaning provocatively against the door to his office, a finger resting on her slightly parted lips, and a pointy red shoe that matched her nail polish dangling off of one raised foot. "Don't be late." She blew him an air kiss and twirled away, almost knocking Anne down in the

113

process. "Sorry," she giggled.

"Good morning." Peter waved her in. "I just got off the phone with Kevin and a few others from Energix. They may need to issue some additional stock to stay afloat."

Paige's new husband was wasting no time in trying to right the financial ship.

"I think that will be a tough sell, given their current financial predicament."

"That's what I thought. Issuing more stock now will just cause the share price to drop further." Peter studied her for a moment. "I want to convince them to issue new debt to tide them over."

"Same problem. Their tenuous financial condition means they'll have to pay very high rates."

He tapped his index finger on the desk. "They need cash to strengthen their balance sheet so they can restore their investment-grade ratings."

Borrowing more money won't help. She shifted in her chair, studying the harried-looking man on the other side of the desk. Why was he so concerned about helping Energix preserve its financial integrity? The underwriting fees might be an incentive, but this sort of deal-making was typically the purview of an investment banker, not the head of fixed-income trading. Nonetheless, she had one idea she thought was worth sharing. "Maybe they could merge with another energy company."

"Hmmm." He stopped the nervous tapping and leaned back in his chair. "That might actually work." His lips twitched as he appeared to consider the proposition. "I wonder if Dynamic Energy could be enticed."

It was an interesting choice of words. As if the goal was to lure them into a trap rather than create a mutually beneficial partnership.

"Why don't you touch base with them and see what they say?"

She blinked. *Me?* Not that she was hung up about job descriptions, but this was getting pretty far afield from her stated responsibilities. She was beginning to regret having made the suggestion at all. Especially since it would have been easy enough to keep her big mouth zipped shut. "I think someone in the mergers and acquisition group should take the lead on this."

He waved his hand dismissively. "They won't understand the nature of the situation."

Why not? This seemed like exactly the sort of situation that an experienced dealmaker would be perfect at handling. He must have seen the look of consternation on her face.

Peter fixed his steel-gray eyes on her. "Frankly, I want to keep it low-key. I have a swap deal bubbling in the background related to wind farms in California." His lips twitched again. "Well, the equipment associated with them, actually."

Wind turbines? I thought the swap deals were related solely to oil barges floating around the Caribbean. Every sentence he uttered made her more and more uncomfortable. He was up to his ears in god-only-knows-what and the last thing she wanted was to get blindly wrapped up in whatever he had going on. "It might be a good idea to run the merger idea past Energix before we worry about who might actually handle the transaction."

He nodded approvingly as his finger found the intercom button.

"Yes?" Twinkle-Toes peeked into his office, her plunging neckline leading the way.

"Would you please get Kevin on the line?"

"Right away." She flipped her hair behind her shoulders and wiggled back to her desk.

Peter gave Anne a thumbs-up signal. "This could be a great solution for Energix as well. And the sooner I can get these swaps sorted out…" His voice trailed off as he gazed toward the trading floor.

"What's the rationale for investing in the wind farms?" Anne tried to keep her voice light and casual. "Don't you still own the oil barges?"

He stiffened. "For now. But if we can arrange a cash infusion, then the wind farm swaps will replace those rusty old boats."

How would that fix anything? Energix would still be on the hook to buy the wind farm equipment back at some point. "Why not sell the oil barges to a third party and release Energix from having to buy anything at all? Given their financial situation—"

Peter's phone rang loudly.

"The contract doesn't allow that." He lifted the receiver and put the call

115

on speaker.

"I like it," Kevin said once he had been briefed on the idea. "Who on your end can take the lead on facilitating the talks?"

"I'll work with Anne to make it happen." Peter peered over his glasses at her. "It will be an opportunity for her to broaden her skillset."

Something was off. She was being used as a pawn. Or set up to fail. She wasn't sure which. "I appreciate the vote of confidence, but I think someone in the Mergers group should spearhead this."

"No," Peter said sharply, surprise evident on his face. "I want you to do it. Report your findings directly to me."

"I agree." the acting CFO's voice echoed down the wire. "And the faster we can get something in the works, the better."

She put her hands up to stop this train of conversation. "Wait a minute. This isn't my area of expertise. A merger of this nature should have seasoned professionals shepherding the entire thing from start to finish."

Peter jerked a thumb toward the door. "Your colleagues out there would give their right arm for an opportunity like this." His eyes narrowed. "Don't be a fool. You're shying away from the gift of a lifetime."

She felt a pang of panic shoot from her heart down through her stomach. Was she committing career suicide by refusing to take this on? If she made him angry, he could make her life difficult going forward. And there was no question this was an incredible chance to be front and center of a major business deal. It could propel her to the top ranks of Spencer Brothers in record time. And yet, she didn't have the first clue about how the mergers and acquisition group operated, or even what floor they were on. Putting her in charge simply didn't make sense.

"It will give us a chance to work together," Kevin jumped into the ring. "Keeping the whole business in the family, as they say."

As in the mafia? Anne became even more certain that she should avoid getting roped into finding a suitor for Energix.

"Peter, you know she's engaged to Alex Hunter, my brother-in-law?"

Anne looked at the small gray box in disbelief. Why was Kevin mentioning any sort of personal connections? It was irrelevant information. Or should be.

"Of course." Peter's mouth widened into a smile that made him look like a shark. "That's why Anne's the best person to handle these negotiations."

Why? Because it would be easy for her to confer with him if need be?

Peter's mouth twitched. "I trust her to keep things quiet, but I also know she's thorough."

Malleable is probably what he was thinking. Like his long list of past girlfriends. Young, impressionable, and eager to please. Except she wasn't. She pulled her shoulders back and looked directly at him. "The most important thing here is to assemble a high-powered team that can make this merger happen. I'm happy to brief the M&A group on everything I know about the financial situation so that they can get up to speed as quickly as possible, but that team will need to broker the deal."

The smile left Peter's face. "You're making a big mistake."

Maybe. But she didn't think so.

Kevin coughed, and there was the sound of papers shuffling in the background. "I'll let the two of you discuss this on your own. Meanwhile, I need to get back to sorting through the *debris* that my predecessor left behind."

Anne was surprised at the impersonal way in which he referred to the former CFO, a man who had at one time been his good friend and boss, was romantically involved with his wife's best friend, and belonged to the same exclusive country club that he and Peter both did.

"That reminds me," Peter addressed the grey box on his desk. "I wanted to caution you about some of his tactics." His gaze shifted up to her. "And you too, Anne."

"I think I've already seen enough of his creative accounting," Kevin snorted. "Not much at this point would surprise me."

"He's desperate," Peter said.

"Of course he is." Kevin's voice boomed at them, as if he had shifted too close to the microphone. "The guy is out of a job and under investigation by the SEC for fraud."

"It's worse than that." Peter stroked his chin. "He wants to rewrite history and claim that Fernsby was the architect behind the financial transactions with the Caribbean entities."

"Well, he's got to point the finger somewhere." Kevin's voice sounded matter-of-fact, betraying no hint of whether he thought it unscrupulous. "Strategically, it makes sense. A dead man isn't in any position to argue."

Peter cocked his head at the speakerphone. "Pretty convenient, wouldn't you say?"

"Fernsby's heart attack, you mean? I don't think he exactly planned it."

Peter leaned forward and dropped his voice. "The medical examiner thinks Richard was poisoned."

Anne's eyes widened in surprise.

"Poisoned?!" It sounded like Kevin had spit out his coffee. "Where did you hear that?"

Peter picked up his gold Cross pen and twirled it back and forth in his fingers. "I got it on good authority from someone I know at the police department." He paused and balanced it in his open palm, a few inches above the top of his desk. "That's all I can say."

Except that he'd already said enough. *Richard Fernsby was murdered?* No wonder the police had been milling around at the funeral. Anne felt her stomach sink. *And I'm a potential suspect.*

"They're waiting for toxicology results to come in." Peter turned his hand sideways. The pen slid through his hand and clattered loudly on his desk. "It will be a couple more weeks before they have anything official."

Which explains the delay in releasing the body. Perhaps Brigitte was right to be concerned. The police would leave no stone unturned while investigating the murder of a major corporate executive, upping the chances that her mother's expired visa would be noticed.

"Well, I'll be damned. You're not seriously suggesting that my former boss had anything to do with Fernsby's death, are you?"

"Why not?" Peter scoffed, as if Kevin had just asked the stupidest question ever. "He was at the wedding. The two of them could barely stand to be near one another."

The image of Richard knocking into the ex-CFO at the wedding suddenly popped into Anne's mind. The reedy man had looked both angry and surprised. And then there was that odd way he had locked eyes with Käthe.

The scowl on Peter's face was replaced by a look of intense concentration. "Maybe the fraudster saw his chance to eliminate a prime witness and at the same time make Fernsby the fall guy."

"With poison?" she murmured.

The senior VP fixed his gray eyes on her, as if suddenly remembering she was in the room. "Or, maybe it was planned. Either way, he was in a precarious situation once Fernsby had turned on him."

"That's putting it mildly," Kevin's voice crackled through the speaker. "His goose was totally cooked. Now that Fernsby's out of the picture, he can claim he was just following orders."

Peter nodded slowly, a sly smile on his lips. "I think that's exactly what he intends to do, which means he's going to be looking for allies."

"Well, he won't find any over here," Kevin said confidently. "He knows I'm up to my ears trying to fix the mess he left behind. But he might try to enlist you Peter, since you were involved in the oil barge deals."

"He already has." Peter's face was inscrutable. "That's why I mentioned it." His telephone buzzed. "Just giving you a heads up so you aren't surprised if he reaches out."

Really? Was that the only reason? Anne found it hard to believe that the executive sitting opposite her had anyone's best interests in mind, except for his own.

Peter's eyes bored through her as his phone buzzed again. "I suggest that you don't talk to him if he tries to call. The man could very well be a murderer."

On top of being a thief.

Twinkle-Toes opened the door. "Sorry to interrupt. Steve Warnock wants to see you." She looked almost apologetic. "Right now."

Peter nodded and looked down at his phone, as if debating whether to say anything more.

"I've got to go as well," Kevin beat him to the punch and clicked off.

Peter stood up and buttoned his jacket. "Anne. I'd like you to reconsider.

You can give me your final decision tomorrow."

* * *

"Why you?" Alex looked at her quizzically. The sun shone through the long office windows, making his sandy brown hair almost glow.

"That's what I'm trying to figure out," Anne replied, still reeling from the meeting that had ended just minutes before. "I have no experience in this area at all." She tapped her foot nervously on the floor. "Even Kevin was on board with the idea, which is weird because he was questioning my qualifications for being an equity fund manager the night we all had dinner at your parents' house."

"He was just commenting that you were young for such a senior type of position, that you've moved up quickly through the ranks."

"I got the distinct impression that he thought I was in over my head." She frowned. "So why would he be okay with me being the point person on a critical merger that could make or break his company?"

"Kevin's in the middle of a firestorm over in Energix-land." Alex picked up his Diet Coke and took a quick sip. "He just wants a solution to his problem. I'm not surprised that he's willing to go along with whatever Peter suggests. He doesn't have the time or energy to figure out who might be a better person for the job."

Anne sank deeper in her chair. "But Eckert does."

Alex set the soda can down. "That's what I'm finding strange about all of this. You're no longer in his group. Officially, you no longer report to him." He put his hands behind his head and leaned back in his chair. "Why is he so insistent that you be the one to take this on?"

"I feel like it's tied up somehow with these weird swap deals. I couldn't get a straight answer as to why he won't just sell the barges. He mumbled something about it not being allowed by the terms of the contract."

"I'd like to see the terms of that contract. It doesn't sound standard to me."

"Nothing about this situation sounds standard to me." She locked eyes with him. As a corporate lawyer at Spencer Brothers, he could pull the file.

He shook his head, obviously reading her mind. "I checked. We don't seem to have a copy up here. But don't read anything into that. It just means our group wasn't involved in the legal work."

She took a deep breath. "I told him no. And that's what I intend to tell him again tomorrow."

"I think that's the right answer."

"He's not going to be happy."

Alex shrugged. "That's his problem."

Except that Peter was a senior-level manager who could probably get her fired, in which case it would be her problem. "I wonder if I should start looking for a job outside of Spencer Brothers."

Alex's hands flew up into the air. "Hang on. You don't know what's going to happen here. He might back off once he knows you're firm."

"He might," she allowed. "And then, I can continue on my merry way while this whole thing blows over. But if it doesn't..." She paused as she started to question whether a new job was even a real option. She had only been in her fund manager position for a few months. Outside of Spencer Brothers, she was probably seen as a novice who had been promoted before her time. A few negative words from him to his well-placed buddies on the street and no one would touch her with a ten-foot pole. "He could destroy my career."

Alex regarded her for a moment. "What do you think about moving to London?"

She blinked. Was he serious? And yet, there was nothing joking in his manner. "Can you practice law there?"

"I'm sure I could."

It would be exciting to live abroad for a few years. She had always envied a college friend who had spent an entire summer backpacking around Europe before starting her first job.

He gazed at the lawbooks lining his shelves. "There are probably some hoops I'd have to jump through in order to get myself called to the bar. The good thing is that I'm already a citizen."

But she wasn't. "I'd have to look into getting a green card."

He smiled. "Probably simpler to apply for a UK spouse visa."

121

Her diamond engagement ring sparkled under the ghostly fluorescent lights, reminding her that she was in a partnership with a man who saw a roadblock as a challenge that could be turned into an opportunity. It was a far cry from her last boyfriend, an academic, who had told her that she was nothing special (everyone's a vice president on Wall Street) and that his career had to take precedence regardless of what happened with hers (of course they would move to Podunk, USA, if he got a faculty appointment of some sort, even if it paid a tenth of what her job paid). In time, he would have been an albatross around her neck. Thank God she had dumped the guy, freeing herself to find Alex.

The tension she had been feeling was gone. "It's probably time we set a date."

"No date required. Just say the word, and we can hop a plane to Vegas."

"You know what?" She leaned over and grabbed his Diet Coke. "I might just take you up on that offer." As she took a quick sip, she was struck by the narrowness of her thinking, as if a wedding had to be planned many months in advance or this employer was the only one in the universe. If Peter made life difficult, she could find another job.

She handed the drink back to him. "And I'll stop catastrophizing about the many ways that Eckert could take me down."

"Good." He studied the top of the can for a second and then shrugged and took another swig. "So, what was the second thing you were going to tell me."

"Oh!" She had been so caught up in the Energix saga that she had almost forgotten. "The medical examiner thinks that Richard Fernsby was poisoned." She paused briefly to let the information sink in. "I guess that means the yellow police tape will be staying up for a while longer at the house in the Hamptons."

14

What part of no don't you understand?

New York City

Two days later

"Glad I caught you."

Anne looked up from the financial statements she had been studying to see Peter Eckert stride into her office.

"Have you given any more thought to my proposal?" He shut the door, but remained standing, watching her like she was a bug under a microscope.

"I'm flattered." She forced herself to look directly at him. "But I'm not the right person for the job."

For a moment, the only sound she could hear was the clock ticking rhythmically on her wall.

His lips twitched. "I thought with some time to think things over, you might change your mind."

You thought wrong. She shook her head.

"I'm sorry to hear that." His gray eyes stared at her, unblinking. "You're throwing away a plum opportunity."

From her vantage point, it looked like she was avoiding a train wreck. This supposedly *plum* assignment had nothing to do with her formal responsibilities. Moreover, she had no experience with mergers and no contacts or colleagues that she could turn to for guidance.

"Okay," he finally said. "I understand."

And yet his disapproving tone suggested he didn't understand at all.

"I think you're going to regret this." He turned on his heel and wordlessly exited the room.

* * *

That afternoon, Jennifer sat down in the chair opposite Anne and pulled a chocolate bar out of her bag. "What did you do to piss Eckert off?"

"Nothing." Anne set her pen down and revised her reply. "I mean, he has no right to be angry…oh hell…" She buried her face in her hands. "What's he saying?"

"That you cost the fixed income division a ton of money by dumping Energix's stock last month."

Anne lifted her head and sighed. "Seriously?"

"I'm afraid so." Jennifer broke off a piece of the bar and handed it to her. "I overheard him complaining to one of the salesmen about how short sellers had taken the company down. He even went so far as to mention you, specifically, by name."

Anne made a face. "Sounds like he's taken a page out of Richard Fernsby's playbook."

"That approach didn't work for Fernsby." Jennifer shrugged. "Probably won't do much for Eckert either." She took a bite of her chocolate.

"Eckert may be aware that I closed out a large chunk of my short positions last week," Anne mused aloud, careful not to add that she had booked an enormous profit with the transaction thanks to the dramatic drop in share price over the previous month. "But, it's not my fault the company is crashing and burning. They've been hiding losses and misrepresenting their financial condition for months, maybe even years. It was only a matter of time before their little charade caught up with them."

"I know." Jennifer's gentle, brown eyes studied Anne. "So, why is Eckert suddenly blaming you?"

The million-dollar question. What's his angle in all of this? Anne sighed and laid her cards on the table.

"Whoa!" Jennifer immediately reacted to the role Peter Eckert wanted Anne to play. "Asking you to find a suitor for Energix and to broker the deal? That doesn't make sense at all."

"That's what I told him." Anne bit her lip, certain she had done the right thing, but unhappy about where it had gotten her.

Jennifer crossed her arms. "There's more to these swap deals than meets the eye. If we could get our hands on the contracts, we might be able to suss out what it is."

An idea suddenly flashed into Anne's mind. "How about if we pay his girlfriend—oh, I mean," her mouth quirked into a sly smile, "his secretary a visit?"

Jennifer's eyes twinkled mischievously. "What exactly do you have in mind?"

* * *

Anne and Jennifer rode the elevator in silence down to the trading floor, quietly mulling their plan. After a quick glance toward Peter Eckert's office to verify that his door was shut, they made their way to Jennifer's cubicle and set to work creating a diversion. Anne watched while her comrade-in-arms typed, peeking around the corner again to confirm that Peter was nowhere in sight.

"Sent." Jennifer stood up. "Wait here while I jiggle the printer."

Anne tapped her foot nervously on the dull, brown carpet, surrounded by six equally nondescript cubicles that housed the rest of Jennifer's co-workers. They were strategically placed on the far edge of the trading floor, within easy reach of the traders, but outside the main area of action, their occupants important only when information was required and then forgotten the moment a trade had been executed. Such was the life of a bond analyst on the trading floor: tolerated but not embraced as one of the

NOT ACCOUNTING FOR MURDER

team and never credited unless there was a problem and the traders needed someone to blame.

"Ready?" Jennifer gave a stiff nod, like an army sergeant starting a mission.

Anne glanced one last time over at Peter Eckert's office on the far side of the floor. "Let's do it."

The background hum became louder as they rounded the cubicles and headed toward the fifty-plus people talking, yelling, and swearing while phones rang endlessly beside them and bonds were frantically bought and sold for Spencer Brothers. The trading floor. The core of activity, it was like a beehive, with everyone assigned a role buzzing away. Anne instinctively responded by going on full alert, ready to respond to any question from any direction.

"Moving back down here?" One of the traders called out, his hand covering the mouthpiece of his phone.

"Not a chance," Anne replied. "I've done my time." Her eight years on the trading floor as an analyst supporting the trading operation had been a great opportunity to learn about the bond trading business and, often, even fun. At the same time, it was exhausting to advise the intensely competitive, hard-nosed traders who destroyed anyone who got in their way.

"Bummer." A small vein pulsed on his forehead. "I could use your help with some airport bonds."

These guys were friendly when you helped them or provided the answer they wanted to hear and downright brutal if you happened to be the bearer of bad news (with a slew of expletives thrown in for good measure). There was a good reason they tended to burn out in their mid-thirties.

The trader returned to his phone conversation. "What? I'm telling you! It's a bargain at fifty-two! Hang on a sec." He turned in his chair, his starched white shirt straining to remain buttoned across his mid-section. "Hey, Jennifer?"

"I'll be back in a few minutes," she called over her shoulder without breaking her stride.

Anne gave him a sympathetic shrug and sped up to her compatriot's side.

Twinkle-Toes was studying her aqua-blue nails when Jennifer and Anne arrived at her polished, wooden desk. She glanced up and blew a big bubble. "Can I help you?"

Jennifer pointed toward a nearby room that housed photocopiers, printers, and other administrative materials. "I sent something to the printer, but now it's jammed, and the document is kind of sensitive." As she appealed for assistance, she crumpled her shoulders and sighed in a way that made her look and sound like a dejected puppy. "Normally, I would ask my admin to help, but I'm not sure where she is, and I hate to leave it just hanging in there." She sighed again, this time accompanied by a look of frustrated desperation. "Could you help me?"

"Of course." Twinkle-Toes closed the bottle of nail polish and placed it carefully to one side. "That printer is so annoying."

As soon as they were out of sight, Anne opened the top file drawer behind the unsuspecting secretary's desk. To her surprise, it was nicely organized, with color-coded folders clearly labeled and everything filed in proper alphabetical order. *Twinkle-Toes did this?* Perhaps she was smarter than she looked. Anne began working her way through the drawer, starting with the A's. In a matter of seconds, she felt a jolt of adrenalin as her eyes spotted the word *Energix* in neatly typewritten letters. She slid her fingers between the file and its adjacent neighbor and began to ease it out.

Wow. That was easy.

"Hey Anne," a male voice boomed out, causing her to jump and bang her hand against the side of the cabinet.

She turned to see a salesman she had been friendly with when she had worked on the floor. "Oh, hi." She smiled, her heart thumping loudly.

"Long time no see. Hope things are going well in your new job." He gave a thumbs-up and continued on his way.

"Thanks." She glanced around to make sure the coast was still clear, grabbed the folder, and slipped it between two others she was already carrying. *Success!* She breathed a sigh of relief and then leaned against the wall, trying to look nonchalant as she waited for the two women to return.

"What are you doing here?" Peter Eckert materialized from his office like an unsettled ghost.

Anne managed to maintain her casual pose and produce an exasperated sigh. "I need to buy a birthday present for my secretary." As she rattled on about how she hoped his admin could help her in this endeavor, she felt his eyes boring through her, the hint of a scowl on his face. She felt a rush of panic. Did he suspect that the Energix file was hidden between the two decoys? It was all she could do to keep herself from glancing down to confirm that the label was hidden. "I can just come back later when—"

"Peter. Do you need something?" Twinkle-Toes came rushing over with Jennifer close behind.

His face became blank. "No. I just wanted to give you these." He set a stack of folders on her desk.

Jennifer waved a single piece of paper dramatically in the air. "That was the weirdest thing. I had to send the print command like three times."

Anne took a couple of steps away from Peter.

"Thanks so much for your help." Jennifer's smile looked genuine. She was a natural at this.

Twinkle-Toes gave her shoulders a little twist and nodded dramatically toward the supply room. "That printer needs to be replaced."

Peter's eyes briefly looked toward the room but came back and roved up and down his admin's shapely figure.

"I need to run." Anne gave a small wave to the group and made a beeline for the elevator.

* * *

"How are we going to put this stuff back without anyone noticing?" Jennifer stared at the Energix papers splayed across Anne's desk.

"I'm thinking we can just slip the folder into the middle of that big pile of stuff Peter gave her."

"Hopefully." Jennifer bit her lip, for the first time looking nervous about what they had done. "But her desk looked pretty neat before we got there. The pile might be gone by the time we're done."

"Then we'll just leave it sitting on her desk. With any luck, she'll just assume Peter put it there." And if that didn't look like it would fly, Anne was confident they'd come up with something else that would work. "I'm not worried about it." She moved the wind barge contract to the side and stared at a second one labeled Enchanted Power. "I thought he hadn't bought these." And yet he had, a good eight months earlier, on December 31, 1989, when everyone else was out celebrating the start of the new year.

Jennifer looked puzzled. "I haven't heard a peep about wind farms from any of my trusty sources on the trading floor."

Anne pointed at the termination date of the contract. "Maybe that's because he sold them back to Energix in April."

"Wait a minute." Jennifer looked back and forth at the two contracts. "April 12. That's the very same day that he purchased the oil barges. And for the same amount. It's like a wash, one sale replacing the other, but no net change."

Ann furrowed her brow. "Earlier this week, he told me that he wanted to sell the oil barges back to Energix and purchase the wind farms again. Only he neglected to mention the *again* part. It's like he's playing musical chairs."

"But why?" Jennifer walked around the desk and sat down in the chair opposite Anne. "What good does all this buying and selling of these two sets of energy assets do?"

Anne leaned back in her chair and rested her head in her hands. "Peter probably collected fees for each of the transactions, and Energix—" she paused. What did Energix get out of these deals?

"I suppose the very first sale of the wind farm made their bottom line look better." Jennifer popped the lid on her Dr Pepper can.

Anne shrugged. "So what else is new?"

"Fair enough." Jennifer took a swig of her soda. "It seems like Energix has been inflating their numbers for a while now."

And yet, this transaction somehow felt different. It involved Peter Eckert. And it had occurred on the very last day of the year, as if it was a desperate attempt to accomplish a specific goal. "There's something about the timing of these wind farm deals…" Anne searched her mind, trying to think of what would matter to the manager of a Fortune 500 company at the end of the year. And then it hit her. "Bigger profits mean bigger bonuses."

Jennifer's eyes widened. "But that would mean—"

"This whole wind farm business was designed as a way to inflate their year-end numbers so that the executives could line their own pockets."

"By sucking the lifeblood out of the company," Jennifer snorted. "It's the epitome of selfishness, especially when the company's in the toilet."

As if that mattered to a bunch of elitist profiteers. They probably thought they were the smartest guys around and *deserved* to be paid four hundred times what the average worker made. From what Anne had seen, none of the C-suite types had any concept that they had arrived at their lofty positions through a combination of luck, ambition, and politics, with talent playing a very limited role.

"If we go with the greedy-set-of-jerks theory, I can see the point of selling the wind farms at the end of the year," Jennifer took a sip of her soda and set the can on Anne's desk. "But what about the April set of transactions? They don't help the bottom line since the sale of the wind farms was offset by the purchase of the barges. And if the *Wall Street Chronicle* gets wind of Eckert's back-and-forth buying spree, Spencer Brothers is going to look like a huge, blood-sucking rat."

Anne shuddered for a moment at the image of an overgrown rodent feasting on the remains of god-only-knows-what in the New York streets below. "What if Energix hid the cost of the wind farm purchase in April by transferring the asset over to their handy-dandy company in the Caribbean?"

Jennifer nodded slowly. "Then it would appear, once again, like they had made a big profit when, in fact, there was no real sale."

Anne bit her lip. Indeed, it would make the first quarter finances look great to investors, even if it had, in fact, been a terrible quarter.

"But if we're right, this charade can't continue forever." Jennifer flipped her long, wavy brown hair behind her shoulders. "It's like a Ponzi scheme. Eventually, it will topple on itself. Eckert, of all people, must know that."

"That's why he was so excited about the idea of a merger. It would be a straightforward way to get extricated from this mess."

"But didn't he say he still wanted to purchase the wind farms again? Even if there were a merger?" Jennifer interlocked her fingers and tapped her thumbs against one another. "Why continue to perpetuate this monkey business of back-and-forth-sales?"

"Maybe he's getting something *personal* out of it. A benefit of some sort..."

Jennifer paused her tapping. "The only thing I can see is that he's delaying the inevitable. This house of cards is going to fall. It's only a question of when."

"I'll bet Eckert had no idea the company was in financial trouble when he purchased the wind farms. He probably thought he was just providing the equivalent of a short-term loan and that they would all walk away a little richer." Anne's eyes narrowed. "But it wasn't just a loan. He was parking their wind farms, temporarily, which allowed Fernsby and his cronies to defraud their investors. And he collected fees for his service." Anne put air quotes around *service*. "Legally? He could be in pretty hot water, along with anyone else who was party to this deal."

Jennifer began gathering the key papers of interest into a small pile. "We need to make copies of this stuff before I take it back down."

"No problem." Anne smiled. "Our copiers don't ever malfunction."

Jennifer stood up and opened Anne's office door. "I have to say, I felt badly when Twinkle-Toes started pushing Eckert to buy a new printer. I mean, that one does have problems, but—"

"Well then, why?" They turned right and headed toward the closet where a single photocopier and printer resided. "You said it's been getting worse and worse."

"I know," Jennifer allowed, "but it's not quite as bad as we were making it out to be."

Anne lifted the lid and set the first document down on the glass. "Come on. It's a drop in the bucket." The copier hummed and began to grind. "A new printer won't even make a decimal point in Eckert's budget." She set a second document on the glass. "Meanwhile, it will make things easier for everyone who relies on it."

"What will?"

Anne whirled around at the sound of her secretary's voice.

"Oh—" Jennifer waved her hand vaguely. "A new printer. Down on the trading floor." She turned and pointed at the shiny new one that had been delivered just a few weeks earlier to Anne's group. "Have you been happy with the one you got?"

Anne pulled the photocopies out of the tray and curled the entire stack into a cylinder in an effort to hide them from her admin's prying eyes.

The secretary shrugged. "It's fine." She reached out to take the papers from Anne's hands. "I can copy those for you."

Anne tightened her grip and heard them crackle beneath her fingers. "No need. We'll take care of it later." She took a step toward the door.

"Are you sure?" The young woman furrowed her brow, obviously surprised that Anne didn't want her help.

Jennifer leaned forward and lowered her voice. "It's actually something for the trading floor." She looked downright apologetic. "Anne was just trying to help me out."

"That's okay." The secretary shrugged. "I don't mind."

Anne groaned inwardly. Usually, her admin had the motivation of a dying turtle, and now she was acting like a volunteer for the Red Cross, ready to help everyone out.

Jennifer put up a hand. "You're so nice to offer, but I don't want to add trading floor stuff to everything else you already do." She gave a small wave and slipped around the corner.

"She's right." Anne smiled and sailed out the door behind her.

* * *

"He could be charged with securities fraud," Alex said as he poured them each a glass of wine that evening. "You need to make sure that nobody else knows about those copies you made."

Anne looked at him in alarm. Was he suggesting that her actions were somehow illegal?

"It could put a target on your back." He handed her one of the glasses.

"How do you know Eckert isn't the one who killed Fernsby."

Eckert? No way. She had worked with the man for eight years. He was many things, but not a killer. Alex must have seen the look of disbelief on her face.

"You don't know who you can trust."

"With the SEC investigating Energix, it seems like it's only a matter of time before everything comes to light anyway." She swirled the wine in her glass. "So even if I have copies—"

Alex's eyes narrowed. "It's possible that just a few people know what actually happened in those transactions. If one of them decides to destroy the evidence…then your little reproductions could become very inconvenient…" His voice trailed off.

"Which makes Fernsby's death look *way* too convenient."

"Sure does."

"It seems like Eckert has the most to lose if this charade gets out, not the recently fired CFO." She inhaled the bouquet of her wine and took a sip. Refreshing, with an oaky vanilla character. "What I still don't understand is why he wanted me to oversee a potential acquisition." *Or Kevin,* Anne almost added, catching herself just in time from dragging Alex's new brother-in-law into the discussion.

"Eckert doesn't want the guys in the mergers group to find out about his swap deals."

"But how is that any different than me knowing about them?" She set her glass down and picked up a cracker.

"He probably doesn't think you'll recognize the significance of what he did."

In other words, Eckert had underestimated her. Anne's stomach sank as she took in his words. Her former boss, a senior executive at the corporation, believed that she was incapable of putting two and two together. She took a deep breath and squared her shoulders, firm in her resolve that she would get to the bottom of these deals and show Eckert how very wrong he was.

Alex shook his head. "When will he ever learn?"

When indeed?

15

Tennis Anyone?

The Hamptons

One week after the funeral

"Game, set, and match!" Kevin lobbed the extra tennis ball high into the air as he and Paige approached the net to shake hands with Anne and Alex.

"Finally!" Anne breathed a sigh of relief. They had been on the court for a good hour and a half with the hot sun blazing and hardly a trace of wind. She was ready for a large glass of ice water and a chance to rest.

"That last point was a killer." Alex wiped the sweat off of his forehead. "I thought the game would never end."

Kevin laughed. "Kind of like the situation at Energix. Sometimes, I think we'll never claw our way out of that mess either."

"Things can't be that bad," Alex said breezily as the group walked toward the side of the court to retrieve their belongings.

"Actually, they kind of are." Kevin grabbed the two nearest tennis balls and popped them into the can. "We got a formal preservation notice from the SEC on Friday."

Anne took a sharp breath. It wasn't every day that the regulators instructed a company like Energix to preserve *all* documents or other pieces of evidence that might be relevant to an ongoing investigation. This sort of official communication was the first step in a possible criminal prosecution for fraud or other financial misconduct. *Not a good sign...*

Alex bent down to pick up his racquet case. "It confirms that they've opened an investigation." He straightened up and zipped his racquet inside. "Given the recent drop in stock price, it's not all that surprising."

"True," Kevin said slowly, drawing the word out for emphasis. "But, I can only imagine what's going to happen next."

Alex shrugged. "You'll probably be invited for an interview of some sort so that they can get a better understanding of how the company got into its current state." He sounded casual, but his rigid stance and tight expression told another story. Anne sensed he was uncomfortable with the conversation, or perhaps recognized that Energix's situation was more precarious than he was letting on.

"That's what our general counsel said as well, but I'm not sure he's ever dealt with something of this nature before." Kevin ground the top of his shoe into the green clay that lined the court. "Do you have any experience with SEC investigations?"

Alex paused before responding. "Only in an advisory kind of way. Never as the target." He looked directly at Kevin. "It would be a good idea to retain separate outside counsel."

"We're going to do that."

"Immediately."

"But shouldn't—"

Alex waved his question aside. "I wouldn't wait. Not even a day. The SEC has a lot of power and unlimited resources at their disposal. From the very start you want to be working with someone who understands how those guys think so they don't decide to throw the book at you."

"That's all we need." A rivulet of sweat dripped off of Kevin's chin and he looked rather pale, as if the long match was finally catching up with him.

"I'm sure everything will work out fine," Paige chirped as she took the tennis ball can from her new husband and inserted the remaining ball. "And anyway, it's not like you caused any of the problems." She snapped the cover on top and threw her tennis bag over her shoulder.

"Right." He mumbled something under his breath and began to struggle with his racquet cover, as if trying to jam something into a case that had been designed for a smaller size. "What the—" He caught himself at the sound of a warning squawk from Paige and continued trying different angles.

"Is it fully unzipped?" Anne finally asked after he gave the racquet a particularly strong jerk that produced no obvious traction.

He paused to take a closer look. "Maybe that's the problem." With the pouch properly open, his racquet slid in smoothly, and he proceeded to zip it up with a series of short, agitated tugs. He brushed a wayward lock of hair off of his forehead and scanned their faces. "Lunch, anyone?"

* * *

Most of the tables had already been taken as they settled themselves down on the brick patio overlooking the inviting, turquoise pool.

"Perfect tennis weather," Paige commented as she waved to family friends sitting at some of the nearby tables.

"Lovely indeed!" came the replies. "Good to see you too, Alex. Enjoying life in the Big Apple?"

Anne had visited this exclusive club a number of times and yet continued to find herself in awe of the place. Nestled on nearly four-hundred, private acres with numerous, large trees scattered throughout the property, it felt serene. And comfortable, despite being located in the middle of a densely populated, northern New Jersey suburb.

Eventually, the pleasantries strayed to questions about the wedding that had just happened. (How was the honeymoon?) and the one that was yet to be planned (Any thought about having the reception here?).

"They haven't even set a date," Paige explained with an exaggerated shrug of her shoulders.

There was no question in Anne's mind that it would be a lovely place for a reception. The clubhouse had large gabled windows and multiple chimneys poking out through a gray slate roof that exuded a sense of stately charm mixed with a casual elegance. Inside were several large rooms with couches and overstuffed chairs arranged in conversation groups that would be perfect for mingling, and outside, there was space on the lawn for a large tent and dancing. And then, there was a picturesque stone path that beckoned down to a small pond surrounded by wildflowers and colorful grasses.

"Time to get hopping!" an elderly couple winked.

"That's what I keep telling them." Paige shook her head and shrugged, as if Anne and Alex were a couple of recalcitrant children.

The combination of friendly people and lovely surroundings was beguiling. Seductive, even. And yet, Anne knew that the club was highly discriminatory. Membership was by invitation only. To be considered, a person needed to obtain six letters of recommendation from current members, and even then, admittance was not guaranteed. Her family, which included a Jewish grandparent on her mother's side, would never have made the (unofficial, but fully enforced) pedigree cut. There was no way that she was going to get married at an establishment that wouldn't allow her family to be members because they supposedly belonged to the *wrong class of people*.

Paige beamed at Anne from across the table. "I know my mother would just love it if you had the reception here."

Alex gave his sister a warning look. He had dropped his junior membership when he was in law school because of the club's prejudicial practices. The only reason he and Anne spent any time at this elitist establishment was because his sister and parents remained active members, and it was their preferred place to socialize.

"We'll let you get back to your lunch," Paige closed off conversation with the other tables when a waitress arrived to take their orders: a mimosa for her (just one, since she was pregnant), a whiskey sour for Kevin (after that tennis game he needed something bracing), and water for Anne and Alex (evidently, the only ones feeling a bit dehydrated.)

"I'll be back with everything in just a minute." She left some rustic Italian breadsticks on the table before disappearing through a wall of French doors on her way to the kitchen.

"Have you heard the latest about our former CFO?" Kevin picked up one of the pencil-sized sticks of crisp, baked bread and dipped it into the accompanying bowl of rosemary-seasoned oil.

"Kevin!" Paige said through gritted teeth. "I thought we agreed you wouldn't bring that up *here*." She gave a surreptitious glance around to see if anyone was listening.

"Relax." He placed an arm on her shoulder and gave a gentle squeeze. "Everyone at the club already knows." He nodded toward Anne and Alex, sitting opposite them. "It's just these city-folk who have no idea."

City-folk?

He leaned back in his chair with a self-satisfied grin on his face that Anne found incredibly annoying.

"How about telling them after we—"

But Kevin couldn't wait to spill the beans. "Don's wife kicked him out of the house yesterday." He chuckled. "She *threw* his clothes out of the second-floor window while their children stood by watching."

Anne was confused. Why did either of these two care about the ex-CFO's marital squabbles? And why did Kevin seem almost gleeful about it? "Was it something to do with Energix?"

"That was my first thought as well. But, no." Kevin raised an eyebrow pointedly. "The reasons are a bit more *tawdry* than that."

"Kevin!" Paige looked around the patio, like a sentry guarding the palace. "You're talking about my best friend!"

Best friend? The only time Anne had ever seen the ex-CFO's wife was at the wedding and she'd never heard Paige talk about doing things socially with the woman, like meet for lunch or coffee. Or even a game of tennis. Ever.

"Maybe she should have thought of that before leaping into the fire," Kevin tsk-tsked.

Fire? Anne glanced at Alex, whose face remained impassive. Was he even listening to this weird interchange?

"At least keep your voice down," Paige pleaded, with yet another furtive glance at the nearby tables.

Kevin lowered his voice a few notches to a raspy whisper. "Truth be told, Don was a total moron! In his initial statement to the police, he claimed he was with his wife during the time they think Richard was killed...except, he wasn't."

He lied. That might be a reason to send the guy packing. Anne glanced at Paige, who was practically cringing in her seat. *What is going on with her?*

"Bad luck for him," Kevin said, sounding anything but sympathetic. "When the men in blue dropped by yesterday morning to confirm his whereabouts, his wife immediately began asking the obvious. *Why did Don say he was with her when he wasn't?*" He drew his lips down in an exaggerated grimace. "I gather the conversation went downhill from there."

Alex leaned forward, for the first time looking interested. "She thinks he killed Fernsby?"

"No!" Paige immediately seemed to regret her vehement reply. "Don has an explanation for where he was...it's just that he...he..."

Uh-oh. Whatever it was, she was clearly struggling to spit it out.

"He was trying to protect someone."

Kevin set his drink down with a loud clunk, causing the ice cubes to rattle and a bit of his drink to spill over the side. "The only thing he was trying to protect was his own reputation."

Paige opened her mouth and shut it again. Anne's interest was now fully piqued. She wasn't sure she had ever seen Alex's sister at a loss for words.

"He was gallivanting with another woman," Kevin explained, more loudly than seemed necessary.

An affair. With one of the guests at the wedding. That would be a good reason to kick the guy to the curb.

Kevin raised an eyebrow pointedly. "You'll never guess with who."

Anne's mind immediately began whirring. *Horse-Lover? Couldn't be. How would they know each other?* She continued searching for alternative candidates. *One of the other bridesmaids? Same problem.* The only person she had seen him interact with that day was Richard Fernsby and there had been no love lost there. *But what about...*

"Here you go." The waitress set their drinks on the table. "May I take your lunch orders?"

Anne's train of thought was temporarily suspended as she grabbed the menu and quickly reminded herself which sandwich she wanted to try (the avocado BLT with mashed avocado and jalapeño-herb mayo on rye).

Paige gave an approving nod upon hearing Anne's order. "I'll have the same."

Kevin waited until the waitress disappeared and then leaned forward and whispered, "Käthe."

The Diamond Goddess. Anne felt like kicking herself. It should have been obvious that the two were embroiled in a torrid love affair. She'd seen the way Käthe had rushed in, concerned, after the bumping incident with her father and later, the two of them lingering close to one another near the punchbowl. How could she not have recognized that they were mesmerized with one another?

"What?" Alex choked on his water. "Are you sure?"

"Positive." Kevin crossed his arms and looked smug as he surveyed the table. "Of *all* the people he could have gotten involved with, he chose the boss's daughter. And not just any boss, but the one who happened to be the CEO of Energix. Can you believe it?"

Or, perhaps, she chose him. Either way, a relationship between the two would have been fraught with peril: on the one hand, Don was her father's right-hand man, so there was the potential for abuse of power (one word to Fernsby and Käthe could probably have gotten him fired); and on the other, there was the obvious breach of trust (the guy was married with two young children!). And then there were the ethics associated with the blatantly fraudulent representations he had made to the financial community as CFO of Energix. Between Don and her father, the Diamond Goddess seemed to be surrounded by some real losers for men!

"Interesting, huh?" Kevin took a big sip of his drink and leaned back in his chair.

Alex looked directly at his sister. "Did you know?"

She nodded, her face grim.

"What about Richard? Did he have any idea that his own daughter was having a fling with the company CFO?"

She nodded again, a red flush rising on her face. "But Brigitte had no idea. Until yesterday."

Interesting. Käthe's father knew what she was up to and yet he hadn't elected to share that information with her mother. It suggested there might have been some cracks in the husband-wife relationship. Or that it wasn't one based on honesty.

"I'm surprised that Richard—" Alex began.

"He didn't approve of office romances. At all." Paige sighed and gave a resigned shrug. "The fact that it was his own daughter who was flouting the rules just made the situation all the more upsetting."

Anne stifled a nervous laugh. Fernsby may have defrauded investors and siphoned money from a struggling corporation into his own bank account, but on the subject of corporate love affairs, his moral compass (supposedly) remained intact, at least when it involved his own family. She glanced at Alex to see if he had caught the incongruity, but his face was inscrutable.

"Their entanglement probably complicated Richard's decision to hand Don his walking papers." Kevin's lips curled upward in what could only be a sneer.

Or perhaps that's the real reason he let the man go. Rather unceremoniously, in Anne's view. And then a darker thought occurred to her. *Had Richard attempted to separate the two love birds, thereby providing the impetus for his own murder?*

Alex must have been thinking along the same lines. "Fernsby's death is certainly convenient for Don. Not only does it make it easier for him to cover his financial tracks, but it also clears a path for him and Käthe."

Paige gave her brother an appraising look. "You're thinking about that weird clause in her trust fund. Aren't you?"

Her money came with strings? Anne tried to keep her face impassive despite being extremely curious what sort of unusual provisions were attached to Käthe's inheritance.

Alex nodded. "What if Richard threatened to revoke her status as the beneficiary unless she ended things with Don?"

It would certainly make it harder for the guy to get his grubby little mitts on her assets, if that was his main goal. But to kill Fernsby in cold blood? That would be a pretty major step to take without being absolutely certain Käthe actually wanted to marry him. Anne did her best to continue keeping her face expressionless as she listened intently to Alex and Paige slowly expose the Diamond Goddess's private financial affairs.

"She would have told me if Richard had said anything of the kind." Paige was rock solid in her reply. "And no matter what Käthe did, Brigitte would never have allowed him to cut off their only child. She wouldn't have stood for it. Not in a million years."

Alex nodded. "You're probably right. And I don't think Richard would have tried to control Käthe in that way either." He picked up his water and gave it a jiggle, causing the ice cubes to tinkle against the glass. "I wonder what prompted the police to question Don's alibi in the first place."

"Maybe they already knew there were some inconsistencies in his story and wanted to see what else they could shake out." The words were out of Anne's mouth before she had thought carefully about whether to wade into the conversation.

Kevin wagged his finger up and down. "That's exactly what happened! Evidently, he and Käthe didn't bother to get their stories straight before talking to the police the night of our wedding."

Which suggests they didn't know that Richard had been murdered. Or, maybe things happened so fast, or differently than they had expected, and they didn't have a chance to get aligned.

Kevin continued to gloat despite Paige's glum face beside him. "Don must have been shocked to open his front door yesterday morning and see those same two detectives who were hanging around the funeral asking to be let in. And then to learn that they wanted to talk to him and his wife—" he coughed, "—soon-to-be *ex*-wife—" he coughed again, not quite hiding a grin, "—about what he and his little sidepiece were getting up to."

"His sidepiece?" Paige glared at him.

He raised both arms to the sky, looking exasperated. "Don was always acting like he was this morally superior being, and now we learn that he was the king of hanky-panky who thought nothing of a roll in the hay with the master's favorite daughter."

Paige blinked and then opened her eyes wide in what looked like *the most-severe-stare-ever*, communicating what appeared to be a warning that he better cease and desist or else he might be sleeping on the couch. Permanently.

He rearranged his face and dropped the swaggering tone, finally sounding more like the highly-paid corporate executive he was. "Before the brouhaha with Käthe erupted, I wondered whether Don might have had something to do with Fernsby's death, simply because of his activities at Energix."

"Käthe says he wouldn't hurt a fly," Paige immediately countered.

Kevin rolled his eyes. "Of course she'd say that."

"And she swears she was with him the entire time in question, which also puts him in the clear."

Unless she's lying to protect him.

"Another obvious possibility is Peter Eckert." Paige pointed the finger at Anne's co-worker casually, as if accusing people of murder was a normal thing to do. "Käthe says that he's the brainchild behind all of the financial stuff that went on." She studied Anne, as if gauging her reaction.

Eckert? He was calculating. And self-serving. But Anne never would have pegged him as a cold-blooded murderer. She shrugged and gave what she thought was a bland reply. "Anything's possible."

"My point exactly! We've known Peter for years through the club, and yet maybe we don't know him at all!" She raised one hand in the air, like a fiery minister preaching from the pulpit. "What if he decided to take Richard out of the picture so that he could blame everything on Don?"

Kevin looked dubious. "Seems like it would make more sense to pin any questionable wheeling-dealing on the dead man rather than the one who's around to point the finger straight back."

A well-reasoned comment from Kevin, finally!

"And," he added with a quick glance at Anne, "word on the street is that Richard was going to leave Don twisting in the wind with the SEC."

"Well—" Paige gave her shoulders a little twist and settled more deeply into her chair. "For Käthe's sake, I hope those rumors are unfounded."

The table became quiet for a moment.

"How's she doing?" Alex finally broke the silence.

Paige shook her head, a pained look on her face. "Not well. She's still very much in shock over her father's death. And now that it's becoming clear he was murdered…" She blinked, looking like she might even shed a tear. "I mean, she's devastated."

"Probably not thinking clearly," Alex said slowly.

"She's a mess." Paige sighed deeply and rubbed her forehead, as if she was starting to get a migraine. "And then yesterday, Don showed up at her place in his new Ferrari. He wants to move in and, once his divorce is final, get married."

Whoa. Even before the papers have been drawn, the guy is already well along the way to his next gig. It certainly showed gumption. And drive. All of which suggested he wasn't a helpless bean counter who was easily pushed into errors of judgment by some tough Wall Street trader trying to make a fast buck. Don Chalmer, ex-CFO of Energix, was clearly a man who went after what he wanted and was perfectly comfortable pushing any obstacle out of the way. Did that include murder?

"I think she's thrilled that he's finally come clean with his wife, but with everything else that's happened, she's feeling pretty overwhelmed."

Anne looked at Paige in disbelief. "She needs time to process her father's death before trying to evaluate a marriage proposal." *Especially one coming from some guy who's just been fired from his job, is under investigation for financial wrongdoing, and is probably in the midst of a mid-life crisis. And, the poor girl needs to be absolutely certain that he's not the one who killed her father!*

"We all saw her at the funeral." Alex's tone was delicate. "She's obviously very vulnerable right now. I think you should encourage her to hold off on making any major life decisions for a while."

For at least six months! Maybe even a year.

"I'm worried about that as well." Paige pursed her lips. "It's too much, too soon."

"Exactly." Alex paused and then pressed on. "There's also a longer-term question to consider. What if Don ends up being criminally indicted? Does she really want to be married to someone behind bars?"

Kevin was no longer smirking like a clueless frat boy. He took a large gulp of his drink and wiped his forehead as if he was suddenly feeling hot.

"That won't happen if Eckert is responsible." Paige tossed her hair back as if that would somehow fling her brother's comment away. "And she's convinced—"

Alex waved his hand dismissively. "Those accounting entries didn't post onto the ledgers all by themselves. Someone gave the order and Don was the person in charge of that. Even if Eckert came up with all of the ideas, which I'm not sure I believe, Don likely has some culpability."

"But—"

"The one thing we know for sure is that the police went to Don's home yesterday to verify his story and it didn't check out. We haven't heard the same thing about Eckert."

"Wait a minute," she corrected him. "Once it became clear that the police actually *needed* to know his whereabouts, he admitted that he and Käthe had slipped away during the critical hour so they could have some private time together."

The man was having a romantic interlude with his mistress while his wife hung around, alone, in the party tent?

Paige must have seen the look of disgust on Anne's face. "It's not what you think. They just took a long walk, away from the party, so Käthe could calm down. She was very upset about the way her father treated *you* at the reception."

"As she should have been," Alex said, his voice terse. "He was beyond rude. If I'd been there, I'd have given him a piece of my mind." His eyes narrowed. "Instead, I was running around doing…I don't know…whatever needed doing."

"It's probably better that you weren't there." Paige gave a weak smile. "You didn't have enough crayons to explain to Richard how much of a prick he'd been." She took a sip and set the frosty glass on the table.

145

Anne looked down at the placemat in front of her, trying to keep her emotions in check. At the time, she had been so worried that everybody thought she was to blame for Richard's eruption that she had somehow brought the whole thing on herself. And yet it was becoming clear that many of the people within Fernsby's orbit thought that he had acted like a total jerk. There was something freeing in that knowledge, as if a huge weight had been lifted from her shoulders. And she felt a sense of optimism that perhaps Alex's parents felt the same way, too.

"Did Käthe confront her father? Point out that he was acting like a—"

"No." Paige shuddered. "But his outburst was the last straw. He'd been erratic all evening. And don't forget, she knew her mother was already talking about getting a divorce. I think she was also struggling with the whole Don-being-married thing, especially since he was attending the wedding with his *wife*."

Yeah, Anne felt like saying, *I imagine it's pretty inconvenient to see the cuckolded spouse in person. Makes it harder to pretend they don't exist. Or that their feelings don't matter.*

Paige looked around the table. "It's incredibly sad that my best friend and wonderful maid of honor was in tears at the wedding. And it's particularly upsetting since it was thanks to her own father. But to Don's credit, he saw she was in pain and tried to comfort her." Paige put a hand on her heart as she pronounced her verdict. "I feel sorry for his wife, but I also feel for Käthe. She was dealing with so much at that moment."

And yet, if Kevin were to do the same to her, Anne was willing to bet Paige would be feeling a whole lot differently about the situation.

Alex took off his sunglasses and rubbed a spot on one of the lenses. "How old are the children?"

Paige looked at Kevin, a quizzical expression on her face. "I think the oldest one—"

"He's five," Kevin jumped to her rescue. "And the younger one is two or three."

"Hmmm." Alex put his glasses back on.

"Don will make sure they're well provided for." Paige's face relaxed as the conversation appeared to shift to more mundane financial matters.

"I expect he will." Alex's tone was even. "Though he does seem to have gotten tired of his first wife fairly quickly. Käthe might want to take note…"

Anne was shocked to find herself wanting to add, *Or, at least make sure he signs a prenup.*

16

When the Cat's Away

New York City

A few days later

"Sorry to interrupt," Anne's secretary leaned in through the partially open door. "There's a woman in the lobby who's asking to see you." She glanced down at her notepad. "A Brigitte Fernsby?"

Anne blinked. *Here? At the office?*

Her secretary stared at her, a bored expression on her face. "Should I tell security to let her up?"

"Yes. Thank you." *I bet she's looking for Alex. She probably ran into a problem reaching him and figured I could bring her to his floor instead.* Anne took a final sip of her Coke and eyed the phone. *Should I call him to let him know she's arrived?* Before she could decide, there was a knock at her door.

"Me again." It was her secretary. She strode into Anne's office and set a prospectus on her desk. "These are the financials on Lightfoot Apparel that you requested. I'm going to take a coffee break with Vanessa." She pointed at Anne's sneakers, strewn haphazardly behind the door. "You might want to move those. They're kind of in the way."

Anne popped the offending footwear into her bottom desk drawer, dumped her empty Coke can into the trash, and then rearranged the papers on her desk into several neat piles. Satisfied that her office looked presentable, she picked up the phone to call Alex and immediately set it down again as a shadow darkened her doorway.

"Good afternoon." Brigitte greeted her warmly. She dropped into the chair on the opposite side of Anne's desk and placed two large bags from Saks Fifth Avenue on the floor nearby. "I'm sorry to drop by unannounced, but I was in the city doing some shopping. I thought it would help take my mind off of things."

"Retail therapy," Anne said gingerly. "Did it help?"

She looked directly at Anne, a slight frown on her face. "No. Not really."

Anne was struck by the deep blue color of Brigitte's eyes and her smooth, porcelain skin. While it had some fine wrinkles, she had aged beautifully. Someone who didn't know better might think she was in her forties rather than the sixty-plus years that she had to be.

"Oh," Anne said, unsure what else to say.

Brigitte fussed with the diamond bracelet encircling her wrist. "When I was in the store, I look at the shoes and try to choose. Should I buy? Should I not? I can't decide. My mind keeps jumping to my husband fixing his tie just before he got out of the car at the reception and then his body, lying lifeless in that boat. And then I find myself staring at those damn shoes."

Anne bit her lip, feeling a mixture of pity, horror, and deep sadness for the bereaved woman. Losing your lifelong partner had to be one of the worst things that could happen to someone, especially when it was unexpected and you had no time to prepare emotionally.

Brigitte let go of the bracelet and rested her arm on her lap. "One moment he's alive, and the next he's gone. In an instant, my life is completely changed. It doesn't seem real. Ja?"

Anne cast about for a reply, something that didn't sound like it had been recycled from a dime store condolence card. "It's going to take time before things start to make sense again."

Brigitte waved her hand dismissively, her bracelet casting fiery flashes of light. "That's what everyone says. But I think they're wrong." She leaned forward and peered at Anne. "I don't need time. I need answers. So I can understand. That's why you and I, we must talk."

Anne blinked. *About what?*

"So, I march straight over here and find your office. You understand? I hope that's okay."

"Of course," Anne said, not understanding at all. In fact, she was beginning to wonder about Brigitte's overall mental state.

"Those two policemen." Brigitte looked quizzically at Anne. "Who were at the funeral? Ja?"

Anne nodded, a feeling of dread starting to take hold.

"They say my husband was poisoned."

She wants to discuss her husband's murder? With me?

"At first, I didn't believe them. It seemed so preposterous. But they insist that the medical examiner is confident. He's just waiting for the results of some tests to come back from the lab before issuing his report. So now, I need to know. Who would do such a thing to him?"

Anne searched her mind for a way to respond to the grieving woman. She wanted to be sympathetic, but what could she do? Brigitte needed to see a professional who specialized in providing support to someone newly widowed. "I'm not sure how I can help," she said as gently as possible.

Brigitte's head moved left and right, her eyes sweeping Anne's office. "You specialize in financial matters."

Wait. Is she looking for help with managing her assets?

Anne nodded slowly. "That's right."

She fixed her gaze solidly on Anne. "You knew to sell your Energix holdings shortly before the stock tumbled."

Oh no...she holds me responsible for her net worth going down the drain!

Anne forced a smile, trying to maintain her poker face.

"That tells me you're sharp, and you know how to get to the bottom of things."

"Or maybe, just lucky," Anne said drily.

Brigitte gave her a knowing look. "I don't believe luck had anything to do with it."

Anne shifted uneasily in her chair, unsure where the conversation was heading.

"Look." Brigitte frowned. "I know my husband blamed you for the price drop in a very public manner. He was...how do you say? All bark and no bite. But deep down, he knew it wasn't your fault."

Really? Then why did he mention me by name to every reporter he could find and threaten to sue both my employer and me? And let's not forget the lovely spitting incident at the wedding, where he later likened me to a heartless, yellow-eyed predator.

A small smile crept across Brigitte's face. "He was afraid of you. Most of the analysts were putty in his hands, but you...you were different. You questioned what you saw. That's why I'm asking for your help. I want to know who's responsible for Energix's financial problems. I think that must be the person who killed my husband."

Finally, Anne understood the real reason for this unexpected visit.

She tilted slightly forward, her diamond earrings flashing as they caught in the bright fluorescent lights. "How did you know that something was amiss?"

Where to even begin? The sky-high earnings estimates? The odd footnotes in the year-end financial statements? Richard's refusal to provide the first quarter financial results and his bullying response to reasonable questions?

"I noticed some unusual accounting entries."

Brigitte's dazzling blue eyes were, at the same time, discerning. "Unusual, how?"

Anne hesitated. She felt comfortable providing general facts, but was cognizant that her employer was Spencer Brothers, not Richard Fernsby's widow. "I'm limited in what I can discuss."

Brigitte nodded, her eyes glued to Anne.

"What I can say is that when I started probing more deeply, I became concerned Energix might not be well-positioned going forward." She felt sheepish as she tiptoed through the remainder of her canned response. The elegant woman in her office was searching for answers to basic questions. And yet they were answers she couldn't, in good conscience, provide.

"Everyone seems to think that Don was the mastermind, my late husband included. At least, I assume he did, since he fired him." She paused. "But I'm starting to wonder. What do you think?"

"I'm not sure," Anne said carefully.

The contrast between Brigitte and her late husband was jarring. She wanted to understand what Anne had found, whereas he had done everything in his power to bury it. Of course, the circumstances had changed with his death. Even so, Anne was fairly certain that Richard would be turning in his grave if he knew his wife was chatting away with his nemesis about how she had unearthed the financial problems at Energix. It was almost as if the two were polar opposites and yet they had, by all accounts, been happily married.

Brigitte nodded at the newspaper that sat folded on the edge of Anne's desk. "You've seen today's front-page story? Even Don's wife thinks he's responsible."

Anne nodded. It had led with a salacious headline:

Energix CFO played around with more than the company's coffers and his wife isn't having it.

The gist of the article was that Don's soon-to-be ex-wife was now reportedly cooperating with the SEC (presumably) to take him down. Somewhere near the middle was a crack about Käthe, in which she was referred to as the ex-CFO's play bunny. *Will she remain steadfast?* the writer had asked.

Brigitte toyed with her gold earring. "Don's wife is angry, as she should be. He's treated her terribly. And yet, Käthe thinks she's in love with the man." She sighed. "I need to know. Did he kill my husband to cover up his financial mess? My daughter says no. She says Peter Eckert devised some swap deals that he doesn't want anyone to know about. The police should be looking at him. But I don't think they have the expertise to follow the money."

She had a fair point. Even the so-called experts had failed to see through the lies and distortions at Energix until it was too late. Why would two homicide detectives, who had no financial training at all, be able to do any better? *Although, they could contact the SEC regulators and see what they have to say...*

Brigitte waved her hand dismissively. "Personally, I don't think Don Juan's smart enough to figure out how to squirrel money away so that nobody knows about it. His idea of a swap deal is putting on a new pair of underwear. But Peter—" she gave a knowing smile, "he knows what he's doing when it comes to structuring financial transactions."

Her candor was jolting, but also refreshing. And Anne agreed. Peter certainly had the financial smarts. But what would be his motive for killing Fernsby? To hide something about those swap deals?

Brigitte leaned forward in her chair. "Don and my husband were avoiding each other at the wedding. I don't see how he could have poisoned Richard. But Peter was talking with my husband throughout the evening. He had many opportunities."

As did almost everyone who interacted with him at the wedding. Anne shifted in her chair. "Have you mentioned your suspicions to the police?"

"No." She shook her head, her face grim. "What if I'm wrong?" She paused. "Maybe I underestimate Don."

And then there was the illegal immigration status of her aging mother to consider. Every time the detectives showed up at her house, there was some risk they'd notice the little old lady who had overstayed her visa, so keeping those visits to a minimum might also be a factor in her mind.

Brigitte tapped the top of Anne's desk. "I want your frank assessment of what really happened at Energix. We can keep it between just the two of us. Make it our own secret." She smiled weakly. "It's something I need to know."

Anne had to hand it to her. The woman was shrewd. And probably right. If they got to the bottom of who profited from Richard's death, they would also find his killer. She took a deep breath and looked squarely at the grieving woman. "If you think it's all about following the money, what about Käthe's trust fund?"

Brigitte cocked her head, clearly surprised by the question.

"I understand there was a clause that allowed Richard to revoke her inheritance."

"No." She shook her head firmly. "That's not correct. He didn't have the power to do that alone. It required *both* of our signatures."

"Did Käthe know that?" *And, perhaps more important, her boy-toy?*

"Of course." Brigitte drew herself up. "And she knows I would *never* agree to something like that. *Never.* And now that Richard's gone, I intend to have that clause removed entirely. I'm not sure why I allowed it in the first place."

"What if Don somehow got the idea—"

She shook her head, a disgusted look on her face. "No. He knew as well." She arched a brow. "He had the gall to ask Richard about the terms of Käthe's trust fund at some point. I forget the details. But it came up in the context of transferring a fairly large asset into her name."

Don Juan sounds more and more like a treasure hunter...

She gave Anne an appraising look. "These are good questions. That's why I want your help."

The two sat in silence for an interminable minute.

She stood up. "I've taken enough of your time."

Anne did the same, handing Brigitte her two bags. "Don't forget these."

"Thank you." She gave a pleasant nod. "For everything."

Anne smiled. "I'm glad you dropped by."

"If you learn anything, please tell me what you *can* about the swap deals. If it leads to Peter..." She left the rest unsaid as she turned to leave Anne's office.

If it leads to Peter, it means my colleague is a murderer.

* * *

"She came to the office?" Alex looked perplexed. He had been in the middle of quarterly filings when Anne knocked on his door, clearly happy for any excuse to take a break. "Why?"

"She wants to know who killed Richard." Anne pulled a chocolate bar out of her bag and broke it in half.

"You've got to be kidding me," he snorted as he reached out for one of the pieces. "You're not a detective."

"True." She arched an eyebrow playfully. "But I am a financial sleuth."

He cocked his head sideways, a look of consternation on his face. "Meaning what exactly?"

"She knows I dumped the Energix stock before it totally tanked." Anne held her Coke can to the side as she pulled the tab off of the top. "She wants me to use my superpowers to figure out the true architect behind all of the financial maneuvering."

He rolled his eyes. "How about the guy who's been seducing her daughter? As the former CFO of the corporation, he seems like a pretty good candidate."

Anne put up a hand. "She doesn't think he's got the smarts."

He raised an eyebrow. "Has she told her daughter that?"

Anne shrugged. "No idea. But, Brigitte doesn't strike me as the type to hold back."

"That's the understatement of the day." Alex chuckled. "Tell me. How did she seem?"

Anne hesitated. She respected the woman and didn't want to sound like she was tearing her down. "A bit all over the place, but, who wouldn't be in her situation?"

"I know." He shook his head. "She and Richard were like the Rock of Gibraltar. Solid. You could always count on them. It would be hard enough to have your husband die unexpectedly, but to come to terms with the idea that he was murdered. I mean, that's a lot."

"And yet, I feel like she's going to be okay in the long run."

Alex nodded. "Me too."

"It's interesting. When she first arrived at my office, it was really obvious that English wasn't her first language. She probably felt a bit awkward showing up the way she did. But by the time she left, it was more fluid, less broken, and she seemed relaxed. I feel like our chat may have done her some good."

"I hope you're right."

"Whenever I talk with her, I feel a sort of camaraderie. Almost a bonding. She's smart and funny and..." And she, too, had been snubbed by her in-laws for no good reason, but of course Anne wasn't about to say that. "I don't know. I just really like her."

He nodded. "I've already told you she was like a mother to me. Maybe we can come up with some way to include her more explicitly in our wedding. Assuming we don't elope." He winked and swiftly swiped her Coke.

"Hey!" Anne pointed.

He gave the can a bounce, feeling the heft. "There's plenty left." He waited for her to nod and then took a sip. "Getting back to Brigitte and her impromptu visit." He set it back down. "If not Don, then who—" He stopped abruptly as the realization hit him. "She thinks it's Eckert."

"Yep." Anne peeled the wrapper off of her chocolate and took a bite.

"And she wants you to look at those swap deals that Käthe keeps going on about so that she can understand what he's been up to. Am I right?"

Anne nodded, letting the chocolate melt in her mouth.

"Hmmm." He leaned back in his chair. "I have to admit. Those contracts you found were a bit strange."

"I know. And Eckert's way too cagey about them." She narrowed her eyes. "There's something off about the whole business."

"With this SEC investigation going on in the background, there's even more impetus to understand the deals." He lowered his voice even though the door was shut, and they were the only two people in the room. "We received a formal notice of retention from the regulators this morning. I just finished briefing our very unhappy CEO a little while ago."

Her eyes widened. Spencer Brothers was getting pulled into the fray, which meant the aperture was widening. Or, perhaps, the noose was tightening. She wasn't sure which.

Alex put on his corporate lawyer hat and laid out the plan for addressing this latest development. "I'm going to be sending a note to all of the Executive VPs advising them that we've been put on notice to retain any and all documents related to transactions with Energix. They can choose how to cascade the message down through the organization." His face was serious, and his tone matter-of-fact. "Failure to comply can result in criminal penalties of up to twenty years. This is *not* something that anyone should screw around with."

Twenty years! Anne took another bite of chocolate and washed it down with a swig of Coke. "Eckert won't be able to keep the details of those swap deals hidden for long."

He snapped his fingers. "Actually, that reminds me. I tried to look up the company that runs those wind farms to get an idea of the size of the overall operation. I couldn't find anything registered under the name of Enchanted Power. Do you recall if the contract listed them as doing business under another name?"

Anne tried to visualize the purloined pages in her mind. "I'm pretty sure there was just the one company with a physical address listed at the very top. I'll check when I get back to my office. If nothing else, the local tax authorities can tell us how much acreage they have."

His phone rang. He glanced down at the number and made a face. "I've got to take this."

As Anne turned to leave, she found herself fixated on the name of the wind farm. Enchanted Power. It sounded almost magical. Like it belonged in a fairy tale.

17

On Par to Execute

New York City

Later that afternoon

"Your phone's been ringing off the hook," Anne's secretary greeted her with a pile of pink messages. "There's some news about Meadow Lake Textiles that must have come out over the wire. At least ten brokers have called asking whether the fund still holds it."

No. Thank goodness. She had dumped that loser the previous month after an odd conversation with the treasurer of the corporation. He had laid out their new strategy for boosting sales, and the longer he talked, the more concerned she became. By the time he was through, he no longer looked like a hard-working man in a slightly crumpled suit. Instead, all she saw was a washed-up snake oil peddler hawking junk she couldn't get rid of fast enough.

"Thanks." Anne nodded and disappeared into her office. But instead of calling the brokers back, she opened her credenza and pulled out the photocopies of the swap deal. Indeed, the company name was Enchanted Power, and the address of record was on Wild Horse Drive in Palm Springs, California. Five minutes later, she was standing in front of the librarian in the corporate library.

"Oh yes," the bespectacled woman chirped pleasantly. "We have maps for every county in the United States and most cities. Which one were you looking for?" She trundled over to a set of file drawers and pulled out five different options. "These have different levels of detail," she explained. "Have a look and see which one suits your purpose."

Anne thanked her and spread them out across a large oak table in the center of the room. She quickly found the corporate address on the street map index for one of them and then looked at the corresponding location on the map. It was in a residential section of the town, overlooking a golf club called Desert Willow Resort. She looked at the index again to confirm the address and then back at the map. The area was completely residential. Perhaps this was simply the corporate office? There was no place for a wind farm unless the windmills were all over the green...

"Can I borrow this?" Anne held up the map she had been studying.

"Of course." The gray-haired woman smiled as she pushed a notebook toward Anne. "If you'd just sign here..."

* * *

Anne practically ran to her office. She pulled out the photocopied contracts and jumped to the section where the wind farm was described:

It comprises 250 turbines spaced at least 1000 feet apart, occupying a total of 4000 acres.

No address. Just the physical description, which left one key question. Where were these turbines actually located?

* * *

"Anne." Kevin's concerned voice crackled down the telephone line. "Is everything okay?"

"Yes. Yes." She hadn't meant to alarm Alex's new brother-in-law. "This has nothing to do with family. I have a quick work-related question for you."

"Oh." He paused. "Okay." His tone became more formal. Distant even. "What can I do for you."

"I'm following up on some paperwork associated with the wind farms that Peter Eckert wants to purchase."

There was a long pause. "Wind farms?"

"They're owned by a subsidiary of yours called Enchanted Power."

"I don't recognize that name," he said slowly. "Are you sure Energix is the parent company?"

Positive. But she wasn't about to let him know that she'd seen the contract. Made a copy of it even! She had no idea if she could trust him. His role in all of this wasn't clear to her.

"No." She sighed for dramatic effect. "That's part of the problem. It appeared in a database we keep." She rolled her eyes silently. Hopefully, if any part of this conversation made its way back to Peter, she'd be able to claim that the garbage she was spewing had gotten garbled somewhere along the line between his secretary and the other support staff. "Someone seems to have made a clerical error and listed a residential address in Palm Springs, California, as the location."

"The only thing I know of in Palm Springs is the Desert Willow Golf Resort." He sounded like a puffed-up bird as he provided the name of the private club. "It's a pretty exclusive place with some fairly big Hollywood names on the membership roster."

Not exactly where you'd expect to find the corporate headquarters of a wind farm.

"You know," she paused. "That name rings a bell. But I'm not sure why." She held her breath, waiting to see if her shot in the dark would yield anything useful.

"Maybe it has a tiny windmill or two on the back nine," he chortled. "That might count as a wind farm." He laughed again, louder and longer, evidently finding his joke highly amusing.

She let her breath out slowly. Not what she was hoping for.

"Actually." His voice became more serious. "Alex's parents have probably mentioned The Desert Willow to you at some point. The Fernsbys have a membership there. And a big house that overlooks the course on Wild Horse Drive. It's supposed to have a spectacular view of the eighteenth hole."

Bingo. Richard must have listed his California vacation home as the corporate headquarters for the wind farm business. But why?

"Once a year, Richard would charter a private jet and invite the executive team to join him for a few rounds of golf," he chattered on. "From what I heard, they'd stay up half the night, bonding over cognac and cigars. It sounded like a great time."

I'll bet. Anne shifted in her seat. Evidently, he knew all about their fun executive retreats, and nothing about the business being conducted there. Convinced she'd learned everything she could, she wrapped up the call. "Well, thanks for everything. I've taken up enough of your time."

"My pleasure. Sorry I couldn't be more help. And good luck getting that database straightened out!"

"Sounds like we'll need it," she replied cheerfully, crossing her fingers that that little piece of fiction didn't come back to bite.

She hung up the phone and leaned back in her chair. Did he really know nothing about the existence of the wind farm business? Or was he lying to protect someone? And where were those turbines actually located?

* * *

Anne glanced at the clock. *Five o'clock already!* She dialed Alex's number and tucked the receiver under her chin as she pulled her sneakers out of the bottom desk drawer. "Hey. I completely lost track of the time. Meet you down in the lobby?"

"I'll be down in a sec." He sounded exhausted. The quarterly filings seemed to be taking a huge toll. The night before, he had described them as dreary and mind-numbing, the absolute worst part of corporate law. If push came to shove with her job here at Spencer Brothers, maybe pulling up stakes and moving to London would be a good change for both of them. As he clicked off, he added, "I just need to check one small thing."

She grabbed her coat and headed toward the elevator. The floor was empty except for another money manager chatting with his secretary down at the far end of the hall. As she waited for the car to arrive, her mind drifted back to the swap deals. Energix had sold them to Spencer Brothers and then bought them back, so there had to be a record of them in their ledgers. How could Kevin not know anything about them? It made no sense.

The elevator dinged, and the door opened a moment later.

"Hello, Anne." Peter's haunted eyes peered out at her from within the car. "Giving up for the day?"

She did her best to smile as she stepped inside. "Finally. Looking forward to a quiet evening. How about you?"

The doors shut, and the elevator began to descend.

"I'm going to have a whiskey sour and watch the sun set."

Alone? Or will Twinkle-Toes be joining you?

His lips twitched. "Maybe take an evening stroll in the park after dinner."

Anne vaguely recalled hearing that he had a penthouse apartment on the Upper West Side overlooking central park. *It cost a mint*, one of the traders had said. *Yeah. But I hear the girls love it*, another had responded. And then both had laughed in a way she found particularly grating.

"Should be a great night for stargazing as well," she said mildly.

The elevator slowed down and came to a stop. She glanced up at the lighted panel and groaned inwardly. They were stopping at the 5th floor. It was going to be a slow ride. Even worse, the doors opened to an empty hallway. *Seriously?* A moment later, they closed again; the elevator bumped and began slowly moving.

"Things seem to be heating up with the SEC." Peter suddenly seemed closer to her, as if he had shifted his position while her attention was diverted. She could smell garlic on his breath and gave an involuntary shudder.

"Oh really?" She tried to sound nonchalant as she stepped back a few inches to have a bit more space between the two of them.

"Alex didn't tell you?" His voice was raspy.

She shrugged, keeping her face impassive. "Why would he?"

"I just figured that the two of you wouldn't keep any secrets." The corners of his mouth turned up in a smile that looked a lot like a sneer.

She shifted her briefcase from one hand to the other and widened her stance, immediately feeling stronger and more grounded. "We try to keep work at work."

He nodded slowly. "Hmmm."

Was that a *hmmm, good idea?* Or was he hmming to indicate he didn't believe her? She looked over at the elevator panel again, wondering how much longer before reaching the lobby, and did a double-take when she saw the number ten, glowing in red. "You've got to be kidding me!"

"What?"

"We're going up instead of down!"

The elevator glided to a stop and the doors opened to an empty corridor. *Should I just exit and wait for the next one?* As she started to move toward the front of the car, he mirrored her motion, effectively blocking her way. The only way out was to force her way past him and risk looking rude, unless she could come up with a good excuse. *What if I say...*

"I'll get it." He reached over and pushed the button for the lobby, firmly, and waited for the doors to close. "Hopefully that will do the trick."

As he turned to face her, she felt almost sick. Why hadn't she pushed her way past and gotten off when she had the chance? Now, she was stuck riding all the way down with him.

Peter looped his thumbs through his bright red suspenders and gave them a little snap. "Looks like we may have found a potential partner for Energix."

"That was fast."

"And easy." His lips twitched. "I'll be happy to get those oil barges off our books." He cracked his neck once on each side, and his tone became almost taunting. "Too bad you missed out. The commissions will be enormous."

Assuming the deal actually goes through. Once this buyer has taken a closer look, they may have second thoughts. She smiled politely, feeling the elevator come to a halt. "Glad everything worked out."

The doors opened, and she practically sprang out of the cramped, airless space, breathing a sigh of relief to be free. She stepped a few feet away and looked around the open expanse of the lobby. *Where are you, Alex?* She did a full 360 and came face to face with Peter. Her stomach sank. He was like an annoying mosquito, buzzing around her ear. And yet she didn't dare swat him away either.

"Hey." He snapped his fingers, as if suddenly remembering something. "I've been meaning to ask you about Energix's financial statements."

She eyed him warily, wanting nothing more than to be rid of the guy.

"When you went through the details…those footnotes you mentioned…I'm just wondering…Did you see any mention of the oil barges?"

She shook her head. But as his gray eyes studied her, she saw something that looked almost like fear. It piqued her curiosity. Why did he even care?

He swallowed. "What about the wind farms?"

What indeed? He'd given her an opening, and she pounced on the opportunity to learn more. "Not a peep. Which is kind of surprising when you think about it."

"Really?" He furrowed his brow. "What makes you say that?"

She shrugged, doing her best to appear casual. "It's kind of a cutting-edge technology, at least in the US. I would think they might want to advertise the fact that they're developing alternative energy sources that could help reduce our reliance on oil from the Middle East."

His lips twitched.

She put on her eager-beaver smile and hit him with the million-dollar question. "Do you recall how many windmills they're running or where it's physically located? It would be interesting to learn more about how much power the farm can produce."

The color drained from his face. "It's not large at all…just ten or twenty turbines, I believe…"

"Oh really? That's it?"

"Yeah." His lips twitched. "They sit on a small farm in central California, somewhere. I think it's just a test operation, more than anything. I'm not sure they even—"

"Sorry I'm late." Alex suddenly appeared at her side. "Evening." He gave Peter a perfunctory nod.

In reply, the stoop-shouldered executive half-raised his hand as if barely able to wave goodbye, turned on his heel, and shuffled off.

"What did *he* want?"

She arched an eyebrow. "Funny you should ask."

18

The Early Bird Catches the Worm

Short Hills, NJ

Later that week (Saturday night)

"Nobody is to bring up *anything* that might be at all stressful," Kevin said by way of greeting. His head shifted back and forth as he eyeballed each of them, sternly. "She needs to remain calm and relaxed."

Anne and Alex both nodded, fully aware that Paige had been instructed by her doctor to remain on full bed rest due to a complication with her pregnancy.

The lines on his face eased, and his mouth widened into a welcoming smile. "We'll be having dinner out back." He glanced down at the bottle of red wine they had brought as a gift and gave Alex an approving nod, the sort that indicated he recognized a fellow connoisseur. "Good choice. This should pair well with the steak."

Alex winked at Anne as his brother-in-law led them through the living room out to the patio. *Score!* They both knew the vineyard was one of Kevin's favorites and had chosen that particular wine accordingly.

Anne slowed down to admire the elegant wainscoting that bordered the floor, ceilings, and windows. "I love the woodwork."

Kevin nodded as he surveyed the room, a look of satisfaction on his face. "The house has good bones. Paige hasn't had a chance to meet with the decorator yet, but I'm sure it's going to be terrific when she's done."

No doubt it would look like it belonged in one of the fancy interior design magazines that featured the world's most beautiful homes.

"As you can see, we're still getting settled in."

Anne smiled. "Fortunately, there's no rush."

"Exactly right." He nodded, his face somber. "The most important thing right now is her health."

Through the windowpanes that took up virtually the entire back wall, Anne saw that Alex's parents had already arrived. She took a deep breath and mentally braced herself for another long evening with the disapproving future-in-laws. "I bet her mother will be happy to help."

"I'm sure she will."

His voice was flat, yet Anne was fairly certain she detected a slight hint of mockery.

"She's already made a number of suggestions."

Yep. It was clear she wasn't the only one who found the woman meddlesome and annoying.

Anne pointed toward the lush green lawn that was shaded by large trees and bordered by rhododendrons in the back. "That'll be a great yard for kids to play in. And the stone wall that goes along the one side is so picturesque!"

Kevin turned toward Alex with a mischievous smile. "Now that you're getting married, you really should take a look at moving out here as well." When Alex didn't reply, he gave Anne a conspiratorial wink. "Paige can give you some tips when you're ready to buy."

Like how to blow our entire budget and then some.

"They're here!" Paige exclaimed as they stepped onto the patio. She was propped up by a couple of large, fluffy pillows atop a tufted chaise lounge chair.

A carefree golden retriever padded over towards them, its wagging tail just missing a wineglass perched near the edge of a small table. "Bailey!"

Alex bent over to scratch the dog's ears. "Are you taking good care of Paige?"

The dog lifted her head and beamed at him adoringly as if to say, *Of course. That's what I excel at.*

"I'm so glad you were able to make it." His mother greeted him with a big hug and quick kiss on the cheek and then turned toward Anne. "Lovely to see you too, dear." With a tight smile firmly fixed on her lips, she went through the motions of an air kiss. Anne did the same, trying to appreciate the woman's effort to be welcoming, even if it was superficial and somewhat half-hearted.

"How are things?" Winston Hunter III stepped forward and shook his son's hand. "Everything going well?" He placed his arm lightly on Alex's shoulder and turned to address Anne. "Say, can I talk you into letting this guy loose for a round of golf this weekend?"

"Dad!" Alex looked exasperated.

"Just kidding." His eyes crinkled as he smiled. "I know you manage your own social calendar."

Was that a veiled way of saying they think I'm keeping him away from them? Anne glanced over at her future mother-in-law, who was watching the exchange. It was obvious she ruled the roost at their house. Perhaps his parents assumed that Anne did the same.

"Actually," Alex's tone softened. "I was wondering if you'd like to hit the links on Sunday. With Richard gone, I thought you might be short a person."

A cloud passed over the older man's face. "Indeed, we are." He blinked and looked away, clearly still grieving the loss of his friend. "You'll make the perfect fourth."

"Great. I'm looking forward to it."

Anne sat down next to Paige and touched her gently on the arm. "How's the patient?"

Out of the corner of her eye, she saw Kevin visibly tense. *Did I just screw up by acknowledging she's got a serious medical condition? But...give me a break! Not only is she lying down on a specially arranged couch, but we're all gathered solicitously around her.*

"I'm resting comfortably, just like the doctor ordered." Paige appeared to be at ease and sounded cheerful. "I can't believe I've got five months of this to go. I sure hope you'll be visiting often."

"Of course!" Anne replied, wondering how they would possibly pass the time. Play cards? Chat about possible suspects in Richard's murder? Unless that was one of the many topics that was supposed to be off the table. "Maybe we can organize a small housewarming party and show off your new home."

"That's a great idea." Paige beamed. "We could do an afternoon tea…with scones and clotted cream." She dropped her voice to a whisper that only Anne could hear. "And mimosas, of course."

For just the guests, I hope. Anne couldn't imagine that the obstetrician (she was fairly certain she had been told it was a he) would approve of his convalescent drinking champagne, even if it were diluted with a splash of orange juice. Anne squeezed her arm gently. "We can do whatever you want."

Some sort of signal passed between Paige and her mother, followed by the two of them turning toward the house simultaneously and motioning to a person who was (evidently) within. A moment later, an attractive blond woman emerged through one of the doors and began setting up the table for dinner.

"I'm not sure what I'd do without Elżbieta," Paige announced once she'd returned to the kitchen. "Käthe was the one who insisted I hire someone. Even made all the arrangements. She was *so* right. The woman's been a godsend." As she looked around the group, her eyes suddenly widened in horror. "Dad! Careful! These chairs tip easily if you lean too far back."

There was a bang as he brought the chair forward, followed by some scraping as he adjusted its position to better face the group. "When she met us at the door, I thought I heard a Slavic accent. Where's she from?"

"Poland." Kevin flicked a ladybug off the table. "Growing up, most of our maids were Polish as well. My mother always said they were the best." He nudged Alex with his elbow. "The only thing I ever noticed was that they tend to be *very* pretty." He raised his eyebrows pointedly, setting Anne's teeth on edge.

Seriously? Is that the best you can come up with as a conversation piece? It was

169

as if Anne was back at work, standing in the middle of the trading floor, listening to the salesmen and traders make crude jokes. She glanced over at Paige, who was twirling a lock of hair between her two fingers. *Are you feeling the least bit bothered that you married this potato-head?*

"Unfortunately," Kevin blathered on. "Her English is kind of so-so." He made a face and mimicked someone using sign language.

Alex's eyes slid over to Anne and then back again to his new brother-in-law.

"The good thing is that we manage to understand one another, eventually."

Well, thank goodness for that! Anne felt like saying. *Just imagine the alternative.* Given Paige's physical state, Kevin might be forced to pick up the phone and book a different cleaning service! Or worse yet, he might have to actually help with the dishes!

Paige leaned back and yawned. "It's hard to find good domestic help these days. I'm starting to think I might keep her on after the baby's born."

Kevin tilted his head, as if this was the first time he was hearing the idea. "I thought we were going to hire a nurse for the first month and then bring on a proper nanny after that. From that school you told me about. The one that trains and certifies them?"

His wife looked at him like he was an alien from some distant planet. "Of course. And in addition to that—"

"But if we have a weekly person come in to vacuum and—"

"Oh, please." She sighed. "You're always tied up with one thing or another at Energix, how would you know what's required to run an entire house?"

The Battle-Axe fixed her eyes squarely on Kevin. "Elżbieta seems to be unusually good at what she does."

"Exactly!" Paige straightened out her napkin. "I'm sure I can use an extra pair of hands." She looked around the table, as if daring anyone to challenge her. "So, why not?"

Why not, indeed? As long as frat-boy remained gainfully employed, they could probably afford to cover the cost. And even if Energix went to hell in a handbasket, they could rely on Paige's trust fund to pick up the tab. Anne caught a glance with Alex just as he raised an eyebrow.

Elżbieta returned laden with their first course and a carafe of ice water on a large silver tray. As she arranged the salad plates around the table, Anne inhaled the scent of fresh, warm bread. One thing she knew for sure: dinner was going to be tasty, even if the conversation that accompanied it went flying off the rails.

Paige leaned forward to let Elżbieta prop her up a bit higher on the pillows and then back again so she could arrange the bed tray above her lap. "Kevin— tell them about Energix."

Everyone froze at the look of alarm on her husband's face. With its stock in the toilet and the SEC investigation looming on the horizon, presumably, this was not a topic he wished to broach.

"Nothing's definite yet, so we really shouldn't—"

"They've found a buyer!" she gushed, cutting him off mid-sentence. "They might even change Kevin from acting to permanent CFO."

"CFO of Energix!" Her father raised his wineglass in the beginnings of a toast. "Impressive indeed!"

Kevin put up a hand to stop him. "Let's not get ahead of ourselves." He gave a brittle laugh. "It hasn't happened yet."

"Of course." The older man lowered his glass. "Don't want to count your chickens and all that, but it sounds like things are finally looking up, which is good news." He nodded. "Good news indeed."

"Well, I…uh…I certainly…"

"He's always waiting for the other shoe to drop." Paige rolled her eyes.

"Just being cautious, dear."

Prudent, more like. At the very least, a promotion would depend on the whim of the new guy in charge. It might even require approval of the board of directors. There was no guarantee it would happen, regardless of whether he did everything perfectly right.

Kevin picked up a forkful of salad. "There are a lot of moving pieces. A new president. Two completely different management teams, which will need to be merged into one. Things may remain in flux for some time."

At least he understands the lay of the land.

"You're absolutely right, my boy." Winston Hunter III was clearly all in.

"Just do what you can to keep that ship moving in the right direction." He broke off a small piece of his bread and casually slipped his hand to the side so that Bailey could easily grab it.

"My plan exactly."

Presumably, that meant he would do everything in his power to bring in a boatload of money to keep the company from drowning. *At what cost*, Anne wondered. And was it realistic?

"If the merger isn't actually public—" Alex stopped as Elżbieta leaned over to top off his water glass.

"That's a good point." Kevin put on his professional business face and voice. "I'm glad you mentioned it."

Indeed. Nobody should be discussing this topic at all. But instead of cutting the conversation off at the knees, Kevin simply took another bite of his salad. Anne watched his square jaw move systematically up and down, grinding the mixed greens down to smithereens. *I guess you aren't going to bother explaining why.*

Alex broke the silence by spelling it out for everyone. "Kevin probably isn't at liberty to discuss a potential partnership that's still being negotiated."

"That's exactly right." He picked up his napkin and dabbed lightly at his chin. "I can't say anything more until the deal is concluded, but—" he paused dramatically and gave a smile showing his shiny white teeth, "I'm optimistic about the company's future. Very optimistic."

You can't be serious. And yet, from all appearances, he was. *Have you forgotten about the SEC investigation looming in the background?* It was all Anne could do to keep from pointing that out.

Winston Hunter III picked up his fork and pushed the cherry tomatoes, one by one, to the side of his plate. "I'll be glad to see their share price rise again."

Kevin swiveled his head around to look directly at the old man. "You kept your holdings, then?"

"Of course."

He owns Energix stock?! Anne glanced over at Alex, who sat completely still, eyes riveted on his father.

"I'm not some nervous nelly who follows the whims of the crowd." He pushed his salad aside and began to butter his bread. "Before he died, Richard told me not to panic. 'Just give it some time,' he said, and things would turn around. He assured me that the underpinnings of the company are fundamentally solid."

And you believed him? She bit her lip. *Like all the other investors who lost their shirts.*

"Obviously, your presence on the senior management team has also made me feel better about the investment in the long run."

Kevin sat up a bit taller. "I appreciate your confidence, sir."

"Not at all. Not at all." He set the butter knife down.

"Dad." Alex rubbed his forehead. "I didn't realize you owned any Energix stock."

He shrugged. "I picked it up a few years ago."

"But not a significant amount. Right?"

To an outsider, Alex sounded simply curious, but underneath the calm facade, Anne sensed anger. And why not? His own father had been taken in by Richard's financial machinations. And now his brother-in-law appeared to be taking over the role of Chief Charlatan.

The patriarch waved his hand vaguely, sprinkling small crumbs on the table as his dinner bread fanned the warm evening air. "Not really."

Out of the corner of her eye, Anne saw Kevin flinch at the reply. *The old man owns a ton of it.*

Evidently, Alex was thinking along the same lines. He intertwined his fingers in his lap and slowly tapped his thumbs. "How big of a hit did you take with the recent drop in price?"

After a long moment, his father finally replied. "I don't recall the exact amount."

The thumbs went still. "Ballpark figure, then."

The patriarch tilted his neck sideways and adjusted his tie. "It was noticeable."

Noticeable? What is that code for? Twenty thousand dollars, or are we talking about something in the millions?

Kevin made a grim face. "Same for us as well. All my stock options and...you name it. Everything was affected."

Technically, what frat-boy said was probably true. However, Anne distinctly recalled Paige saying that they had sold a large chunk of their Energix holdings to pay for the house, which meant, at the very least, they had minimized their exposure. Unfortunately, it didn't sound like her father had done the same.

"Of course, they're just paper losses." Winston took a bite of his bread and set it down, appearing unfazed. "When the stock bounces back, all those naysayers will be eating their hats."

Oh my God. Talk about swallowing the bait. Hook, line, and sinker. Anne shifted her gaze down and studied the china pattern running around the edge of her plate to hide the shock she imagined was visible on her face.

"That's exactly what I expect as well!" Kevin was suddenly brimming with excitement.

Seriously? She glanced sideways to see if he was for real.

"With a new partner, we'll be able to get our finances back under control. In fact, we're poised to jump in several new directions that could be very exciting technologically. One of the things we're considering is harnessing the natural power of wind."

But you're already invested in wind turbines. In fact, you sold a bunch to Spencer Brothers at the end of last year and then bought them back again. He must have seen the look of consternation on her face.

"That reminds me." He pointed his fork at Anne. "I checked up on those wind farms you were asking about. Even looked through old contracts." As he waved it back and forth, a drop of salad dressing flew onto the table. "We don't own any. Never did."

Anne froze as she tried to make sense of what she was hearing. *Don't own any. Never did.*

"It's an interesting idea, though. Like I said, something we might want to pursue in the future."

"I could have sworn Peter mentioned—"

"You must have misunderstood."

Anne blinked. She'd seen the sales agreement, even made a secret copy for herself. How could he have no knowledge of the transaction? The money had flowed from Spencer Brothers onto the Energix corporate ledgers. But it had happened while Kevin was just a footman to the former CFO.

"What about your former boss? Could he have—"

He shook his head. "We've been through the files. There's nothing there."

Which suggested that the ex-CFO, in conjunction with Richard Fernsby (conveniently deceased), had cooked up the wind farm deal on the sly. And now, nobody left at Energix was even aware of the arrangement.

"That's interesting," Anne said evenly. "Thanks for checking."

"I was curious too. As you can imagine, I've been working day and night to wrap my arms around the financial situation." He jumped as Elżbieta dropped a serving spoon on the ground, making a large clank.

She curled over as if trying to make herself invisible. "Sorry!"

"It's very complex," he continued, as if explaining some difficult concept. "But things are starting to come together. I fully expect that we'll emerge even stronger than before."

And if you believe that, I have a bridge to sell you. Anne glanced over at the maid, who was bent down near the dog, holding the spoon in one hand so Bailey could give it a good lick. Was she just trying to be nice to the dog, or was this her way of intentionally lurking in the background to hear what was being said?

"Okay." Alex arranged his hands to signal a time-out. "I know I always sound like a stiff-necked lawyer, but—"

"That's because you are one," Paige said in a sing-song voice.

He looked directly at his sister. "Given that Kevin is an executive at Energix and he's married to you, *we*—" He made a circle with his finger to indicate everyone sitting around the table. "—all need to be careful about the trading decisions each of *us* makes when it comes to the company stock."

She raised both of her arms in a gesture of frustration. "Which means what, exactly?"

"Mom and Dad shouldn't be buying or selling Energix stock based on any...*tips*...or other information from Kevin. Honestly, they shouldn't own the stock at all. If it ever recovers—"

"What do you mean, *if?*" She looked incredulous. "Kevin's been instrumental in finding a buyer. Once the sale—"

"And that's exactly my point." He eyed her severely. "The fact that there might be a merger is inside information. The only reason Kevin knows about it is because he's privy to behind-the-scenes discussions that are occurring within the company. Or maybe he's even the one arranging the transaction."

"Not singlehandedly..." Kevin mumbled.

Alex kept his gaze focused solely on Paige, ignoring the interruption. "Whatever the case, you and Kevin can't be telling anyone else anything about it. At all. And mom and dad can't be making investment decisions based on that information either." He shifted his attention toward his father. "Right now, there's an active SEC investigation going on, which makes it all the more important that none of us do anything that gives even the *appearance* of impropriety."

"As a financial professional, I am fully aware of insider trading rules," Kevin sniffed, his tone bordering on condescending.

"Then why risk—"

"Don't you think I have an obligation to do anything I can to help my wife?" His calm veneer had been replaced by a taut, barely contained fury. "She's in a fragile state in case you haven't noticed."

As if on cue, Elżbieta scurried over to adjust the pillows of her charge.

"I think it only right," he spat, "to let her know about important developments at work that might make her feel better about the future. Or would you have me keep her in the dark to satisfy some archaic rules that were written to go after the likes of Michael Milken or one of the other junk bond traders?"

"Of course not!" The Battle-Axe set her fork down loudly and glared at her son. "Paige was just sharing some good news with the family. It's not like she's running around, willy-nilly, telling her friends."

Alex stared at his mother. "I'm not saying she is. But even with us—"

"What? Are you saying she can't trust members of her own family?"

"That's not the point."

"Then, what *is* your point?"

Anne saw her fiancé take a deep breath and knew at once he was figuring out how to change tack.

"I suggest you sell the stock once it gets back to an acceptable price, so there's no question about you being fed information on the side."

"On the side!" The lord of the manor drew himself up stiffly. "You make us sound like a bunch of dodgy Wall Street swindlers."

Alex put up his hands, and Anne was afraid that he might finally lose his cool. But when he spoke, his voice was calm and reasonable.

"I'm just saying that you can protect Paige and Kevin from ever being accused of improperly sharing information with you by dumping the stock and never buying it again, regardless of what happens to the price." He shook his head. "There are millions of other investments out there to choose from."

"I already own many of them." Winston arched an eyebrow and crossed his arms.

"Exactly." Alex mirrored his father in response. "So, it should be trivial to replace your Energix holdings with one of those instead."

A tense moment ensued in which nobody said a word.

"Wine, anyone?" Elżbieta pointed toward a chilled bottle of white sitting in a marble cooler to the side. "Or I can bring out the red, if you'd prefer."

And with that, the standoff between the two men was broken.

Later, as Anne tossed restlessly in bed, one thought kept coming back into her mind. Throughout the evening, Elżbieta's English had sounded perfectly fine. Was there any chance she could be an undercover SEC investigator?

19

Financial Trust

New York City

The next morning

"They only do stuff like that in the movies," Alex said dismissively when she asked about SEC investigational tactics.

They were finishing up a leisurely Sunday morning breakfast in their New York apartment with the luxury of no pressing plans for the rest of the day. Even so, Anne felt like a slug as she poured her second cup of tea. They had dropped into bed close to one in the morning after what seemed like an interminable drive from Paige's house the night before. And then, because of the stagnant summer night (or perhaps pent-up stress from socializing with his family, she couldn't be sure), she'd had a sleepless night.

"Really?" She gave him a quizzical look. "I thought—"

"Okay. Fair enough. It's occasionally done. But you need a court order... and a very good reason...I mean, installing a person undercover in someone's home? That's a big deal."

"I guess you're right." She stirred a spoonful of sugar into her tea. "Probably the kind of thing they do when they're going after the head of a major crime organization. And even then, I imagine they'd want to place their mole in the home of the kingpin himself, not some random lieutenant."

"Exactly." He snapped his bacon in half. "Why would they use that kind of firepower on Kevin, of all people? It's pretty clear he has no idea what's going on."

Anne nodded as she blew on her hot tea.

"I about dropped my fork when he said that Energix had never owned any wind farms!" Alex snorted. "Blimey! Everyone and their brother knows about those swap deals. Talk about clueless!"

She burst out laughing and struggled to keep from spitting her tea. "Obviously, he's been kept in the dark. But how would the SEC know that?"

"Oh, please." Alex rolled his eyes. "After a few minutes of chatting with him, I think it would be pretty obvious."

Ouch.

He scraped the last of his eggs off the plate. "If the SEC were going to pull a stunt like that on anyone, they'd go after the guy who was CFO at the time all the financial stuff went down."

Or Richard Fernsby, if he weren't already dead.

"I still don't understand how that silver-tongued lothario managed to worm his way into Käthe's heart."

"You think the guy's just using her?" Anne took a sip of her tea, savoring the full-bodied, slightly bitter aroma of the English Breakfast blend.

"I don't know." Alex picked up his empty cereal bowl along with the plate and took them over to the sink. "Sleeping with the boss's daughter when he has a wife and two young kids at home? I mean, maybe his marriage was on the rocks, and it was love at first sight with Käthe…" He turned on the water and gave everything a quick rinse. "But more likely, he's an opportunistic jerk who saw a ready-made meal ticket."

And decided to sample the buffet.

Alex scanned the dishwasher, looking for an open spot. "Not only that, Dapper Don seems to be one of the key players in all of the financial problems at Energix." He shifted a few plates around to make some space. "I know his love life is completely unrelated to whatever financial games he might have played, but, taken together, he just seems like an unethical scumbag.

Honestly? I'm surprised that Brigitte hasn't come out more strongly about him."

Käthe's mother was a bright, determined woman. If she thought there was even a chance that Don was toying with her daughter's affections, there was no question in Anne's mind that she would cut the guy to ribbons. "Brigitte must think he actually cares about her daughter. And Käthe certainly seems to be smitten with him."

Alex straightened up, plate still in hand, and closed the dishwasher door. "I give up."

"On the dishwasher? Or Käthe." Anne pushed her chair back and joined him by the sink.

"Both. I don't understand her fascination with the man." He jerked a thumb toward the dishwasher. "And we need to remember to turn this thing on when we go for our run along the river."

"Where's Elżbieta when you need her?" Anne set her plate on top of Alex's bowl and wrapped her arms around him.

"Hopefully," he whispered, "not eavesdropping outside Kevin's study door."

* * *

Short Hills, New Jersey

A week later, Anne strode into the living room of Paige's new house with Käthe by her side. They stopped near the antique mahogany table that was being used as a sideboard for their impromptu housewarming party and smiled at the women gathered around the food.

"What are you hiding behind your back?" Perfect-Teeth looked back and forth at them as she poured the last of the mimosa out of a hand-blown glass pitcher.

Paige craned her neck around the pile of gifts on the coffee table and then reclined again on her comfy couch with a knowing smile. "I can make a pretty good guess."

The dog lifted her head, evidently sensing that something interesting might be about to happen. Perhaps some food might find its way down to the floor?

"They're up to something." Pearls-Galore tottered away, drink in hand, and settled herself into an oversized chair. "I don't know what they've got brewing. But they look like a pair of evil twins."

Evil twins?

Perfect-Teeth tapped her glass lightly. "Someone's been watching too many horror movies lately."

Horse-Lover let out a cackle that echoed loudly around the room.

With a look of chagrin, Pearls-Galore immediately backpedaled. "I just meant…like *two peas in a pod.*"

"As in boring clones?" Horse-Lover chuckled. "That's even worse!"

At least she doesn't think one of us is morally corrupt! And it was true that they both wore their hair the same way and were dressed in sheath-style dresses (one in navy and the other in cerulean blue), but in Anne's opinion that's where the similarity ended. The only diamond she wore was her engagement ring, whereas Käthe practically glowed with her sparkling hoop earrings, emerald and diamond frog pendant, and double-stranded tennis bracelet fully encircling her wrist.

"That's not what I was saying at all! I was simply noticing how alike—"

"Don't worry about it," Käthe dismissed her friend's floundering with a quick wave of her hand. "You're absolutely right." She smiled. "We do have something up our sleeve."

The room went silent with an air of expectation, and for a moment, Anne felt a sense of déjà vu.

She was an outsider, surrounded by Paige's closest friends. Except the previous times Anne had attended gatherings with these women, she'd been a last-minute addition, trying to find a way to fit in. This time she was the hostess, the person organizing the event. Even though the party was being held at Paige's new house, she was fully in charge. With all eyes on her, she nodded to her partner in crime.

"We can't find Elżbieta anywhere," The Diamond Goddess announced somberly. "The kitchen's empty, and there's no sign of her out on the patio." She raised a hand dramatically to stop the ensuing groans. "Fortunately, with a little bit of sleuthing, we were able to locate the key components."

"Thank God!" Pearls-Galore flopped back against her chair.

Käthe whipped out a bottle of champagne from behind her back and set it on the table while Anne did the same with a container of orange juice.

A chorus of cheers made it clear the party would go on.

"It's not quite as elegant to pour the two separately—" Käthe pretended to warn her haute couture friends, "—but girls—" she brought the back of her hand to her forehead as if she might faint, "—we'll just have to cope!"

Horse-Lover stepped forward, empty glass in hand. "Maybe the new housekeeper is *keeping* Kevin company in one of the bedrooms upstairs."

Wait, what?! Anne blinked and then stared as the woman's mouth widened into a smile that looked like a leer. *Did she actually just say that?*

"He's at the club, practicing his swing." Käthe's gay tone was at odds with her glare, which looked capable of vaporizing whatever stood in its path.

There was an awkward silence as the guests took turns casting furtive glances in Paige's direction, all painfully aware that the whole point of the party was to cheer the poor girl up with a fun and friendly afternoon.

"Come on!" Horse-Lover spread her arms wide as she appealed to the slack-jawed group. "Lighten up! I was just kidding! We all know that Kevin only has eyes for Paige."

You actually thought that was amusing? If she hadn't realized it before, Anne definitely knew now why she had a visceral dislike of the awful woman.

Käthe whispered through clenched teeth. "Remind me again why she's here."

In fact, Anne had gently floated the idea of dropping the killjoy from their guest list by reminding Paige that she had a tendency, as of late, to drink to excess. *Remember how she threw up in the Bachelorette party limo? It ruined your favorite shoes. And at the wedding send-off, she tripped and fell against your mother, almost knocking her off the cliff.* But Paige had insisted. *If she finds out we had a party and she wasn't included...I don't want to deal with the fallout.* Anne hadn't been willing to push the point, and now there was a chance the little troublemaker could end up ruining the party.

Horse-Lover popped the cork and twirled the bottle in her hand. "Anyone else want a top-off?" She looked down at the baleful dog, watching her attentively. "Not you."

Perfect-Teeth took the opportunity to steer the conversation elsewhere. "Hey Paige. When are you going to open those gifts?"

Anne mouthed to Käthe, *I'll get the dessert.*

* * *

Anne carefully lifted the triple-tiered chocolate cake out of the box and set it on the ornate blue and white porcelain cake plate that was sitting beside it (undoubtedly Spode, possibly an antique, definitely a disaster if dropped). She took a deep breath. *So far, so good.* Now, all she had to do was to get the entire stack from the kitchen to the living room still in one piece. With a single swoop, she picked it all up and inched her way across the floor, making sure she kept everything level and balanced.

You've got this, she told herself, as she turned left and entered a dark, narrow hall. *Just don't trip over the dog.* The hardwood floor was more slippery than the kitchen tile, so she slowed even more, still feeling confident she had everything well under control.

And then she heard the small squeak of a floorboard from somewhere behind.

She froze, her nerves taut, and forced herself to turn around. Nothing but an empty hallway. Had she imagined it? She couldn't be sure. It was an old house, after all. Maybe it tended to creak and groan as the structure shifted slightly throughout the day. She started to turn back and then stopped when she heard it again. A squeak followed by the muffled sound of something, perhaps a drawer, being softly closed, coming from behind her on the left.

Someone was in Kevin's office.

He's back already? Maybe he'd like to join us for a few minutes and have some dessert. As she stood there debating whether to knock on his door, she saw the brass knob slowly rotate and heard a single click when the latch finally released. She stepped back to have more space between him and the cake, and yet the door itself remained closed, as if he was listening for who might be out there before actually exiting the room.

Why is he taking so long?

After a moment, a small crack of light appeared around the edges, and the door began to slowly open.

Okay, Mr. Stealthy. This is getting weird.

Anne tiptoed away from the office, glancing back just in time to see a shadow silently cross the threshold and stop short at the sight of her.

"Elżbieta?" She almost dropped the cake.

The flustered woman stared, muscles tense and eyes wide, looking like she might flee at any moment.

"What are you doing?"

"I was…I was checking to see if the room needed dusting." Her accent was stronger than in previous conversations and there was a shrillness to her voice. "Here. Let me help you with that."

For a brief moment, Anne had forgotten about the cake and the expensive platter it was resting on.

Elżbieta nodded toward a marble-topped table just to Anne's right. "You can set it down there."

Once the cake was safely positioned, Anne turned to face the wayward maid. "We were looking for you a while ago when we ran out of mimosas." She nodded toward Kevin's office. "Were you in there the whole time?"

"No." She spat the word forcefully. "I was probably upstairs cleaning one of the bathrooms."

"That might explain it," Anne said slowly, trying to decide what to believe.

Elżbieta smiled innocently, and a dimple appeared on each of her rosy cheeks. "Or it might have been when I was putting the suitcases away in the attic."

Something about the multiple explanations just didn't sit right.

She pointed at the chocolate fenceposts that ran along the bottom tier of the cake. "It's cute. Don't you think? And this is incredible." She pointed at the small chocolate creation topping the cake that was a mini-version of

Paige's new Georgian-style brick house. "Hopefully, it tastes good, too."

Before Anne could ask her anything more, Elżbieta picked up the towering platter and perched it on one arm. "Let's not keep the guests waiting," she called over her shoulder and, in a flash, disappeared down the hall.

* * *

"Did you tell my sister?" Alex glanced at Anne as they sat in his BMW, waiting for the light to turn green.

"I never got a chance. Elżbieta stuck to her like Velcro until you arrived."

The light changed. He shifted into first gear and began to accelerate. "I wonder how Käthe found the woman in the first place."

"Don got her name from someone he used to work with." At least that's what Käthe had said when Horse-Lover had asked. *That new maid of yours...Elza...Eltza...whatever her name is...*She'd prefaced the question with her annoying cackling laugh before crumpling into one of the wingback chairs with a loud burp. *Where did she come from on such short notice?* Soon after, she'd demonstrated her incredible sense of tact by pointing at the maid while she was tidying up and announcing loudly, *I'm not sure I'd want someone so pretty living under my roof.* With a hard face, Käthe had whispered, *I could just kill her.*

"I hope somebody actually called a few of Elżbieta's prior employers for references." He checked his sideview mirror as he merged onto the highway. "It could be she has sticky fingers."

Anne bit her lip. Between Paige's sterling silver collection (flatware, serving platters, and a particularly elegant Tiffany tea set) and her jewelry (casually stowed in a box on her dresser), the woman would have quite a bit to choose from if she was, indeed, a thief. "That would be awful."

"I'll give Kevin a ring when we get home. Let him figure out if they've got a problem." He glanced in his rearview mirror and then signaled to switch lanes. "Otherwise, how did it go?"

She stared out the front windshield, watching the first drops of rain hit and splash across the screen. "Pretty well. I think. But let's wait to hear what your mother has to say after she talks to Paige."

20

The Panic Button Gets Pushed

New York City

The following Thursday

"She's a mole," Kevin screamed into the phone. "Why else would they come after me?"

Anne just happened to be in Alex's office, dropping off some papers for his review, when the frantic call from Kevin had come in. The SEC had raided Energix's corporate headquarters and all he could do was stand by idly, watching them tear the place apart.

"Now they're starting in on my secretary's file cabinet! By the time they're done, this place will be in shambles!"

Alex held the receiver some distance from his head to keep his ear from being blown out. Consequently, Anne had no difficulty hearing Kevin's nonstop spewing, even though she sat on the other side of his desk, a good three feet away.

"Wait a minute," Alex said calmly. "The subpoena is requesting access to Energix's financial files. That's not targeting *you*, in particular."

"They might as well be," he huffed. "You should see the state of things over here! The contents of my credenza are spread out as far as I can see and they're inspecting every nook and cranny they can find. Even checking my pencil drawer, for God's sake."

"Probably just looking to see if Dodgy Don left anything behind before he was sacked." Alex switched to speakerphone mode and set the receiver back in its cradle. "Just so you know, Anne's here with me, so I just put you on speak—"

"More likely, they're acting on a tip they got from Elżbieta!"

"The only way they could do that is if there was something incriminating for her to find at your house."

That shut him up for a moment.

"Regardless," Alex continued in his reasonable, lawyer-like tone, "you might want to consult a law—"

"Of course there was nothing for her to find!" Kevin's voice ranted down the line. "Still, what's to keep her from manufacturing something just to make me look bad."

Alex rolled his eyes. "Okay. Now you're starting to sound paranoid. Look—"

"I should have fired the little snake the moment you told me she'd been snooping around. But, oh no! Your sister wouldn't hear of it. Wanted to give her another chance. And *stupidly,* I—"

"Listen." Alex tried again. "Given this latest development—"

"What am I going to say to Paige? Don't worry? This kind of thing happens all the time?"

"You can figure that out once—"

"Do you really think she'll buy that?" Kevin scoffed. "Because I sure don't. Her medical condition is already touch and go as it is. This search and seizure event could be the thing that sends her over the edge!"

"Okay. Let's get a grip here. The SEC investigation is old news. Everyone knows they're looking into the financial transactions that took place *before* you were CFO. It shouldn't surprise anyone that the regulators decided to pay Energix a visit and take a look at the files."

"Even so," Kevin murmured. "The newspapers are going to have a field day. Especially the *Chronicle.* Have you seen the kinds of articles they've been running?"

Anne glanced at Alex. They both had. Truth be told, some of them were rather funny. *How Energix oiled those greasy executive palms...The Energy Company that Wore No Clothes...Is Energix running out of gas?*

"Probably." Alex shrugged as he addressed the small, gray box on his desk. "But you can get in front of the whole thing by telling Paige first. That way, she won't be surprised when the story comes out."

"Right." Kevin made a choking sound and then lowered his voice to a whisper. "but what if…" His voice became unintelligible.

Anne and Alex both leaned forward, straining to hear.

"…the thing is, I'm kind of starting to get worried." His voice suddenly boomed out, causing them both to jump backward in their chairs. "It's not like I orchestrated *any* of this...and yet now I have to field all these questions...half the time, I'm not sure what they're looking for…"

Anne almost felt sorry for the guy now that his cocky attitude was gone. He sounded stunned and bewildered, as if he had been rattled to the core.

"Obviously, I don't want to appear uncooperative, but let's say I was *vaguely* aware…"

She gave Alex a warning look. From her perspective, Kevin was treading on dangerously thin ice. He responded with a single, firm nod that said he completely agreed.

"What if," Kevin coughed, "theoretically...what if I saw a few questionable entries slide by my desk?"

Anne made a motion as if slitting her throat. *Cut him off.*

"Am I oblig—"

"I can't advise you on corporate matters that relate to Energix," Alex said firmly. "I work for Spencer Brothers, and frankly—"

"I know. But as a family member," he wheedled, "you can at least offer—"

"No. I can't." Alex looked askance at the phone. "What do the Energix lawyers say?"

"Why would I possibly care?" Kevin snorted. "They're the ones who let this whole search happen in the first place. Part of complying with the SEC and all that garbage. It's not like those twerps have my best interests at heart."

"Then you should consult with a private attorney—"

"The thing is—" Kevin barreled ahead. "I might've...I don't know...I'm afraid I screwed up."

Uh-oh. What has Frat-boy done?

"All the more reason—" Alex began again.

"I *never* should have listened to Eckert. But he was so adamant!"

Alex's eyes widened. "How does he fit in?"

"I think he's the one who killed Fernsby. To hide his involvement in the swap deals."

Alex shook his head, clearly unable to follow the logical train. "What does that have to do with the SEC investigation? I thought you were worried about what to tell the regulators who are busy tossing your office."

"He's the one who told me to shred all of the paperwork. Make all of it disappear."

You've been shredding corporate documents? Ones that you were specifically instructed and legally required to preserve? You're even stupider than I thought.

"Wait a minute." Alex looked incredulous. "You're saying Eckert instructed you to destroy financial records?"

"Otherwise, he said everything would come back on *me*."

"Hang on. He doesn't work for Energix. Why would you listen to anything that snake had to say?"

"Because he and Dodgy Don, as you call him, have been working together all along. They were ready to tell the SEC that I, *alone*, had booked the phantom swap deals at Fernsby's behest. That they had no idea what I was up to."

Smart. Gang up on the little fish and serve him up to the regulators.

"So, I took one of the junior accountants aside and had him re-book everything. Plus, I made sure we pulled all of the contracts—"

"Stop!" Alex shouted into the speaker. His calm composure was gone. "Don't say another word. You need to get a lawyer. Someone who specializes in security law. And don't say anything to anybody about what you might or might not have done. Not to Paige. Not to me. Not your favorite co-worker.

Nobody. Is that clear?"

After giving Kevin the name of someone he knew, Alex hung up the phone. He stared at Anne, his eyes wide, face white, and clenched hands shaking. "How could he have thought that shredding corporate documents was a good idea?"

What could she say? *Your sister married a gullible idiot?* Or better yet. *Maybe he thought it's only illegal if you get caught?* Instead, she opted to be sensible and hopefully comforting. "He must have panicked and figured—"

"In what universe did that make any sense at all?" Alex threw his arms in the air. "Especially after receiving an official preservation notice from the SEC just a few weeks ago? The letter specifically instructed him and his cohorts to preserve evidence, meaning do NOT destroy, alter, or delete any documents that might be relevant to an SEC inquiry." He narrowed his eyes. "What part of those instructions did that wanker not understand?"

Presumably, a rhetorical question. "Obviously, Kevin didn't think through the conseq—"

"He could go to jail for what he's done." Alex leaned over his desk and buried his face in his hands. "And Paige will be… I don't even want to think about it."

Devastated. Beyond belief. But then she'll bounce back with the help of her friends and find someone new. Someone handsome and charming who checks all the right boxes. And after that, she'll move on to her next adventure and we'll never speak of it again.

"Blimey!" He gave his desk leg a slight kick. "How could he have been so stupid?"

Because he was a two-bit player who managed to get in way over his head. "Maybe things aren't as bad as—" She caught herself trying to make Alex feel better by making light of the situation and instantly shifted gears. "Who am I kidding? The guy pretty much admitted he was aware of Energix's creative accounting practices."

"Yep."

"Let's face it. He probably even helped to grease the wheels a bit. And then he managed to dig an even deeper hole for himself by trying to cover his tracks."

"Yep, again."

"It's probably only a matter of time before the SEC uncovers his part in this whole sordid mess."

Alex slowly raised his head. "The thing that really gets me is that he *knew* it was a sham, and despite that, *encouraged* my father to stay invested in the stock. What he's done is beyond the pale."

No question, it was despicable. And incredibly short-sighted. How did he think he would face the old man when the game finally ran its course?

"This is going to kill my parents. They think Kevin's the greatest thing since sliced bread."

The Battle-Axe will survive alongside the lord of the manor, but Kevin's another story. She'll rip him to shreds and leave his carcass to rot on the rocks. "I'm not convinced."

"What's there to—"

Anne waved her hand dismissively. "I think the family's in for a rocky ride, but they're resilient. They'll come through in the end. Kevin, on the other hand..."

"He's toast." Alex clamped his lips together so tightly that they virtually disappeared. "My sister should just dump him now."

Who'd blame her? Boy was she smart to make frat-boy sign that prenuptial agreement! Anne shifted in her chair. "One thing to consider is whether you want to try to soften the blow by telling either her or your parents what you've learned. The stock is virtually worthless at this point anyway. So financially, they've already taken the hit." It was just the emotional one that was still yet to come.

He took a deep breath and let it out slowly. "Any meddling by me could just make things worse."

A fair point.

"Probably best to let nature take its course and then do my best to help reassemble the pieces of their lives after everything comes crashing down."

Totally agree. "Then that's the plan." Anne wanted to come over to his side of the desk and give him a big supportive hug and yet she remained firmly planted in her seat, cognizant that they were in his corporate office where anyone could walk in at any moment. Always appear professional in the workplace, as if they were just friends. It was one of their unspoken cardinal rules. Nonetheless, she wondered, *is this the time to make an exception?*

Alex gave a rueful smile. "The thing that surprises me the most is how easily Eckert was able to manipulate him."

She shrugged. "He's a salesman at heart. An expert at reading people. He knew exactly how to play on Kevin's fear of getting caught."

"I think it's about time he started to feel some of the heat himself." Alex pressed the button for his secretary. "Would you please get Peter Eckert on the phone?"

Anne put up a hand. "Wait a minute! What are you going to say? *I hear you pressured Kevin to shred some incriminating documents? I'm going to report you to the SEC?* Let's just slow down and think this through."

Alex stared at her for a long moment. "You're right." He pushed the button again. "Forget that. I've changed my mind."

"He's not available anyway," his secretary replied. "Took the day off to play golf."

* * *

"This is a better idea," Alex said as they rode the elevator down to Peter Eckert's floor. "I'm glad you reached out to Jennifer, and she's willing to help."

Anne smiled. "Undercover missions are right up her alley. I think she missed her calling and should have joined the CIA."

"You're sure she'll stay on the sidelines? Not do anything rash?"

"Positive. She's just there to provide cover if you need it. You, on the other hand, are the prime player." She eyed her fiancé sternly. "Make sure you stick to the script."

He gave her an exasperated look. "Give me a little credit."

"I am!" She reached out and squeezed his shoulder. *Otherwise, we'd be in our offices, doing something more in accordance with our regular jobs.* Truth be

193

told, she had been shocked when he'd picked up the phone, ready to flip off and say the first thing that came into his head. He'd always been Mr. Calm-And-Controlled in the years she had known him before they'd begun dating, the epitome of taking setbacks in stride. And that same predictable, unruffled manner had continued throughout their entire courtship. Until now. Clearly, the Energix drama had struck a very deep nerve.

The doors slid open to the trading floor. Anne gave him a thumbs up and headed over to meet Jennifer, who was milling around one of the salesmen's desks a short distance away.

"Hey there!" Anne greeted her old colleague with a friendly wave. "Any chance you could give me some advice?"

"Of course!" Jennifer smiled widely, as if Anne had just paid her the biggest compliment in the world. "I'd be happy to." The two stepped over to a spot just around the corner from Peter Eckert's office where they could stand within earshot, pretending to be engaged in a conversation, ready to jump in if necessary.

"Good afternoon." Alex greeted Twinkle-Toes with his winning smile. "I'm following up on a matter with Energix."

She paused her nail-filing and looked up at him with a warm smile. "Sorry. Peter's not in today."

"Maybe you can help me instead."

"Sure." She gave her shoulders a little twist. "What do you need?"

"I recall that Peter purchased some…" He paused and pretended to look quizzical. "…oil barges, I think it was? Could you please pull the files?"

"Hmmm." She opened her desk drawer and carefully placed the nail file inside. "I should probably check with Peter first." Her grin turned sheepish. "He can be a bit of a stickler about procedure, if you know what I mean."

"Right." Alex nodded sympathetically. "When will he be back?"

"Tomorrow."

"Oh," he said with a pained look.

"He gets an Academy Award," Jennifer whispered. "That pitiful expression is perfect!"

"The thing is—" He leaned forward and lowered his voice, as if taking her into his confidence. "I'm in a bit of a pickle here. Something has come up on the legal front that needs an immediate response. I really need to see whatever Energix files we might have. Today."

Her eyes widened. "I don't think that's possible…" She glanced back at Peter's door. "It's unfortunate that he's not around, but…"

"Perhaps you could just take a peek, given the circumstances?"

She bit her lip nervously. "I really shouldn't."

Alex studied her for a moment. "I hate to pull rank, but do you recall a note I sent out a week or so ago?" He paused. "About preserving correspondence and other information associated with the company?"

She opened her mouth and then stopped.

"It was sent to all of the senior managers at Spencer Brothers, including Peter Eckert."

"Yes." She nodded slowly. "I do, but—" Her head darted around, like a cornered cat looking for a way to escape. "Peter would really be the best one—"

"Actually—" He put up a hand to stop her. "I'm fairly certain Steve Warnock would disagree. I guess I can always ask him to call down here directly…"

Wham! Now that he had pulled the CEO card, there was no stepping back.

Twinkle-Toes looked like the air had been sucked out of her. The friendly smile had been replaced by a look of anger mixed with fear. Anne wondered if he should have held that zinger back.

He shrugged. "It's up to you. But I need access to any information about Energix that's being stored down here," he finished firmly.

She sank back in her chair and sighed. "There are no Energix files." Her voice was dull, and she looked as if her spirit had been zapped.

"Oh, please!" Jennifer hissed under her breath. "We've already seen the damn file. Cough it up, already."

Shh. Anne mouthed as she gave her friend a warning look.

He narrowed his eyes. "I was in a meeting with him a few weeks ago in which he said—"

Twinkle-Toes waved her hand dismissively. "I should have just told you that from the start." She stood up, pulled her short skirt down a millimeter, and then opened the drawer and pointed. "See for yourself." She stepped aside to let him take a closer look.

After running his fingers along the tabs, he straightened up to face her. "What happened to them?"

It's not there? Anne raised an eyebrow.

"I don't know." Twinkle-Toes spoke quickly, her eyes looking everywhere except at Alex. "Maybe there never were any." She gave a small shake, as if trying to rid herself of the entire conversation.

"Hang on. You must have some idea—"

"I…you'll have to ask Peter." Her voice sounded vaguely shrill.

Alex studied the defeated woman for a moment. "Right. That's it, then. Thanks for your help."

"Anytime," she squeaked through pursed lips.

* * *

"So now the contracts have gone missing on both ends." Alex spat the words out as they glided in the elevator back up to his office. "Peter Eckert is starting to remind me of a mafia clean-up guy, the one who disposes of bodies and removes all traces of a crime."

"The fixer. Except—" Anne locked eyes with Alex.

"He didn't quite get everything though, did he?"

She blinked with feigned innocence. *Thank goodness I made that copy.*

Alex winked. "Good work, Sherlock."

The car came to a rest, and the doors slid open. "I wonder if these wind farms even exist." More to the point, Anne wondered, *Did they provide a motive for murder?*

21

A Lady Scorned

New York City

The following day

"It was all because of that little stunt you guys pulled yesterday." Jennifer plopped herself down in the chair opposite Anne. "Poor little Twinkle-Toes was so unnerved by Alex's request to see the files that she tried to reach Eckert and tell him what had happened." She shrugged her shoulders theatrically and looked up toward the sky. "If only Peter had ignored his pager."

"But how did she find out?"

"He didn't bother getting out of the jacuzzi, if you can believe it." Jennifer arched an eyebrow. "Evidently, there was a whole lot of splashing and giggling in the background when he returned Twinkle-toe's ever-so-urgent call."

"You've got to be kidding me." The guy was not only arrogant but totally tacky. "So, who was he with?"

"One of the new salesgirls. Hired a month or so ago. You probably haven't seen her since you don't work on our floor anymore." Jennifer pulled a candy bar out of her bag. "Tall, willowy blonde thing. Very pretty, except for her chin. It's kind of twisted in an odd sort of way." She clucked her tongue. "Men. They can be such muttonheads."

Indeed, they can. Kevin's face immediately popped into Anne's mind as someone eminently qualified to join that club.

"But I think Peter's playing with fire." Jennifer wrinkled her nose. "Sleeping with women who report to him? Again and again? It's so inappropriate. And now Human Resources can't pretend they aren't aware."

Anne looked skeptically at her friend. "Unless his behavior truly impacts the bottom line negatively..." She pursed her lips, leaving the rest unsaid. On Wall Street, all that mattered was how much money you produced. If you cost the company more than you brought in, then you'd be out in a flash. But a lawsuit or two? Not a problem if you were a big producer who made it financially worth their while.

Jennifer gave a dejected sigh and sank down in her chair. "You're right. Nothing will change."

"Probably better that Twinkle-Toes found out. At least she won't waste any more time on the loser. Although, at the same time, it's kind of sad. She told my admin that she fully expected him to propose to her any day."

"Hah! No way that was going to happen." Jennifer snorted. "Obviously, the poor girl had no idea what sort of reputation he has." She motioned with the chocolate. "Do you want some?"

Anne shook her head.

"Oh my god. You should have seen her. She was livid. Storming around her desk. Telling anyone who'd listen that she was *done with the man*." Jennifer made air quotes. "The traders were taking bets on whether she'd quit on the spot. If he'd been in the office, I think she would have strangled him with her bare hands." She took a bite of her Hershey Bar and asked again. "Sure you don't want any?"

Anne shook her head. "I already had a Milky Way just a few minutes ago."

Jennifer flipped her hair behind her back and sighed. "But I feel kind of sorry for her too. She was clearly shocked out of her socks. I guess she thought he actually cared about her."

"I'm sure she's not the first..." Anne rolled her eyes.

"And won't be the last..." Jennifer did the same. "But one thing about Twinkle-Toes is she's determined to get out of Peter's clutches as quickly as possible. First thing this morning, she marched down to Personnel and demanded a transfer to another department. From what she told everyone afterwards, she didn't mince words either."

"Good for her. Why stay in the employ of your former boyfriend while he skips around the trading floor with his new sidepiece?"

"I'm with you." Jennifer nodded. "Although it was naïve of her to get involved with him in the first place. He's what? Twenty years her senior? Never married? Obviously not gay. Why would he suddenly decide to settle down with her?"

"Or anybody, for that matter." Anne shrugged. "Hope springs eternal?"

"Yeah. Well, now that that delusion has been crushed beyond recognition, she's clearly on the warpath. Didn't even bother to finish out the day." Jennifer chuckled. "Around lunchtime, she packed up and headed out, claiming she had a migraine. Meanwhile, his phone was ringing off the hook."

"Serves him right. What did Prince Charming do?"

"Nothing. He just grabbed one of the sales assistants and told her to take over, cool as a cucumber. Then he shut his door and disappeared. He's probably happy to have Twinkle-Toes out of his hair. Or, at the very least, he doesn't really care."

Anne narrowed her eyes. "That kind of says it all, doesn't it?"

Jennifer nodded. "Aren't you glad you no longer report to him?"

"Beyond glad. I'd just as soon see him fired."

* * *

"That explains why Twinkle-Toes dropped by my office." Alex handed Anne a glass of wine and took a seat in the armchair facing her. The subway had been jam-packed during their commute home, and this was their first chance to catch up on the day.

"To file some sort of complaint? Although I'd have thought that was the sole purview of HR." Anne took a sip of her wine and leaned back on the couch.

"No. Nothing like that." He smiled cryptically. "She wanted to bring something else to my attention."

And now you have mine. Anne squinted curiously at him.

He placed a hand on his chest and mimicked an innocent maiden speaking in a high, breathy voice. "After you left, I remembered something I found in Peter's trash can."

"I'll bet she wiggled that big chest of hers and batted her eyelashes as well."

"She did, actually." They both laughed as he gave a semblance of her signature shoulder twist. "But that's not the point."

He dangled a limp hand in the air as if it were clutching something and finished his parody. "Is this what you were looking for?"

"Oh my God. The swap contracts?"

He raised a single finger. "Copies. Not the originals."

"No way!"

"Dumped them on my desk and said she had to run. I was gobsmacked." He picked up the cheese slicer and ran it over the slab of cheddar, making a series of neat slices before placing them on a row of waiting crackers. "Now I know why she decided to turn on him."

"Wow!" Anne paused to digest the information. "She knew all along."

"Of course she did." Alex smirked. "Peter picked the wrong woman to mess with."

"As they say, hell hath no fury…How much do you want to bet her next stop was the offices of the SEC?"

"That's my guess, too." He set the plate of cheese and crackers on the table between them and picked up his wine. "Not only that, I wonder what else she might know."

"Boy. Peter really blew it! His timing couldn't be worse with the SEC investigation swinging into action."

"Not his finest moment. The good thing is that we have no need to mention your possession of illicit copies."

"Is that a legal term?"

"It is, actually. Fortunately, not one that you have to worry about any longer." He kicked his shoes off and pushed them to the side.

"I sense a *but* hiding in there."

Alex sighed as he waved his free hand back and forth. "It's just a lot of work. I'll probably have to meet with the SEC to get in front of this whole swap business. Tell them what we've learned. Make it clear the firm had no idea what Peter was up to. Promise to improve our oversight. Yada, yada, yada."

"But once done, hopefully, they'll just give the firm a slap on the wrist with some minor fines and let that be the end of it. Right?" She searched his face.

"That's the hope." He frowned. "After I've done enough groveling for forgiveness. Except for Peter, of course." He twisted the wineglass in his fingers. "He's not going to be happy at all about being held accountable."

"Hopefully, Twinkle-Toes is transferred before he finds out what she's done."

"Shouldn't be necessary. I've already forwarded everything to our illustrious CEO with the recommendation that Peter be terminated, effective immediately."

Anne breathed in sharply. "With no chance to explain why he might have dumped the files?"

"It doesn't matter why. We had explicit instructions from the SEC to preserve documents and he violated that instruction. He's a liability to the company." Alex looked confused. "I thought you'd be happy to hear that you won't have to deal with that slime ball anymore."

"I am." And yet she felt she found herself imagining his shock as his life blew apart in an instant, in part because he had underestimated Twinkle-Toes. Truth be told, they all had. "I was just wondering from a procedural point of view. If I were accused of something, I guess I'd want a chance to defend myself. But in this case, there really is no acceptable explanation."

"Exactly."

She leaned over and picked up a cracker with cheese. "It's looking an awful lot like Peter killed Fernsby in order to keep the swap deals secret."

"Sure is."

"Well then, aren't you worried that he'll be angry about getting fired? What if he comes after you?"

"Me?" He snorted. "He's more likely to go after Twinkle-Toes. She's the one who gave me the files. And even if he does blame me, what's he going to do? Send a poisoned letter through the mail?"

"The man poisoned a high-level CEO at a wedding. How can you be so oblivious to the risk?" She stared at her fiancé, unblinking. "What if he shows up here?"

Alex glanced around their living room. "He has no way of getting in."

"Or does something drastic at the country club, next time we're having dinner with your family in Short Hills?"

"In front of everyone?" He swirled his wine glass and took a sip.

"Isn't that kind of what happened at Paige's wedding?"

Alex froze as her words sank in. "We don't know for sure that he's the one who murdered Fernsby. It's just speculation on our part."

"Yeah, but he's looking more and more likely."

"Then he'll probably be arrested in the near future."

"We've heard nothing on that front since Richard's funeral. Except for the crime tape around your parents' dock, there's no sign of an investigation."

Alex stood up abruptly. "Peter doesn't scare me."

"The thing is," she said quietly, "he *does* scare me."

22

The Proof Is in the Pudding

The Hamptons

That weekend

"Move it over here," Paige directed from her semi-reclined perch on the sofa. "That way, we can look at the wedding proofs together."

A few days earlier, she and Kevin had decamped to the Hunter family home in the Hamptons with the idea that the sea air would be a pleasant change of scenery. When Alex spoke with his parents, they seemed thrilled about the arrangement, enjoying the opportunity to help oversee their daughter's care. *I wonder,* Alex had said to Anne with an arched eyebrow, *how long do you reckon that'll last?*

She didn't bother guessing and instead responded to his more relevant question as to whether they should join the family over the weekend. (Yes. Paige would probably enjoy their company.) So, now she found herself trying to lift an armchair, which was surprisingly heavy, and instead, opting to slide it (carefully) across the rug. "I hope your mother doesn't mind."

Paige waved her hand dismissively. "She won't care."

If not, we'll know soon enough. After several pushes, Anne paused to give her muscles a break. "I need to do something to beef up these little chicken arms."

"At least they get a chance to be flexed and used, whereas mine are just wasting away." Alex's sister looked down at her stomach and sighed. "I always thought high-risk pregnancies were reserved for women over the age of thirty-five."

Anne smiled sympathetically. "I don't think there are any hard and fast rules on that." She resumed inching the chair across the floor.

"Obviously not, since I'm just thirty-two." Paige leaned forward and stretched. "I'm so sick of being on total bed rest. It sounds ridiculous, but it's exhausting!"

"It doesn't sound ridiculous at all." Anne gave the chair a final nudge and plopped herself down in the seat. "Except for bathroom breaks, you're basically a prisoner of your bed. Or couch, as the case may be." She watched Paige pick up a large navy blue box from the coffee table. "How many photos did you say there were?"

"A lot." Paige laughed as she rolled the container back and forth in her hands. "The photographer told me it would be six weeks before they were ready because summertime is their busy season. But with those two detectives breathing down their necks, magically, they managed to deliver them in less than half that time."

"I guess that's one of the few good things to come out of everything that's happened."

"Except it was still a bit of a hassle. I had to wait for the police to give permission for them to be released. And I'm the bride!"

Do you seriously think that matters in a murder investigation? Anne's eyes widened as Paige set the box down and picked up a second identical one that had been hiding underneath a blanket casually strewn on the end of the sofa. If both were full of pictures, there were a ton of them. "They're just following procedure."

"For some reason, it all feels rather invasive." Paige flipped the lid back and set a handful of prints on the table in front of them. "But I do understand. There could be something in one of these boxes that ultimately leads them to Richard's killer."

A sobering thought.

She squeezed Anne's arm. "You look really good in a couple of them, and there's one of you and Alex that I plan to get framed."

Anne's cheeks flushed at both the compliment and the idea that her future sister-in-law actually wanted to include her in the family photo wall. "I can't wait to see how they turned out."

"Here we are." The Battle-Axe returned, carrying a tray with a pitcher of water and a couple of crystal glasses. "I see you've been doing some rearranging in my absence."

Uh-oh. Anne's pulse quickened. Had she managed, yet again, to tick off her future mother-in-law?

"It was my idea," Paige said firmly. "I think it'll be easier while we go through the photos."

"I'll move everything back when we're done," Anne added quickly.

"It's fine." Mother smiled at daughter weakly, her forehead creased with worry. "Drink up. The doctor said you need to stay hydrated."

Paige rolled her eyes but took the proffered glass after handing the photographs to Anne. "With the amount I've had, I feel like a beached whale."

"You look great," Anne reassured her, although, in truth, she thought Alex's sister looked worn out and rather pale. *How much does she know about Kevin's shenanigans at work?*

"Make sure you rest if you start getting tired." Her mother set a small bowl of nuts on the coffee table. "I don't want you concerned about anything except taking it easy."

Paige gave an exasperated sigh. "You don't need to keep hovering. I'm fine!"

"Of course you are." The matriarch glanced briefly at Anne and back at her daughter, a look of hurt obvious on her face. "I was just trying to be polite."

"I didn't mean—"

"I'll be in the study if you need anything else."

"She's such a worrywart," Paige confided once her mother had left the room.

Not exactly how Anne would have described the woman. But she did seem genuinely concerned about her daughter's health.

"And my father's a nervous wreck." She stretched her arms overhead and looked up toward the sky as if she was at her wits' end. "I'm so glad you and Alex decided to come out for the weekend. I'm not sure how much longer I can stand all of their fretting. I thought it would be fun to hang out here by the beach, but so far, it's been the complete opposite!"

Anne did her best to be supportive. "They just want the best for you."

"I think they're all in a twit about the SEC investigation at Energix. Afraid it's going to send me into a tailspin." She snapped her arms back down and gave a dramatic eye roll. "It's not like I'm some fragile flower that needs to be protected from every gust of wind."

No. But you're used to getting your way. And you haven't had to deal with much disappointment in your pampered life. "At least they care."

"I know." She looked down at her huge engagement ring, moving it back and forth so that it glinted dramatically in the light. "It's just that I've come to terms with things." She shifted her gaze up toward Anne and smiled. "Kevin's a smart guy. If Energix goes down in flames, I'm sure he'll find another job. And besides that, I don't see what good it does to get my knickers all in a twist anyway."

She doesn't have a clue what he's been up to. Or else she's in total denial. Anne nodded. "I agree. Worrying won't change a thing. We all need to sit back and let the chips fall where they may." She nodded towards the photos and shifted the conversation to a lighter topic. "Your pictures, on the other hand," she clucked ominously. "Once you choose which ones you want in your wedding album, you're stuck with them for life. If you fail at this task…"

Paige lifted her hand to her brow, feigning alarm. "The world might stop spinning on its axis!"

After they had been through both boxes of proofs (six hundred!), Anne turned to Paige, a quizzical expression on her face. "There are none of Peter Eckert in here."

"I pulled them out in case Käthe decided to pop by."

"Oh. I didn't realize—"

"She said she might...although she wasn't sure...." Paige bit her lip. "I thought it would be upsetting for her since...I mean, we don't know anything for sure, but it kind of looks like—" She gave a small shrug.

"—like Peter might've killed her father." Anne nodded grimly, wondering why she hadn't immediately realized.

"And then the ones of Richard—"

"I just assumed that the police had held those aside."

"No," Paige said quickly. "I did that. Seeing as they were taken just a few hours before his death..." She grimaced. "I just thought...I don't know...if Käthe does come by, it could be triggering."

"Of course." Again, Anne felt like kicking herself. It should have been obvious. "That was thoughtful of you."

"They're over there," Paige pointed to the center drawer of an antique, burled maple desk on the far wall. "Why don't you grab them, and we can give them a quick thumb-through since she's not here." She rested a finger on her lips. "I think you're in a couple."

"We don't need to," Anne said quickly, thinking she was being sensitive.

"Oh. I thought you'd—" Paige leaned back, looking stung.

Evidently, she wanted Anne to see the pictures. And since they captured the hours before Fernsby's death, it would be interesting to see what they revealed, if anything.

"Are you sure you won't find it disturbing...given...you know..." Anne's voice trailed away as she searched Paige's face.

"This may sound strange, but I find the ones with Richard sort of comforting," Paige said somberly. "You can see that he was having a great time up until the end. Well...up until the spitting incident, anyway."

An image of his bulging eyes suddenly popped into Anne's mind. And his face, dripping with sweat. Or had it looked pasty? She couldn't recall. Did the photographer happen to capture the event?

"And I find that I'm curious to look at the ones of Peter Eckert." Paige looked directly at Anne, her blue eyes firm and unwavering. "I keep trying to find a trace of something on his face. Something that suggests he's about to kill Richard."

Vaguely macabre. But I'm curious, too. Anne stood up. "Okay. Let's check them out."

* * *

"Six hundred photographs?" Alex shook his head as they walked along the beach below his parent's home. "That must have taken all afternoon."

"We finished up just as you returned." She stopped and wiggled her toes in the warm sand. "How did it go with your father?"

"He seemed distracted. I think my parents may have an inkling that Kevin's in deep trouble. Did you get the sense that Paige is concerned?"

"Not about Energix." She pulled the ponytail holder out of her hair and slipped it back on more tightly. "But I have to say, it was a little strange to look at the pictures and think back to that night. The ones of Richard, in particular."

The two began walking, arm in arm, along the edge of the water. "She separated them from the rest of the proofs in case Käthe comes by and wants to take a look."

"Good thinking on her part."

"Mm-hmm. I thought so, too. The thing that was interesting was that it meant they were all grouped together." She stopped and turned to face Alex directly. "Over the course of the evening, you can see his appearance *visibly* change. He gets kind of pale looking shortly after dinner and then in each picture, just looks worse and worse."

Alex tilted his head, as if trying to make sense of her words.

"Honestly?" She shuddered. "I found it a little gruesome to look at those photos. It's like they captured his poisoning in real-time."

He blinked. "Blimey."

"I feel badly that we didn't realize something was terribly wrong. That he was dying." She bit her lip.

Alex pulled her toward him, wrapping his arms around her back, and she inhaled the minty scent of his cologne. "Nobody did," he said quietly. "We all just thought he'd had way too much to drink."

"Except the killer. He knew." She shivered at the thought of someone standing by, simply watching and waiting, while the man disintegrated.

"I still have trouble believing that anyone attending my sister's wedding would be capable of such a thing."

And yet that was exactly what had happened. While the guests happily partied under the stars, Richard Fernsby had collapsed and died in the boat down below.

After a long moment, they slowly disentwined and resumed walking along the hard edge of the sand. When Alex spoke next, his voice sounded brisk and lawyerly. "Was Eckert in any of the pictures with him? Brigitte said he had ample opportunity to—"

"That's what was so surprising. The only time the two of them were together was when they first arrived. After that, Eckert and his date mingled with other guests and, for dinner, sat together at a completely different table, far way."

"Didn't Richard and Brigitte sit with all the *parents*?" He made air quotes.

She nodded. "Yours. Kevin's. Plus, all the associated godparents and that elderly couple who flew in from England for the event." She glanced sideways but didn't change her pace.

He grabbed Anne's arm and gave it a tiny tug. "I hope you don't think anyone in my family killed him."

"No!" She said. *Did that come out a bit too strong?* "I'm just not seeing how Eckert would have had the opportunity."

"What if he slipped something into Fernsby's drink shortly after dinner?"

"From what I can tell, Eckert and Twinkle-Toes danced the night away. And by the time the spitting incident happened, Fernsby was looking pretty green, so I think the poison was well into his system by then, probably slipped into his food or drink at dinner or very shortly thereafter."

Alex pointed toward a series of rock steps that led up to the top of the bluff, and both turned in unison to begin climbing. "That would explain a lot, actually. His erratic behavior as the evening wore on. Why he went off the rails at you. And the weird comment he made afterwards to Kevin about your supposedly yellow eyes."

"Likening me to a snowy owl." It still rankled her, just thinking about it.

"I'll bet the drug caused him to hallucinate or somehow impaired his vision." Alex slowed down as they reached the top, sounding slightly out of breath.

"I'm pretty sure Digitalis does that. And it can cause the heart to stop. When the official toxicology reports come in, we'll know for sure." Anne looked left and right at the rocky path, overgrown with grasses and prickly bushes, wondering which direction to go.

"That way." Alex jerked his thumb toward the right. "Further down, we'll hang a left onto the old cow lane." As he led the way, he resumed analyzing potential suspects. "If it wasn't Eckert, then it's got to be Dodgy Don. He was up to his ears in all the financial troubles at Energix, and then Fernsby hung him out to dry."

"Except, that loser sat with his wife at yet another table, way over on the other side."

"Then maybe he did it immediately afterwards. And the photographer didn't happen to catch him in Richard's vicinity."

"It's possible." She slowed down and tried to choose her next words carefully. "I did notice something sort of odd in the background of one of the other pictures, halfway between dinner and the spitting incident."

"Okay."

"I'm not sure if it's even relevant."

Alex stopped abruptly and turned around to face her. "Out with it."

She took a deep breath. "Kevin appears to be talking to a woman who's holding something pink."

"Maybe a flower fell out of the bridal bouquet?"

"It's not a flower. It's something sort of long and narrow." Anne tried to reconstruct the photo in her mind. "And there's something about her posture and the way her hands are raised. It looks as if she's yelling at him."

He shrugged. "They could have just been joking around."

"Except she's wearing shorts and a t-shirt. She definitely wasn't dressed for a wedding."

"Hmm." Alex picked up a shell and threw it into the water. "That's strange. When we get back, I'll take a look…see if I know who she is."

* * *

"Is it working?" Paige anxiously watched her new husband fiddling with the settings on the VCR.

"I think I got it now," Kevin said confidently. "Just remember. This is the raw footage. The only reason we have the tape is because this is what they gave to the police. Normally, it would be edited down to just the highlights."

As Alex clicked the remote, Anne settled into her chair, ready for a long, boring night.

"Wait a minute." Paige frowned. "You just fast-forwarded past the wedding ceremony."

"We can look at it afterwards," Alex said calmly. "I'm curious what the video from the reception shows."

"But I want to see—"

"And you will. As soon as we're done with this section." He continued past the guests exiting the church and their initial arrival at the house, where they were milling around the lawn, casually sipping cocktails.

"Hang on!" Paige protested. "You just skipped the entire—"

He stopped at the start of dinner and pushed the regular play button. "This is the section where the police will be focusing their efforts."

"The police? I thought we were—"

He put up a hand. "We have maybe thirty minutes before Mom and Dad come in to join us. Let's make sure we don't see anything strange that could be—"

"Strange?" His sister asked in an exasperated tone. "How?"

"I don't know how. But our house became a crime scene, and I think we should make sure that we're not caught off guard the next time those two detectives decide to pay a visit."

"But—" Paige opened and closed her mouth, evidently struggling to come up with a strong counterargument.

"I'm speaking as your favorite, picky attorney right now, by the way."

She rolled her eyes and sighed. "I thought having you hang out with us this weekend would be fun!"

Kevin stood up. "Popcorn, anyone?"

The room remained silent.

"Or something more to drink?"

"Not for me," Anne and Alex both said simultaneously. They locked eyes and laughed.

"Me neither," Paige said through pursed lips, obviously still processing Alex's comments.

As Kevin exited the room, Anne shifted her attention to the screen where Richard could be seen pulling a chair out for his wife and then sitting down next to her. The camera panned around the tent, where the guests were slowly taking their seats. Meanwhile, servers moved in and out of the frame carrying trays laden with salad and freshly baked bread.

Alex looked vaguely surprised as he watched the video play. "Mom. Dad. Everyone looks happy at dinner. Even Richard."

"Of course they look happy." Paige spat at him. "They were celebrating my wedding!" She crossed her arms. "When Kevin returns, I want to rewind the tape to the beginning."

"Give it a rest," he muttered.

Uh-oh. This could descend into World War III any minute. Anne glanced over to see if Paige had heard her brother's snippy comment, but she showed no obvious reaction.

He fast-forwarded through the dinner, stopping just as the guests began to stand up and dance. "There." He paused the VCR, and everyone strained forward in their seats to get a better look. "Don is heading over toward the stage with his wife. And there's Eckert. Up in the far right."

They watched in silence as Peter gyrated with Twinkle-Toes on the dance floor, and Don and his wife wove their way through the partygoers to join them. Moments later, Don began moving his tall, thin body in small, jerky movements, looking awkward and gangly. In stark contrast, his well-coordinated wife flowed easily with the music, appearing relaxed and comfortable.

"I still don't get what Käthe sees in that guy." Kevin set a big bowl of popcorn down on the table and rejoined the group. "He can hardly even dance, much less construct an intelligent sentence."

If that wasn't the pot calling the kettle black.

Alex sped the VCR up slightly and the four continued to be visible, dancing and talking and laughing for a good twenty minutes while the bride and groom worked their way around the tent.

"See?" Paige said primly. "Käthe was right. Don's not a murderer."

No. He's just a cheat and a scoundrel. Not even a particularly good-looking one.

"By the same token, neither is Eckert," Alex said grimly.

"Then who does that leave?" Kevin dropped a few kernels of popcorn onto the floor for the dog and then popped the rest into his mouth.

Alex stared intently at the screen, slowing the VCR down as the camera focused on the dinner tables again. Brigitte was still sitting with Kevin's parents, but her husband's seat was now empty. "Where did Richard go?" he murmured.

Kevin stood up, stray kernels falling from his shirt, and began to swing his arms as if taking a golf shot. "Probably in the bathroom or getting another drink. Maybe we should take a break."

The camera swung over to the bride chatting with her godparents before panning around to a couple of the bridesmaids doing shots with the groomsmen. As Pearls-Galore threw her head back, Anne could just make out the woman in shorts talking with Kevin in the far corner.

"Hey!" Paige motioned for him to move. "I can't see."

"It's been a long day." He smiled at his wife without shifting. "We can watch the rest of this later."

"Let's just finish—" Alex began.

"I'm concerned about Paige's health," he said firmly, his eyes unyielding and his stance suddenly rigid.

"But I'm not tired." She gave Anne a quizzical look that said, *What's up with him?*

"Would you like some more water?" Anne stood up and walked toward the left of the group, to a position that allowed her a full view of the screen.

"I'm turning the VCR off." Kevin swiveled and bent down to locate the power button.

"Wait!" Anne was surprised at how loudly her voice echoed around the room. In the video, the mystery woman was gesturing angrily, and Kevin was clearly arguing back. "Who's that woman you're arguing with? In the upper left-hand of the screen?"

He froze, one hand midair, his head still facing the opposite side of the room.

Alex craned his neck around to get a better look. "It looks like—" he began.

Paige sat straight up. "What's Daisy doing at our wedding?" She leaned back slowly as the woman on the screen flung something small and narrow at Kevin before storming away. Then, the camera panned over to other guests in the foreground, twirling onto the stage.

Kevin stood up slowly, both hands held out as if trying to keep her from throwing a grenade. "I can explain."

* * *

"She's someone we know from high school, but not anyone that my sister or I ever hung out with." Alex paced their bedroom back and forth, trying to make sense of what had just happened. "I had no idea she worked at Energix."

Anne pulled out her vanity case and began hunting for the small pouch she used to store her jewelry. "Interesting coincidence that this Daisy person was let go the same week as the CFO."

"Kevin said it was completely unrelated."

Said being the operative word. Anne paused her rummaging and turned to face Alex. "I can understand she was angry about being fired. Furious even. But to show up at Kevin's wedding uninvited? And throw a raspberry madeleine at him? That's pretty weird." And a total waste of an exceptionally good dessert.

Alex bit his lip.

Now that she had come this far, she laid her remaining cards on the table. "Honestly? I'm not sure I believe his story."

He nodded, a concerned look on his face. "Me neither."

23

The Chickens Come Home to Roost

New York City

A week and a half later

"They just arrested Peter Eckert!" Jennifer's voice screamed down the telephone line straight into Anne's unprepared ear.

She flinched and jerked the receiver away.

"For fraud and money laundering," her co-worker continued at full volume. "Because of those swap deals with Energix."

Anne felt the world shift into slow motion. *Eckert. Arrested. For financial wrongdoing. Not for murder.*

"A bunch of federal marshals came onto the trading floor, flashed their badges, and literally walked him away in handcuffs! His jacket is still hanging on the back of his chair."

"Wow! That seems kind of heavy-handed. I mean, if he was willing to walk out voluntarily—"

"Come on," Jennifer chided, finally lowering her voice a notch. "You know how it is. The perp walk is all part of the show. It tells everyone that prosecutors are tough on crime and that the rich and famous aren't getting special treatment. They're counting on John Q Public to show their appreciation at the next election."

Anne could certainly see the audience appeal. Obnoxious yuppies with their fancy homes and sporty BMWs, accumulating all of that (no doubt undeserved) wealth, finally getting their comeuppance.

Jennifer laughed. "They *love* parading white-collar criminals in front of the cameras."

"The press was there?"

"Are you kidding me?" Jennifer snorted. "They were blocking the entrance to the building. It was a total frenzy. Someone must have tipped them off."

Anne gave a small shudder as she imagined Peter Eckert being escorted out the front door, past microphones, television crews, and pushy reporters looking for a quick sound bite. "Oh my god. Talk about humiliating." And yet, she was pleased that he was being held accountable.

"The whole thing was unbelievable. When they marched him out, the trading floor came to a total standstill. I've never seen the place go silent like that. You could've heard a pin drop."

"Peter can't have had any idea, either. The shock must've—"

"He was white as a sheet. I'm not sure he's going to survive this. I seriously wonder if he'll keel over in that dingy jail cell before he even gets to trial."

"Oh, c'mon. He'll post bail and be out in twenty minutes. But this is definitely the end of his career at Spencer Brothers."

Jennifer chuckled. "I guess Twinkle-Toes didn't need to ask for a transfer after all."

Anne took a sharp breath at the reminder of his jilted girlfriend. "What did she do while all of this was going on?"

"Sat at her desk looking smug as a clam."

* * *

"All the SEC would tell me was that they acted on a tip." Alex leaned back in his executive chair and put his hands behind his head. "And that they have two informants."

"Two?" Anne's mind began whirring. "That could be anyone on the trading floor who happened to be aware of the swap deals. A salesman or even one of the back-office clerks. Besides Twinkle-Toes, I wonder who else had an axe to grind with Peter."

He smiled mischievously. "I've got a strong suspicion that both informants are exes." He made air quotes around *exes*. "As in Peter's *ex*-girlfriend and the *ex*-CFO of Energix."

Anne's eyes widened. "That would give them someone from each company…"

"Indeed." He arched an eyebrow. "A snitch on each side of the financial transactions in question. Both trying to trade their skins for his."

She took a moment to process his words. "If you're right…"

"He's toast."

* * *

"And so it begins," Alex announced, setting the newspaper down on the breakfast table the following morning before heading over to the refrigerator to get a glass of orange juice.

Anne took a sip of her tea and began reading.

The Wall Street Chronicle
Tuesday, August 28, 1990

Spencer Brothers Executive helped Energix Mislead Investors

Peter Eckert, head of fixed income at Spencer Brothers, was arrested on the trading floor as shocked employees looked on. He is charged with fraud and money laundering in connection with the downfall of energy giant Energix. In addition, he is accused of directing others in his organization to shred evidence related to those fraudulent financial transactions.

As she was finishing up, Alex came over and massaged her shoulders. "I think it's safe to say that Twinkle-Toes is informant number one." His thumbs moved slowly toward her neck, gently releasing the knots.

"I agree. How else would they know that he told her to make everything disappear." She leaned forward so he could rub the middle of her back as well.

"It's also clear that they know an awful lot about how the financial transact—" he stopped abruptly as she let the paper slide through her fingers and drop onto the table, landing with a thud on a bowl of soggy cereal and then flipping over in the process. "Oh no!"

Anne groaned inwardly as he snatched the thing up and gave it a quick shake, completely fixated on the bottom corner of the page. She knew that he was persnickety about the state of his newspaper, wanting to only open perfect sheets of crisp paper. "Is it still readable?"

"Uh-huh," he said without looking up at her.

And yet he was still studying the damn thing, giving no attention to her stiff neck. Was this his way of saying he was angry at her? Over something as trivial as a few milk drops on the morning paper? It made no sense. And it was ridiculous. "Are you mad at—"

"Take a look at this." He set it back down on the table and pointed to the far right corner, a smug expression on his face. "Informant number two."

The Wall Street Chronicle
Tuesday, August 28, 1990

The Canary Starts to Sing

Donald Chalmer, former CFO of Energix, has agreed to cooperate with the SEC investigation in return for immunity from prosecution. As part of his deal, he will testify that Spencer Brothers participated in a temporary arrangement called "parking", whereby they purchased three oil barges at Year End 1990 for a fee. This allowed Energix to claim a profit so that the managers could take larger bonuses. Spencer Brothers then sold the barges back to Energix in April, as agreed, which contributed to the big losses taken that quarter. In addition, they knowingly purchased a nonexistent wind farm, in order to further prop up the books.

He sighed. "I better hightail it into the office and get started on damage control."

* * *

"No wonder I couldn't find the wind farms on a map." Anne dropped her quarters into the vending machine slot and pushed the button for a Hershey's chocolate bar with almonds. "They never even existed."

Jennifer ripped the tab off of her Dr Pepper and took a gulp. "I can't believe that Peter Eckert played us like that."

"Not just us. He played everybody." Anne leaned down to retrieve her candy bar from the machine.

"Now that Energix has officially dropped to junk bond status, I'm betting that Spencer Brothers won't recoup a penny from that sham trade. Word on the street is that they're going to be filing for bankruptcy any day."

Anne stood back up and shrugged. "Who cares? We're big enough to absorb the loss. If Spencer Brothers were a small boutique firm, it might be another story."

Jennifer pointed at the candy bar in Anne's hand. "We're splitting that, right?"

She nodded, and the two began walking back to her office. "The people who will be hardest hit are the regular joes who put Energix stock in their retirement fund thinking it was a great investment. Talk about getting screwed over."

"Fair enough." Jennifer allowed. "It'll suck for them. But don't forget, it'll also suck for us too."

As Anne opened the door to her office, she turned to face her friend. "How? We both know that Spencer Brothers will live to see another day."

"Well, *yeah.*" Jennifer crossed her arms indignantly and looked at Anne like she was a total dimwit. "Except for our bonuses! They'll be totally hammered! I was thinking I might buy a new car this year. Something sleek and sporty. Maybe even get a fur coat. Now I'll be lucky if I can buy a new pair of shoes!"

Anne looked at her friend, dumbfounded. "I thought you didn't believe in wearing fur because it's cruel to the animals."

"I don't," Jennifer said primly.

"Well then—"

Her face relaxed into the beginnings of a smile. "I was just trying to make the point that this whole debacle could have ramifications for us as well. That's all."

Anne flipped her hands in submission. "Fair enough. I know that my secretary wants to pay down her credit card debt. She can barely keep up with the monthly payments and is counting on her bonus to knock the principal down big time."

"Exactly." Jennifer flipped her long, wavy brown hair behind her back. "One of the clerks on our floor recently had a baby. She's hoping to use her bonus for a down payment on a house." She eyed the chocolate in Anne's hand. "I need some energy if I'm going to make it through the rest of the day."

Anne snapped the bar in half. *You and me both.*

* * *

"Jennifer's worried that our bonuses will be affected." Anne unlocked the door to their apartment and set her briefcase down on the floor. "She could be right, you know. Depending on how this plays out. Especially if Spencer Brothers is hit with large fines. We could lose some of our clients."

"That's why I told our illustrious CEO that I thought it was a bad idea to deny everything." Alex threw his jacket on a nearby chair and loosened his tie. "But he's of the opinion that you never admit fault. *Make them prove it,* he said. *Nine out of ten times, they can't.*" He shook his arms in frustration. "And, if you can believe it, our outside legal counsel agreed with him."

"Wait a minute. They're going to claim the oil barges weren't actually parked with us? That what Eckert did was totally fine?"

He sighed. "Yep."

"Maybe there's some way to make that work as a legal strategy, but from a PR point of view, it seems kind of risky."

Alex waved his hand dismissively. "It's doomed. I just hope this doesn't end up completely killing the business."

* * *

The following morning, Alex dropped the morning paper onto the table and shook his head.

The Wall Street Chronicle
Wednesday, August 30, 1990

Spencer Brother Goes Toe-To-Toe with the SEC

In a statement today, Spencer Brothers denied that it had allowed oil barges to be parked with the firm, saying, "Spencer Brothers' investment was fully at risk in this transaction. We did not receive any guarantee that Energix or any other entity would purchase the oil barges back."

John Wilhoit, Co-Chief of the Enforcement Division's Asset Management Unit said he could not comment on an active investigation, but that he intends to hold all guilty parties accountable for their role in the Energix financial debacle.

"Maybe Jennifer was right." Anne pushed the newspaper aside and picked up her tea. "Spencer Brothers is going to end up looking as bad as Peter Eckert and everyone else who was involved in this hare-brained scheme."

"Not only that, killing Richard accomplished nothing." He cocked his head, as if suddenly realizing how his words sounded. "Not that I'm advocating the use of murder to achieve financial goals. But presumably, someone wanted him out of the picture so they could hide this financial jiggery-pokery. And yet, it's all coming out anyway. His death was a total waste."

"Unless there's more that hasn't yet come out."

"Like what?"

"I don't know. But what if we're wrong about the motive?"

24

Jailbird

New York City

September 1, 1990

"Let me just grab my sunglasses, and I'll be ready to roll." Anne ran into their bedroom and scanned the top of her dresser. *Not there.* She unzipped her pocketbook and peered inside. *Not there either. Where else could they be?* She walked back into the kitchen and did a full three-sixty, finally spotting them on the counter next to the sink just as the phone rang. She took a step back toward the hallway and yelled out. "Should I answer it?"

"Let it go," Alex called from the front door. "They can leave a message on the answering machine."

Anne glanced at her watch. 8:20 a.m. It was a bit early for a call on a Saturday morning. His family generally adhered to the social rule of no calls before 9 a.m. "What if it's an emergency with your sister?"

The phone rang again, and she heard him sigh. "Ugh. You're right. I guess we better see who it is."

She nearly dropped the receiver at the sound of Kevin's babbling voice. *Police Precinct?* She interrupted the panicked jabber. "When?"

"Last night." Kevin rambled on about a knock on the door by what he thought was the Pizza Delivery guy who instead turned out to be a mob of police officers ready to swarm the house. "Next thing I know, I was handcuffed in the back of a police cruiser!"

"Alex! It's Kevin! Get in here!"

The discombobulated man continued rattling away. "Paige has no idea where I am. She's still in the Hamptons at her parents' house. I'm supposed to meet her there in a little while. She thinks I'm taking care of the lawn guy right now. That's the whole reason I went out to our New Jersey house in the first place."

Anne whirled around at the sound of Alex entering the room. "He's been arrested!"

He grabbed the phone from her hand. "Kevin?" There was a pause, and his eyes widened. "Richard Fernsby's murder?! ... Don't say another word! These conversations are recorded! ... Listen to me. I have a friend from law school who's a top-notch criminal attorney. I'll give him a call. Don't say anything more until I get there. Okay? ... Hang tight! Help is on the way."

When he hung up, his face was white as a sheet. "I need to get down to the station and figure out what the hell is going on."

* * *

A few hours later, they drove to the Hamptons in silence, with Kevin sitting morosely in the back seat of the car. Alex's mother rushed out the door when they pulled into the driveway and stood rigidly on the porch while they unloaded, hands on hips, her face a grim piece of stone.

"You should probably give your mother a heads up before we go inside," Anne whispered. They had just had a few seconds to chat before she jumped in the car, so she had only the barest idea of what had transpired at the station. But she'd heard enough to know it somehow involved Daisy's appearance at the wedding, and it wasn't good.

Alex picked up his travel bag and slung the strap over his shoulder. "Mom—" he began.

"We've done our best to keep Paige calm." She stood at the top of the steps, looking down at Kevin imperiously, like a queen surveying her subject.

"Good," the beleaguered man managed to squeak out.

"We told her you were delayed because the lawn service was late." She deepened her stare. "She has no idea you spent the night in jail!"

Kevin gulped. "Actually—"

She put up a hand and turned away so that he was no longer within her view. "I'm not interested in anything you have to say. My concern is how we're going to manage this…" She squeezed her eyes tight, accentuating the wrinkles on her heavily creamed face. "…this fiasco with Paige."

Alex ascended the steps and stood face-to-face with his mother. "We need to sit down as a family and—" he began.

His mother tilted her head in Kevin's direction while still avoiding a direct view of the man. "You paid his bail, yourself? We said we'd take care of it."

Alex shook his head. "There was no bail."

Her lips twisted. "They let him out on his own recognizance?"

"He wasn't under arrest."

"But when you called—"

"I know." Alex glanced down at his brother-in-law cowering on the flagstone path below. "Kevin was so distraught at being taken down to the station that he didn't realize he was simply being brought in for questioning."

His manner was calm and factual, betraying none of the disgust he had privately voiced a few hours earlier to Anne when he had swung by the apartment with Kevin in tow. *I don't know what my sister ever saw in him. How hard is it to understand whether you've actually been charged with a crime? It's not exactly rocket science!*

"I was in shock." Kevin began to creep up the stairs. "I opened the door expecting the pizza guy, and instead I was greeted by—"

The Battle-Axe raised her hand again to silence him and then addressed her son, her right eyebrow arched up toward the sky. "So, it was just a follow-up interview? To clarify a few things that he previously forgot to mention?"

Alex nodded.

She brightened, almost cracking a smile. "Then it sounds like we don't have to mention a word of this to Paige."

"I totally agree." Kevin stepped onto the porch and wiped his brow.

"Mom." Alex's face was grim as he shook his head. "The only reason they let him go was because they didn't have enough to hold him."

"Because I'm not guilty!" Kevin flashed an angry look at his brother-in-law.

Alex ran his fingers through his sandy brown hair. "We can't keep something as serious as this—"

His mother placed a hand firmly on each of her hips. "But if they've resolved whatever concerns—"

"Exactly!" Kevin waved his damp handkerchief in the air. "There's no need—"

"Nothing is resolved," Alex said firmly. "He's still considered a prime suspect in Richard Fernsby's murder."

Anne took a sharp breath.

The matriarch's face clouded again as she stared at her son. "What are we going to tell your sister?"

"The truth."

* * *

Paige was sprawled on the couch, propped up by several big pillows, with a glass of ice water on the coffee table and a tall pile of books and magazines on the floor below. As she watched the family members getting settled into their chairs, she searched each of their faces, probably sensing the growing tension in the room.

"What's up?" She fixed a wary eye on her parents, who sat stiffly in a pair of matched wingback chairs flanking either side of the fireplace. They immediately looked over at their son, signaling for him to take the lead.

"Alex?" She swiveled to face her brother, who appeared generally relaxed except for his foot, which he alternated between kicking and waving back and forth across the floor.

He spoke in a calm, measured voice. "There's been a development in the investigation of Richard Fernsby's murder."

Kevin shifted in his seat.

She sighed and placed a hand heavily on her heart. "Don't drag it out. Just tell me. Who killed him?"

"We don't know." Alex had circles under his eyes. The stress of the day was clearly taking a toll. "But the police suspect Kevin."

"What?" She laughed in a way that sounded almost like a gasp and looked over at her new husband in total disbelief. "Why would they think that?"

He nodded his head so vigorously it looked like it might fall off. "It's ridiculous. I had nothing to do with his death."

"I know you didn't," she spluttered, wiping a small spray of spit off of her chin. "It was our wedding night. We have a million guests who can attest to the fact that you were at the reception the entire evening. With me!"

"Well, that's the thing," Alex said quietly, barely hiding his contempt. "There was a period of time in which he wasn't with you. Shortly after dinner, before you cut the cake."

She froze, as if trying to reconstruct the scene in her mind.

"It was just a few minutes," Kevin said in a panicked voice. "What you saw on the video."

"What video?" His mother-in-law cast a dagger eye in his direction.

*If looks could kill...*Anne tried to keep her face blank as she observed Boy Wonder experiencing the woman's wrath for a change.

"From the wedding." He sounded exasperated. "But there's no need to get into—"

"This tacky person I knew back in high school crashed the reception." Paige waved her hand disdainfully. "Angry about being sacked the week before. You can see her taking Kevin to task in some of the raw footage." She rolled her eyes. "It's unbelievable what some people will do for a little attention."

"Another boorish American." Her father muttered under his breath, followed by something unintelligible.

Alex leaned forward. "What was that, Dad?"

He fiddled with his collar. "I was just wondering what any of this has to do with Richard's murder."

Good question.

"It's the reason the police became interested in Kevin. Evidently, he neglected to mention that he'd spent any time talking with this mysterious woman who appeared on the video." Alex's jaw tightened. "And then the first time they paid him a visit, he refused to account for his time, choosing instead to slam the door in their faces."

"The officer was insolent and—" Kevin began.

Alex cut him off without so much as a glance. "Which is why the men in blue resorted to their pizza delivery charade the second time around and dragged him down to the station."

"Last night?" Paige looked at her husband in disbelief. "How long were you there?"

His voice quivered as he spoke. "They released me this morning, and we drove straight over."

"I thought you were at the house, waiting for the gardener." She slowly turned toward her parents, her voice becoming flat, as the reality dawned. "You knew."

Her mother flitted her hands back and forth nervously. "We didn't want you to worry. We thought it was all a huge mistake." She blinked and drew herself up tall. "And it was!" She paused again to glance around the room, suddenly looking uncertain. "Wasn't it?"

Paige turned back to face Kevin, fully alert, like a cat ready to spring on a mouse. "Why didn't you just tell the police you were talking to Daisy?"

"I did!" His gaze was averted, looking everywhere, except at his shocked wife. "Eventually! And now, it's all water under the bridge...so we can all move on."

Does he really think he can get her to drop it that easily?

Paige leaned back heavily on her pillows and crossed her arms. "Why the delay?"

"It's just...I didn't think it reflected very well on me that she was so angry... that I hadn't handled her...her separation from the company very well." His speech was halting, and stuttered as he stumbled through his explanation.

"Obviously, no one wants to be let go from their job, but sometimes the blow can be softened...and in retrospect, I didn't do a great job of that." His mouth twisted. "I didn't want to admit that I'd failed."

Paige tilted her head sideways and squinted, looking as if she didn't quite believe him. "You're saying your pride got in the way?"

He sighed, like a downtrodden beggar, and nodded.

"You can't let your job be the only thing that defines you."

Is she actually buying this?

"Tell her the truth." Alex's eyes were hard. "Or I will."

"There's nothing more to tell," Kevin said quickly. "I was talking with a disgruntled employee, which had nothing, whatsoever, to do with Richard's murder. And I had so much going on with the wedding that I just...forgot... to mention it when the police interviewed me that night. Case closed."

Alex looked down at the floor for a long moment and let out a long, loud breath of air. When he raised his head again, his face was tight as he addressed his sister. "He was with Daisy. And as you know, she threw something at him. Except it wasn't a breadstick."

Surprise. Surprise. Anne glanced over at him, expecting to share a smug smile that they had been right to be suspicious of Kevin's little story, but chose instead to keep her face expressionless upon seeing his hands balled up in tight fists that made him look as if he wanted to punch something. Or, more likely, someone.

Paige pulled her shoulders back, evidently bracing for the worst. "Okay," she said slowly. "What was it then?"

Alex practically spat. "A pregnancy test."

It was as if the air had been sucked out of the room.

"I'm not the father!" Kevin shook his arms in a show of desperation. "Daisy made the whole thing up!"

"She invented a bastard child?" Either Alex's father was a bit slow on the uptake or he didn't believe a word that Kevin was saying. Anne studied the old man's face, but his blank expression gave no indication of what was going on in his mind.

"The woman's a bitter, vengeful little snake! I couldn't believe it when she showed up at our wedding telling me I had to pay up or else. All because she was fired? For cause? It's despicable!" He shifted his gaze to Paige and slowly sank down in his chair with the saddest look in his eyes. "I just didn't want anything to ruin your big day."

His spine rounded as he bent over and buried his face in his hands, crumpling into an abject heap of devastation. And yet there was something about the firm way he flexed his shoulders and shifted his feet that suggested his inner core was fully intact and in control. Anne couldn't help but think he was putting on a show.

"Daisy wasn't part of the in-crowd," Paige said slowly. "But she never struck me as being off-the-wall..."

Assuming the mantle of a lawyer, Alex laid out the key facts. "In her sworn statement to the police, she says that the two of them had been in an on-again, off-again relationship for the last two years and that she broke it off about two months before the wedding because that's when she learned he was getting married to you."

"What?" Paige blinked and then clutched her chest, looking as if she had just been stabbed.

"Are you okay?" Anne started to rise from her chair, wondering why Alex hadn't found a softer way to deliver the news.

Paige nodded, but at the same time, she looked pale and trembled. "I'm just trying to—"

"It's all lies! When would I possibly have time to cavort around with a low-life piece of trash like her? And why would I?" Kevin looked at the ceiling, as if beseeching the sky. "Why? When I had someone as wonderful as you?"

Why does anyone have an affair? The excitement and allure of being bad? A need for validation? Commitment issues? Anne stole a glance at Alex's wide-eyed parents, anxiously looking back and forth between their daughter and her new husband, with all semblance of the stiff British upper lip gone.

Kevin turned and pointed a shaking finger at Alex. "How dare you upset Paige with this fictitious crap! You have nothing but the word of a—"

"Enough!" The Battle-Axe leapt up, bringing the conversation to a standstill. She fixed her steely gaze on Alex. "Does this Daisy person have anything to do with Richard Fernsby's death?"

Anne had to hand it to her. Within seconds, she had gotten to the crux of the matter. Had Kevin lied about his conversation with Daisy to keep Paige from discovering his affair? Or had he lied about it because he was somehow involved in Richard's death?

"The police certainly seem to think so." There was an edge to Alex's tone that caused Anne to stiffen. It suggested he knew something and was slowly laying a trap.

"I didn't realize that Daisy was a suspect." Kevin straightened up and crossed his arms, a smug smile overtaking the look of surprise that had been on his face. "But actually, it makes sense. Richard's the one who escorted her off of the premises." He laughed darkly. "And chewed her out like you wouldn't believe."

Gee. Fernsby seems to have a real habit of coming to the rescue. First, saving Alex, the teenager gone wild with an illegal bonfire on the beach, and then Kevin, the philandering groom.

Paige flipped her palms as if giving up on ever understanding his story. "How did Richard know that Daisy was a problem?"

Kevin sighed. "He overheard her threatening to go public with our *supposed* affair and told her to get the hell off the premises. That it was my wedding day, for god's sake! You can't see it in the video, but he practically wrenched her arm out of its socket as he led her away. Honestly? I almost felt sorry for her. But he was right. She had no business being there."

"Obviously, Richard recognized the importance of keeping this whole Daisy business under the radar," Alex said evenly.

Kevin nodded. "At that moment, I could see how he became CEO of a major corporation. Talk about quick and decisive. He swooped in and booted her out of there with no one at the wedding being any the wiser."

"Which is exactly why the police are wondering if you're the one who killed him."

Kevin stared at Alex incredulously. "Why would I do that to someone who had just helped me out of a bind?"

"In order to keep your affair with Daisy a secret."

25

The Grand Finale

Hamptons

A few minutes later

The doorbell rang, catching them all off guard.

"Are we expecting company?" Alex's mother was met with a series of blank stares as she scanned the room.

Anne stood up. "I'll see who it is."

Finally, she'd found a way to be useful. And a great excuse for taking a break from the depressing family forum. With each step, she felt lighter, her body unwinding from the pent-up stress of holding herself tight in order to hide her revulsion at Kevin's behavior. *A two-year relationship with a subordinate at work? While he was in a supposedly committed relationship with Paige?* If he was up to deceiving his fiancée like that, why wouldn't he be capable of murder?

"I'll go with you," her future mother-in-law announced just as Anne was about to disappear through the doorway.

So much for escaping the Hunter clan. She hoped her disappointment didn't show. "Great."

As soon as they were in the hallway, the Battle-Axe pounced. "Did Kevin say anything else in the car ride over?"

"Not a word." In fact, Anne had found the drive long and awkward; her attempt at light conversation met with nothing but a few stilted answers while their charge slumped in the back, staring mindlessly out the window.

"Hmmm." The older woman's lips pulled together, making a thin red line. "What about Alex?"

She shook her head. Alex had spent the majority of the drive with his jaw clamped shut and his hands gripping the wheel so hard that his knuckles turned white. She figured he would fill her in on the details once the two of them were finally alone.

"Oh no," the Battle-Axe murmured at the sight of Käthe's and Brigitte's smiling faces peeking through the window. She stopped short and looked sternly at Anne, her hand slicing through the air. "Not a word of what happened last night. Is that clear?" She smoothed her skirt, put on a big smile, and opened the door.

"Surprise!" Mother and daughter stepped forward into the foyer.

"Oh, my goodness!" Alex's mother exchanged air kisses with Brigitte. "How lovely to see you." She pulled back to admire the widow's earrings. "Are those new?"

"Ach! You see all." Brigitte smiled fondly at her friend. "It's one of the many things I cherish about our friendship."

After the ritual of hugs and compliments had reached its natural end, Käthe held out a box from the village pastry shop. "Raspberry chocolate bars. Paige's favorite." She leaned toward Anne and whispered. "I hope we brought enough. We had no idea that you and Alex were visiting this weekend."

"Oh." Anne waved a hand casually. "It was a last-minute decision. Don't worry about it. We can share." After having their morning run disrupted by Kevin's frantic call, the only exercise they had gotten was climbing in and out of the car. The last thing she wanted was to eat a big sugary dessert while everyone pretended to pleasantly chat.

Käthe motioned toward her mother. "So can we."

Out of the corner of her eye, Anne saw Kevin step into the hallway and stop abruptly.

"Kevin!" Käthe smiled widely and opened her arms as if to give him a hug. Alex's mother froze.

He pointed toward the front door. "I'm...uh..."

"What is it you need?" the matriarch asked through gritted teeth.

The Fernsby women looked back and forth at Kevin and his mother-in-law, no doubt trying to understand why the room suddenly felt electrified.

He pointed again. "Just passing through."

What's going on? Käthe mouthed to Anne.

I'll tell you later. Anne mouthed back.

As Kevin passed by Brigitte, he slowed down and turned to face her. "I just want you to know I had *nothing* to do with Richard's death."

Oh God. What is he doing? Anne took a sharp breath.

The widow furrowed her brow, looking taken aback. "I never thought you did."

Alex's mother put an arm around her two guests and ushered them away. "Let's move into the living room, shall we? I'm sure Paige would love to see you both."

Käthe kept shooting shocked glances in Anne's direction as they walked down the hall. But with the Battle-Axe standing watch, Anne wasn't about to start explaining that Paige's six-week-old marriage was on the verge of coming apart. Or, perhaps Kevin's odd exit meant it already had. She glanced back at the door and saw him sinking onto the porch steps, looking like an abandoned dog. She shivered. So sad. And yet, he'd brought it upon himself.

As the group approached the living room, the exasperated voice of Alex's father reverberated down the hall. "This is exactly the reason you need to have a prenuptial agreement. Good grief! Can you imagine where we'd be if Paige hadn't had one?"

Not that damn prenup again! Anne's heart sank. Thanks to Kevin, the discussion had obviously been rekindled. She took a deep breath and stepped over the threshold.

"Dad! I'm not discussing that anymore. My only concern is what Paige should do now that—"

The old man waved his arms angrily. "Get a divorce, obviously! Which is exactly what could happen to you if—" He stopped abruptly at the sight of the women entering the room. "Brigitte!"

Alex whirled around, his eyes like saucers.

Before anyone could say anything else, Käthe ran over to the couch. "What happened?!"

"He's been two-timing me!" Tears streamed down Paige's mottled red face.

"No way!"

"With Daisy! And she's pregnant!"

Käthe did a double-take. "Are you sure?"

Paige's head bobbed up and down while sobs racked her body.

"Oh my God." The Diamond Goddess's beautiful face morphed into something unrecognizable. She looked both angry and hideously disgusted, as if she had just picked up a dead rodent by mistake. "I can't believe he did that to you."

Paige curled up into a heartbroken mass, quivering on the couch.

"It's been a shock to us all," Alex's father said grimly.

But fortunately, her assets are protected! Anne stared defiantly at him, daring him to say more.

Käthe looked around the room in confusion, throwing her arms to the sky. "How could he? Daisy's such a...she isn't even pretty!" She gave an exaggerated shake of her head. "It makes no sense!"

"I know." Paige sniffled. "And on top of that, the police think he might have killed your father."

Käthe sighed loudly and dropped her arms heavily into her lap. "Why would they possibly think that?"

"I don't know." Paige ran a hand roughly over each cheek in an effort to wipe away her tears, yet the waterfall was nowhere near stopping. "Maybe it's because he lost so much financially when Energix went down the tubes. His 401K. All his stock. And then, when he didn't admit that he'd been talking with Daisy at the wedding—"

NOT ACCOUNTING FOR MURDER

Käthe jerked back in surprise. "She was at the wedding?"

Paige doubled over crying, unable to say any more.

"She made a brief appearance at the reception." Anne picked up a box of Kleenex and set it down next to Paige. "Shortly after dinner. Your father caught wind of what was happening and kicked her out."

"Always the knight in shining armor," Brigitte murmured from the other side of the room. "Up to the bitter end." She took a deep breath and looked down at the ground.

"Oh, Brigitte," Alex's mother placed a hand over her heart. "I'm so sorry you heard any of this. With everything still so raw..."

Anne felt a flutter of astonishment. Was that a glimmer of humanity peeking through the Battle-Axe's armor?

Brigitte lifted her head and smiled bravely. "I'm fine." She slowly surveyed the room, her eyes coming to rest on Paige. "Such a difficult day for your beautiful daughter. But things will get better. I'm sure of it." She turned as if to leave.

"If Käthe's going to stay behind," Alex suddenly called out. "I can give you a ride home."

Brigitte paused and leaned toward Anne. "Such a gentleman. But you know? I think I prefer to walk." She held her elbow out, as if she were a lady from the Victorian era about to be escorted on a stroll. "You join me for part of the way. No? Get some fresh air?"

Anne didn't even hesitate at the chance to escape the oppressive room. "I'd love to."

* * *

"A sad business," Brigitte began as they stepped across the perfectly mowed, lush green lawn. "But I'm not surprised. Kevin's a puffed-up frat boy who probably thinks sleeping around turns him into a man. Just like that imbecile my daughter thinks she's in love with." She flicked her fingers and made a spitting motion. "No wonder Energix had so many problems. My husband was working with Dumb and Dumber."

Anne took a sharp breath. As usual, Brigitte didn't mince words, and yet it was surprising, nonetheless, to hear her attack both men so openly. "Not a big fan, I take it."

"Not really." She stopped short at the sight of the boat dock, quickly averting her gaze from the spot where her husband had died. "But I don't believe either of them killed Richard. The police are …how do you say? Barking at the wrong tree." She turned to face Anne, her sapphire eyes dazzling in the sun. "I wonder about Peter Eckert, though. You've worked with the man. What do you think?"

Anne shook her head. "From the available wedding pictures and video, it appears that the only time he and Richard interacted was when they first arrived, which doesn't give him much opportunity." The two women reached the ocean path and turned to follow it along the top of the bluff. "Plus, I don't see how Eckert benefited. If anything, it seems like Richard's death created a whole lot of problems for him. He had to rely on—" she glanced quickly at Brigitte, "—Dumb and Dumber to help him hide his tracks. Not exactly a winning strategy."

A fit and sprightly sixty-something woman, Brigitte picked up the pace, pounding the sandy track fiercely with each step. "It certainly wasn't that pathetic girl that Kevin managed to get pregnant," she pronounced with a big sweep of her arm. "I doubt my husband even knew her. And she had no idea before she arrived that he would be the one to throw her out."

Anne's thoughts exactly.

"Unless she was trying to kill Kevin and somehow made a mistake and killed Richard by accident instead." Brigitte furrowed her brow, as if considering the idea, before shaking her head. "No. Not possible. She didn't have time."

"Or any obvious reason. Daisy was looking to embarrass Kevin. Maybe hoping to shame him into taking responsibility." Anne felt around her pockets for a ponytail holder to counter the strong wind batting her hair against her face. "Fat chance that was going to happen."

"Ach. I know." She sighed. "It's pitiful. I'll bet she thought he actually cared about her." Brigitte slowed down and looked directly at Anne, her face somber. "So naïve. When will women learn that it's all about collecting those notches on the belt?"

Probably never. Anne pulled her hair back and secured it with the elastic. "What if Kevin didn't trust Richard to keep the pregnancy secret?"

Brigitte waved her hand dismissively. "My husband was the least of his problems. She'd probably already told a dozen of her closest friends. And even hired a lawyer."

"Maybe Kevin panicked? And wasn't thinking straight? In the heat of the moment, he might have assumed—"

She rolled her eyes. "A man who doesn't use birth control with his mistress is too stupid to kill someone. And besides, my husband was poisoned, which means his death wasn't some last-minute idea. Someone planned it."

Anne felt a small chill go down her spine.

Brigitte stared out over the vast expanse of the ocean. "You should probably go back. Join Alex and the rest of the family. No?"

"Probably." Although Anne hated to leave. She was enjoying the feel of the wind on her face and the sound of ocean waves crashing rhythmically on the rocks below.

"But first, let's go down to the beach and feel the water. Ja?" Brigitte smiled as she pointed at a gap in vegetation. "We can climb down along the side over there."

Anne looked at the incline they would be traversing. It was littered with rocks and loose gravel. "Looks a bit steep. Maybe there's a better place farther along."

"It's not as bad as it looks." Brigitte laughed. "If I can do it, you certainly can." She paused. "Give it a try. If you change your mind, we can always turn around."

How could she argue with that? Anne gave a nod and led the way, marveling at the power of the ocean as the waves broke on the beach. "This is beautiful!" Anne called out, trying to make sure her voice could be heard. "Thanks for suggesting we do this!"

"I knew you'd love it," Brigitte called back, followed by something only partially intelligible about the house, her voice drowned out by the surf.

Anne stopped and turned to face her. "What was that?"

"Ach. Just that—" she shrugged, "It was a bit tense back there. No?"

"Hopefully, things have calmed down by now."

Brigitte shook her head. "I doubt it. Alex's parents seem very concerned that you will try to steal his inheritance."

Anne drew back, surprised at the sudden change of subject. She had assumed Brigitte was referring to the drama surrounding Paige, not Alex's financial affairs. And she wondered why Brigitte was driving the conversation in this new direction. "I thought you meant—"

Brigitte gave a sly smile. "It reminds me of my own in-laws. Always assuming the worst. Convinced I was trading my looks for his money because I wanted a secure life outside of East Germany. You will always need to be careful with them."

Anne tensed, uncomfortable with the topic. "Mm-hmm." She turned and tried to decide which way to go next. Below the big rock with the narrow sandy section or over it?

"Go around it," Brigitte instructed, as if reading her mind, before picking up where she had left off. "Fortunately, Alex is strong. He stands up for himself."

He certainly had so far. But now that Kevin had turned out to be such a dud, his parents would be on a mission to make him change his mind. She dug her toe into the sand and inched forward.

"He has solid principles. Like Richard."

On that point, Anne completely disagreed. Richard was an unethical jerk who had lured investors into his web by inflating the net worth of his company and then tried to make a run with the money. But she wasn't about to say that to his widow.

"Of course, under the right set of circumstances, anyone can be convinced to do anything."

Anne recoiled at the odd statement. Was Brigitte trying to justify his behavior? Suggest he had somehow been pressured into duping his investors? Why was she even talking about this?

Anne's foot slipped, and she almost lost her balance.

"Careful!"

She righted herself and stopped to lean against the boulder, no longer finding the scramble down the steep edge of the cliff a fun challenge. Instead, she felt vulnerable.

"We're almost there." Brigitte glided in next to her. "Just a few more steps."

Anne looked at the sun glistening on the water, but instead of feeling a sense of awe or joy at being surrounded by such natural beauty, she felt her knees go wobbly. In that instant she knew that she didn't want to go any farther. That she needed to turn around and get herself on to more solid ground, but that meant she had to squeeze past Brigitte.

"The Hunters don't understand that you and Alex are like me and Richard. He was my whole world. No matter what he did, I would never have divorced him. Not in a million years."

"But at the rehearsal dinner, Käthe said—" Anne swallowed as the realization hit her. *Just follow the money.*

The older woman's mouth twisted. "What did my daughter say?"

"Just that…" Anne blinked as she struggled to come up with a suitable reply. "…that she was worried about you, given everything going on at Energix." Her muscles tensed, ready to spring into action, while she glanced around in search of an alternative route.

"Ach. That's not surprising." Brigitte's voice was smooth. "It's been a difficult last few months." She paused, her blue eyes sharp and unrelenting in their stare. "Is everything okay, dear?"

"It's been a really long day." Anne's heart thumped wildly, and her voice sounded tinny in her own ear. "I should probably go back."

Brigitte's eyes narrowed, and suddenly, the space between them seemed extremely small. "But we're so close."

Anne bent her knees slightly like a skier about to turn over a mogul, and at the same time dug her feet into the sandy embankment to anchor them more securely. "You go ahead. I'll foll—"

"Anne!" She heard Alex's voice faintly in the distance.

Relief flooded her body. She put her hands around her mouth and looked up toward the top of the bluff. "We're below the—"

She felt something brush against her shoulder and, out of the corner of her eye, saw Brigitte's contorted face surging toward her.

26

And Then There Were None

Hamptons

That evening

Between a sprained ankle and what seemed like a million bruises, any small movement sent slivers of pain through her body. Anne winced as she limped over to the chair and gingerly sat down. She glanced at the Hunter family arrayed around the room: Paige sprawled on the comfy couch, her dog Bailey lying quietly by her side, Alex's mother sitting primly by the fireplace, and his father over by the liquor cabinet, studying the rack of wine. If she didn't know better, she might think that nobody had moved and nothing had changed during the time she'd been out and about scrambling on the bluff.

"You should probably elevate your foot," Alex's mother said gently. "Don't you think?"

Anne nodded, surprised at her solicitous manner. "That's what the doctor suggested as well."

As Alex rummaged through a large wooden chest near the fireplace in search of cushions, Paige swiftly launched into the subject on everyone's mind. "I still can't believe Brigitte killed Richard. They always seemed like such a perfect couple."

"Let that be a lesson to us all." Her mother sniffed. "Appearances can be deceiving." She gave her daughter a pointed look. "As we've learned several times today."

No doubt she was referring to Kevin's dalliance with Daisy on the side.

Paige's face reddened. "I can't believe you're—"

"I'm not criticizing, dear. I'm sympathizing."

Her version of tough love? Anne struggled to keep her face expressionless.

"It's just terribly unfortunate that Kev—"

Paige put up a hand to stop her mother from going any further. "I don't want to hear his name mentioned anymore. I'm done with him. He can rot in jail with Brigitte for all I care." A tear rolled down her face that she roughly wiped away.

Anne locked eyes with Alex. *Well, that answers that. Paige and Kevin are splitting up. Can't say I blame her.*

"Let's go with this one." Alex's father held up what was probably a very nice bottle of red wine, but nobody seemed to pay attention.

"What happened with Kev—" the matriarch gave a little shake of her head as she stopped herself and revamped. "—*him* is not your fault. Things like this can happen to the best of us." She flipped her palms in a show of exasperation. "I thought Brigitte was my good friend. And yet she chose to murder her husband at *my* house on one of the biggest days of *your* life." She looked at her daughter beseechingly. "What kind of a friend does that?"

Alex winked as he handed Anne a couple of pillows. *Who indeed?*

Presumably mollified by her mother's explanation, Paige relaxed back on the couch. "Obviously, she was desperate. The fact that Richard happened to die at our house most certainly had nothing to do with us."

An interesting thought. Had Brigitte intended to kill him off at the wedding, or had the timing of the two events just been an unfortunate coincidence? Anne leaned toward the latter, given the vagaries of poisoning someone with herbs harvested from their garden. It had to be difficult to get the perfect dosage. *Although...* She glanced over at her future mother-in-law. It could have been deliberate, a way to thumb her nose at someone she considered overly elitist. Or simply pragmatic, since the wedding venue greatly increased the number of potential suspects.

Alex's mother rubbed her forehead and sighed. "I hate to admit it, but I always envied that lovely landscaping of hers. Little did I know her property was full of poisonous plants."

"Mom." Alex always had to be the voice of reason. "Lots of people have lily-of-the-valley in their yards. You probably have some as well."

"Well, then, it should probably be removed. What if the dog were to get into it?" She gestured toward Paige's stomach. "Or the baby?"

Alex's father pulled the cork out of the bottle and gave it a quick sniff. "I'll instruct the gardener to yank it out the next time they do the lawn." He carefully poured a glass, making sure no sediment escaped the bottle. "What gets me is how ruthless she was about the whole thing. How could she sprinkle poison over Richard's food, day after day, and watch the poor sod slowly sicken?"

"And then to finish the job off at a wedding reception of all places, with a final, fatal dose?" His wife crossed her arms. "It's sociopathic."

"I don't agree." Anne shrugged as the Battle-Axe looked at her in surprise. She was done filtering her comments in an effort to fit in. If her language was too assertive or judgmental, or seemingly uncouth, his parents would just have to deal with it. It was one of the good things she had learned from Brigitte.

"Why not?" Alex's mother asked, sounding genuinely curious.

"A simple label like that makes her sound like a nut job and doesn't give her sufficient credit. What she did was methodical. And calculated. She didn't think anyone would realize he'd been poisoned."

"Good job the medical examiner saw what's what." The patriarch took a sip of the wine and nodded. "Would anyone else like a glass?"

Anne signaled her interest by putting up a finger.

"I'll get it for you." Alex joined his father at the bar and took over the pouring. "You make a good point about Brigitte being shrewd rather than unhinged. For the longest time, she refused to accept the idea that Richard had been murdered. I thought she was in denial. Of course, now it's obvious

246

that it was a strategic move on her part."

"Probably waiting to see who might be a suitable patsy." His father picked up a glass and sat down near his wife. "With everything going on at Energix, there was bound to be someone who could be blamed."

"That's for sure." Alex set the wine bottle down and pushed the cork back into the top. "There were a bevy of candidates who could easily fit the bill."

Anne thought back to Brigitte's impromptu visit to her office. "She made sure that Peter Eckert's name bubbled up fairly early on as a possibility. *Follow the money*, she said. He had *lots of opportunities* at the wedding reception to slip something into Richard's drink."

"No question, she kept pushing us to look into him. Now we know why." Alex handed Anne a glass. "Here. This should take the edge off."

Anne took a sip, savoring the bouquet of redolent blackberries. "Very nice." She glanced at the nearby antique table. "Can you grab me a coaster?"

He gave a thumbs up.

"Käthe kept going on about Eckert as well." Paige narrowed her eyes. "But, of course, she was worried about her boyfriend being accused instead."

Anne swallowed. At the hospital, the poor girl had virtually collapsed upon learning that her mother was responsible for killing her father. "She's going to have a tough time in the next few weeks. Her whole life has been turned upside down."

The room became silent for a moment.

"At least she now knows the truth," Paige said quietly. "I think it's worse to live in ignorance. And it would have been awful if someone like Peter Eckert had been unfairly blamed instead."

Alex smiled wryly. "He has enough problems on his plate. Fraud. Money laundering. There's a good chance he could actually end up spending time behind bars."

His father wagged his drink in the air. "It seems rather unsportsmanlike of her to have suggested him at all. It's akin to kicking a man when he's already down."

"As if anything's fair in love and war." Alex set a small bowl of nuts on the table.

"Brigitte had no qualms about taking advantage of whatever leverage she could find. Even this afternoon. At the beginning of our walk, she dangled the idea of Eckert again. Trying to see if she could pin Richard's murder on him." Anne's eyes widened. "Oh God."

"What?"

"I told her that we'd scoured the wedding video and didn't think he had any real opportunity." She bit her lip.

"That's probably when she decided to frame you." He sat down next to her and rested a hand on her leg.

With that simple comment, I stepped straight into Brigitte's crosshairs. Anne took a deep breath and nodded slowly. "It was shortly afterwards that she suggested we hike down to the water."

"That's just…" Paige shivered.

"Diabolical," her mother said crisply. "I still can't believe I counted her as one of my good friends."

"It shows how desperate she was." Alex's voice caught in his throat. "She had made a beautiful life for herself in the States after narrowly escaping a life of misery behind the Iron Curtain. And then the situation at Energix threatened to upend everything she had worked so hard to achieve." He shrugged sadly. "We all know how driven she was."

"But then to try to pin everything on Anne?" Paige looked incredulously at her brother. "It's so heartless. And beyond that, why would Anne have any reason to kill Richard? Just because he yelled at her during the reception? That seems so far-fetched."

Alex's father set his wine glass down and opened the lid on his prized cigar box. "She also caused Energix's stock price to fall, which ultimately destroyed the company."

Anne stiffened. *Does he actually believe that?*

He picked up a cigar and turned to face her, a smile on his lips. "At least that's what Richard claimed for public consumption. But I think he knew full well that everything was on the verge of being exposed and was looking for a scapegoat. You were the first person to sell, which made you a convenient choice."

"And then he wouldn't let it go." Anne blew a strand of hair off of her face. "First I was a clueless neophyte who didn't know the first thing about investing, and by the time we got to Paige's wedding—"

Alex waved his hand back and forth. "Let's not even go there. The bottom line is that he said some awful things, and Brigitte recognized it gave you a motive for murder."

"Fair enough." Anne took a sip of her wine.

The lord of the manor felt around his pockets for a match. "As you scrambled down that cliff, you had no idea that anything was amiss? That she—"

"None. We were just chatting away." Anne felt a chill as the scene replayed in her mind. Brigitte had been making comments about Alex's family never accepting her. A ploy to distract her while she teetered on the rocks. And it had almost worked. "Until she made a comment about divorce. That's what got my attention."

"Divorce?"

Anne shivered. The moment when she and Brigitte had looked at each other, both knowing the hard truth, would remain forever seared in her mind. It was then that she knew she was in trouble. "She said she would never in a million years end her marriage with Richard."

Paige's eyes widened. "You knew she was lying."

Anne nodded.

"How?" Alex's mother looked back and forth at the two of them.

"Käthe was a basket case at the rehearsal dinner because Brigitte had consulted with an attorney earlier that week *about getting divorced*. With Energix going down in flames, she wanted to protect herself financially."

The older woman blinked and looked away. "Why didn't she just take that route? It would have saved everyone so much grief."

"You're telling me." Anne gestured toward her sprained ankle. "And now she's looking at spending the rest of her life behind bars." So sad. And so avoidable.

"That assumes she recovers from her injuries. A skull fracture, three broken ribs, and a punctured lung?" Paige arched an eyebrow. "Doesn't sound too good to me."

"She's a tough cookie." Alex sounded strangely distant. Almost as if he didn't care what happened next to Brigitte, and yet Anne knew that she had been like a mother to him. He leaned over to scratch the soft fur behind Bailey's ears. "The doctors said they expect her to make a full recovery."

"Hmm." Paige gave her brother a sideways glance. "Too bad she didn't have a prenup."

Not the damn prenup again! Drumroll anyone?

"Although, she's supposed to collect a huge amount on his life insurance policy," Paige grudgingly added. "So maybe it wouldn't have actually mattered."

Alex shook his head. "Not anymore, she won't. That policy was voided the moment she was identified as his killer. And a premarital agreement wouldn't have changed anything with regard to assets deemed to have been obtained illegally. She still would have lost everything." The dog nudged his hand in a bid to convince him to continue petting her. "Okay, Bailey." He gently rotated her collar back and forth, lightly massaging her neck.

Anne rolled her eyes. "Except executives are rarely held accountable when they run a company into the ground. Seems to me that her best move would have been to just sit back and watch Energix crumble. Chances are that Richard would have emerged relatively unscathed."

Alex stopped petting Bailey and squeezed Anne's hand. "I'm just so thankful that you're safe and sound."

"We all are." His mother said, sounding like she truly meant it.

Alex winked at her as if to say, *See? I knew my mother would eventually come around. She just needed some time to thaw.*

"You know. It's funny." As Anne said the words, they sounded bizarre because what she was thinking wasn't humorous at all. "I'm always so alert and careful when I walk in the City. Not making eye contact with strangers. Keeping a twenty-dollar bill in a separate pocket in case I get mugged. I've always thought of the Hamptons as a retreat where we can relax and not worry. And yet—"

Alex didn't wait for her to finish. "And yet you were almost killed while taking a leisurely stroll on the bluff!"

His mother rubbed her hands together nervously. "I certainly hope this mishap doesn't put you off from having your wedding reception here." She looked back and forth at the two of them. "Have you given any thought to a date?"

Anne and Alex locked eyes and after a moment began to laugh. They hadn't set a date or settled on a venue. But one thing was certain, they wanted to keep things simple.

"Mom." Alex sent a warning shot over the bow. "We might just elope."

Acknowledgements

A special thanks to Philip Tracadas for his unwavering encouragement, and to my wonderful critique group: Alicia Richardson, Lynn Long, Tassie Hewitt, Vanessa Rivera, and Mark Anderson, for providing candid feedback and many enlightening (and fun) discussions. I will always be grateful to Harriette Sackler who brought me into the Level Best Books fold with my first novel, and then provided guidance on my second one, even though she had retired by the time it was finished. Ginger Driver, Carol Chenault, and Maneesha Patil have been steadfast friends on this writing journey, reading drafts of both novels and offering many helpful suggestions. And lastly, I want to thank Verena Rose, Shawn Simmons, Deb Well, and everyone at Level Best Books who worked tirelessly behind the scenes to help make this book possible.

About the Author

Rebecca Saltzer worked as a bond analyst on the trading floor at Lehman Brothers in New York City in the financial heyday of the eighties. Like the protagonist in her novel, she sometimes encountered fraud and other questionable business practices, except in real life, none of it led to murder. In 2021, Rebecca received the William F. Deeck-Malice Domestic Grant for unpublished writers. When she's not writing, she enjoys hiking with her two rescue dogs and exploring the great outdoors.

AUTHOR WEBSITE:
  www.saltzerbooks.com/

SOCIAL MEDIA HANDLES:
  Facebook: Rebecca Saltzer
  www.facebook.com/rebecca.saltzer.14/

Also by Rebecca Saltzer

Murder Over Broken Bonds